IF YOU CHANGE
Your Mind

IF YOU CHANGE

Your Mind

ROBBY WEBER

ISBN-13: 978-1-335-42590-4

If You Change Your Mind

Copyright © 2022 by Robby Weber

For questions and comments about the quality of this book, please contact us at CustomerService@Harlequin.com.

Inkyard Press
22 Adelaide St. West, 41st Floor
Toronto, Ontario M5H 4E3, Canada
www.InkyardPress.com

Printed in U.S.A.

Recycling programs
for this product may
not exist in your area.

For Mom.
My best friend.
I'll always want to be you when I grow up.

And for Gabby and Reagan.
My beyond talented and creative sisters.
You inspire me in every way.

AUTHOR'S NOTE

Dear Reader,

My absolute favorite kind of day is one that's sunny and spent with a book at the beach before pizza at dinnertime—when I'm still toasty from the sun, with great music and loved ones—followed by an evening at the movie theater. Somehow, I've been lucky enough to write a story that feels like my favorite kind of day in book form, and my hope is you'll feel the same sense of warmth within the pages that I do on those perfect summer days.

For so long, in film and literature, all of my go-to romantic comedies had been about a guy and a girl, which I didn't have complaints about, but I found myself wanting to write my own, centered around laughter and love just like all of my favorites. I really aimed to create an optimistic book that felt welcoming and, hopefully, comforting, with a focus on relationships and the duality of love—falling in and out of it—along with friendship and family. It was a conscious decision to include many nods to romantic comedies, and to try to tell a story that felt somehow both familiar and fresh, featuring a gay lead.

One of the best lines in the film *Something's Gotta Give* is when Diane Keaton's character says: "People need romance… and if somebody like me doesn't write it, where are they gonna get it? Real life?" It's tongue-in-cheek, and—spoiler alert—she does end up finding romance, after all. In this book about love, with its emphasis on romantic films and its own screenplay that's really a rom-com with a twist, Harry questions if love exists at all outside the movies. I hope you'll take away from this story a firm, lasting belief that the best, warmest kind of love—be it love for family or friends or a romantic partner—doesn't only happen in movies or books at all.

Thank you so much for reading!
Robby

1

WHEN HARRY MET LOGAN

Hot guys are the best part of summer. Pastel ice cream scoops, lemonade-like sunshine, and sea salt–strung hair are staples, but there's something about guys with sandy calves and strong, tanned arms wearing low-hanging swimsuits.

Honestly, I love *everything* about summer. The warmth, the way my mom stocks the freezer with the variety pack of popsicles—cherry for Milly, grape for Lottie, and orange for me. There's new music and the feeling of going into a cold movie theater on a hot day. And, yeah, the guys. Everywhere you look, there's a hot guy. It's like that *Oprah* meme—you get a hot guy, *you* get a hot guy, everybody gets a hot guy!

I can absolutely appreciate all of the six-packs and dimples, but only as long as I keep my eye on the prize and stay focused. My mom always says fortune favors the determined... Or something like that.

And I am determined. I have two weeks and six days to

finish and submit my screenplay before the Reel Sunshine competition deadline, which is totally doable.

My whole future depends on it. No pressure.

Damn, there really are attractive men *everywhere*—lying out at the pool or, past the iron gate and sandy walkway, stretching across the volleyball court down on the beach. It's like in summer, hot guys get even hotter. It's the sweat and the bronzed abs.

I don't do the whole dating thing anymore, so this summer really is the equivalent of scrolling through the Calvin Klein Instagram or something—purely about the visual.

Getting close to a boy leads only to heartbreak, disappointment, and—most importantly—distraction from one's goals. See, most people spend their high school years searching for their great romance. One like in the movies. But I've already had mine, and TSwift's "Death by a Thousand Cuts" was my top song on Spotify last year, so I'm good.

Maybe once I've secured my spot at USC. Actually, maybe once I've gotten an internship at a studio. By then I won't even remember Grant Kennedy or what heartbreak feels like and I'll be able to spend a little bit more time focused on romance.

Well, realistically, I should probably wait until I sell my first script and—

My youngest sister, Lottie, laughs maniacally, and I am snapped to the real world. I watch in horror as she grabs a fistful of Milly's hair and yanks her down into the shallow end of the pool.

"Lottie," I say. "Come on, that was totally unnecessary!"

Lottie, though she be but five, is fierce. And now she has hair that barely falls under her chin because she decided to give herself an impromptu trim with her crafting scissors just before her last day of school. Nana had to give her an emergency haircut. She narrows her eyes at me and then shrugs.

My mother is careening down the path from the club's new restaurant, a tote bag slung over her shoulder with a large silver tumbler in one hand and her phone in the other. I haven't been yet, but the photos I've seen are really cool.

Mom met some local beauty influencers there at the launch event and they've been promoting her products. Really, her company doesn't need much more press since Jen Aniston likes her stuff, but she says it can't hurt to keep reaching the younger crowd.

"Harold," Mom says, out of breath.

She *always* calls me Harold. Even though Lottie and Milly get nicknames and everyone I know calls me Harry, apparently I'll always be Harold to her. Because of this, Milly and Lottie call me Harold, too.

"I thought you guys went to the kid's pool. I was worried for a second you'd disappeared."

Moms are always worried. I'm convinced it's a personality trait that's earned as soon as they change their first diaper.

Sitting in the chaise next to my table, Mom is wearing a white cover-up and big black sunglasses. Under a giant straw hat, her hair is probably tied up into a knot—it's dyed much lighter than Milly's dark brown waves and certainly differs from the more chestnut hair Lottie and I have. Mom lowers her glasses to eye the girls, and then her phone sounds an alert.

"They're at war," I say, gesturing my Spider-Man pen toward my flailing siblings. This pen—a gift Lottie selected for me from her class treasure chest—reminds me of another reason to love summer: the new superhero movies. It isn't *all* about hot guys. Even if most of the heroes are hot. That's a happy coincidence.

"They'll work it out," Mom says, engrossed in whatever email she just got. She quickly responds as two more alerts come through. She doesn't even kick off her flip-flops. She just sits up straight and reads, reads, reads and types, types, types.

For my sisters and me, the Citrus Harbor Beach Club is all palm trees and virgin daiquiris and nighttime Disney movies projected on the screen at the kid's pool. For Mom, it's a blurred background behind her phone—second to the masses of work emails and texts she gets when she tries to relax by the pool with us before she inevitably goes home because she needs her computer.

The club is fun, but there's not much variety or excitement apart from the screaming kids like Lottie, or the guys who could resemble a shirtless Tom Holland if you squint really hard. It's the epitome of our small town's slow pace and fixed reality. When I'm home from college for nostalgia-filled summers, it'll probably be a nice, calm escape from the hustle and bustle of my new Hollywood life.

"I said I want to play 'DANCING QUEEN,'" Lottie shrieks.

"You little gremlin, you scratched me! Do you ever cut your nails?"

Ignoring Milly and Lottie, I look around for Hailey. Behind our table and chairs, up a winding path of rust-colored tile and past the children's pool, cantina, and toddler play area, the two-story clubhouse is like a bright white seaside castle, complete with a courtyard and a big red fountain. It's almost historic looking—Spanish, which is common in Florida, but especially here since we're not far from where Ponce de León first arrived. That's everyone's go-to fun fact. Like, awkward silence? Ponce de León.

Lottie growls: "If you don't play it, I'm gonna scream that you peed in the pool!"

"I would never do that!"

"They don't know that."

Hailey says she's getting snacks and drinks, but there's a fifty-fifty chance she's at the spot with the perfectly placed palm trees, taking First Day of Summer selfies for her Instagram story.

"Would you tell me how to Instagram?" Mom says to me, as if she's reading my mind.

"How to what on Instagram?" I blink.

"How to *Instagram*." Mom sighs.

Lottie cackles again: "Is that a floating turd? Is it *yours*, Milly?"

"You get one song." Milly groans in defeat.

Hailey sits down next to me and hands me a glass, cold to the touch and nearly overflowing with an Arnold Palmer. She sets down a basket of fries and chicken tenders with a little cup of ranch.

As my best friend and fellow admirer of *GQ* magazine covers, Hailey Birch appreciates hot guys as much as I do, which is why it's *almost* a shame she wants to tie herself down with one guy—Justin Andrews. We're only seventeen, after all. But Justin's handsome, motivated, and completely sweet to her. Plus, he always gets me a coffee when he drives us to school. Things could be worse.

It all started when Hailey's Mimi left the Philippines and

moved in with them last summer. She was looking for an excuse to miss Sunday Mass—her parents pretended they hadn't missed in years—so she signed up for a summer-long weekend surf camp, which lead to *many* extra one-on-one surf lessons with Justin.

The rest is history. And Hailey still can't surf.

It's just hard to understand how Hailey is such an effortless beauty—she's wearing a red one-piece, her deep brown skin glowing in the sun and her lush windswept curls falling onto her shoulders—and now her entire life revolves around one guy. But that's her choice and not all guys are Grant Kennedy, so I have to just root for her and Justin.

"Tell me you figured out the big hook for your movie." Hailey nods toward my notebook, dunking a tender, and Mom looks up from her phone to us. Convinced she might meet a Hemsworth at Hollywood and Vine, Hailey wants my movie to be a total blockbuster for completely selfless reasons.

I think marrying a Hemsworth might be the only thing that could distract Hailey from winning Cutest Couple with Justin for the senior superlatives. It's all I've heard about since we got back from winter break and realized we'll be seniors *this* August.

"Justin might have some ideas, he—"

"It'll come to me," I say quickly, not ready to make this conversation about Justin. I *do* hope it'll come to me.

"It definitely will," Mom says. "Although it might not hurt to at least *consider*—"

"Mom, I'm going to win the competition," I say.

Here's the thing.

I sort of screwed up. Really, Grant made me screw up more

than I was already screwing up, but I'm trying to listen to Mom's advice and take responsibility for my actions.

My grades are mostly good—not perfect—and USC is not easy to get into. I always sort of knew I wasn't getting in purely on grades. But then after Grant, it was like my brain just couldn't do school. Or anything really. It was just looping my heartbreak, over and over, with no time for any other programming.

It was only really bad until December, but by then the damage was done. I had C averages in three of my AP classes and my GPA was seriously affected. Plus I'd absolutely bombed the fall SAT, despite months of studying. It was like it all flew out the window.

Young love is a bitch.

Now this contest is literally my only chance at USC, my dream school. The school I've wanted to go to for as long as I've wanted to work in movies, which is basically since I could start writing scripts and making Milly and the neighbors act them out. I've never even imagined myself anywhere else. Nowhere else will get me where I want to be.

There are severable notable (i.e., Oscar-winning) USC alumni on the board overseeing the competition, and if I can win a mentorship, I'm guaranteed a letter of rec that will stand out.

USC is the best of the best. It's in the heart of the film industry and even has its own Hollywood Walk of Fame star. Plus, USC has the First Look Festival for students' work, which has an *industry jury*.

Kevin Feige, aka the *president* of Marvel Studios—who produced the highest grossing film of *all time* before the *Avatar* re-release I don't speak of—applied to USC's School of Cinematic Arts six times before he got accepted. Six!

Let that sink in.

"I want you to win," Mom says. "You've just been struggling with the screenplay for a while now. It's healthy to have options. That's all."

"Who has the time for options?"

"I simply meant USC isn't the only school. What happens if, for any reason, you—"

"I'm going to USC," I say, desperate not to have this conversation with Mom again.

She's always been supportive, but ever since this terrible Grant-induced writing block struck, she's been pushing for backup—more "viable" options. Safer bets, thanks to my guidance counselor calling USC a reach school.

The phrase *reach school* actually makes me want to throw up. Like USC is something I'm *reaching* toward, not something I have. She says I have to stand out from all the killer GPAs and SAT scores with my creative materials.

To name a few, there's an autobiographical character sketch, my essay about my most challenging moment, and my writing sample. Then there are the letters of recommendation. That's where the Reel Sunshine competition comes into play.

I think in my mom's mind, I'm being impractical. A dreamer who screwed up and lost his shot. But I can still make it happen.

"I just need the hook to be *perfect*," I say. "Once I have it, I'm gonna really work my ass off, and it'll all come together."

My mom points to Lottie. "Your sister can hear you."

"It's okay." Lottie smiles. "Vanessa Thomas says *ass* all the time."

Mom only offers her signature exasperated sigh. "Dinner ideas?" she says, and both my sisters turn, alert. "First one to tell me one of their summer reading books gets to pick."

Hailey's face falls as she and I rack our brains— Oh, crap. I know we have to read some books from the '50s or something…

"Miss Spider's Tea Party," Lottie screams with a shit-eating grin. "I want breakfast for dinner!"

"Well, great. I don't want breakfast for dinner." Milly throws herself back into the water.

"Lottie won," Mom says with a raised brow once Milly resurfaces. "If you won, you'd want me to honor that."

"Yeah, I won," Lottie teases, making her way over with a devilish smile. "And you *lost*."

"CHARLOTTE!"

In the pool, Lottie has jumped on Milly's back and wrapped her little arms firmly around her neck.

"AMELIA," Lottie cackles, hanging on for dear life.

"That's it," Milly shrieks, pushing Lottie off her and storming up the steps. It takes her five quick steps to join us where we're sitting, nearly soaking us and the family at the next table, who pretend not to watch her temper tantrum. She wraps a towel over her pink crochet bikini.

"You're going to get my notebook wet," I say, like it matters the blank pages might get a few splashes on them.

Milly rolls her eyes and groans something dragon-esque. "I've had enough of Lottie being a little demon. I'm going to Madeline's and *not* eating breakfast for dinner."

Lottie looks devastated as she walks up behind Milly, her

new bob dripping wet while she unapologetically plucks a wedgie from her Little Mermaid bathing suit bottoms.

"I still can't think of any of our summer reading," Hailey says slowly.

"I only want to play, Milly," Lottie whines with a stomp.

"You want to play guerilla warfare," Milly says with a hiss. "I'm over it."

Lottie looks at me, eyes all big and sad. I frown.

"She's fifteen, Lot," I say pointedly, eyeing Milly. "It's not you. It's her."

Though, to be fair, Lottie might have very well knocked Milly unconscious had their playing continued.

"It's definitely *her*." Milly rolls her eyes and stomps a few steps from Lottie. "But go ahead, Harold, defend your favorite sister like you always do."

"Milly, she's five, you can't just call her a demon. Anyway, like—hello, pot? It's kettle."

"Harold, please, you're not helping. Your sister is just experiencing—"

Milly full on yells, flipping her hair and assaulting us with the heavily chlorinated pool water. She hurries over to snatch her bag before heading up to change, her wet feet slapping angrily against the cement.

"You have to learn when to just let her be." Mom sighs. "She's like a teenage grenade. It's a constant battlefield. Do you want to *make it* to dinner or do you want to risk the minefield because really, it's, like—" Mom mimics an explosion with her hands, and Lottie nods in agreement.

"On that note"—Hailey stands up and smiles—"I have to go take Mimi to get her lotto tickets."

I tell Hailey I'll text her later as I close my notebook and get up, then follow Lottie into the pool. She jumps on my back and nearly sends me hurtling forward.

"You're supposed to wait thirty minutes before you get in the water," Mom says, though it comes out exasperated. She hasn't even opened the book in her lap; she's just typing away at her phone, probably negotiating an international contract or something.

Lottie laughs as she dunks me under. When I come up, I sputter and shake out my hair.

I hear one of the staff members greeting my mom.

With my eyes closed, I remember a moment just like this from last summer: A tall, tan guy with wavy chestnut hair. He was lean and wearing an aqua polo that was tight around his biceps and just short enough that if he reached up, you'd see the golden skin of his stomach. His khaki shorts grazed his thighs, and his boat shoes were worn in, making the leather look soft. Of course, he wasn't just any employee of the club. He was Grant, boy wonder. The hottest guy on the staff. A year older, so he was about to be a senior.

All the girls were always crushing on Grant in school. And I was, too.

When I open my eyes, I don't see Grant. Obviously. Grant's nowhere near here; he's in California with his family living a whole new life.

"Can I get you anything?" the new guy says. He's wearing the same aqua polo and khaki shorts Grant did. Only they don't fit the same. On this guy, the shirt's a little bit looser, and the shorts are a little longer, not brushing the tops of muscular copper thighs but hovering above pale knees.

He has these airy eyes—a cool light blue—and a wide, inviting smile. His hair's dark brown, almost black, and it's tousled haphazardly atop his head. He's wearing tattered blue Vans with white socks that rise to his ankles.

This new guy seems nice, and I have to admit he is cute, but I can't stop imagining Grant over at the cantina, leaning against the bar, probably causing some girls to swoon over his warm golden skin and piercing green eyes. With that, I submerge, letting air out of my nose until I'm sunken, sitting at the bottom of the pool and fighting every urge to scream or feel anything for Grant.

Once Lottie tires out and falls asleep face-first on the pool deck, I figure it's time to get my clothes from the locker room and get ready to leave. Plus, I should spend time working on my screenplay.

The club's locker rooms are super nice: clean with the same Spanish-style architecture throughout the buildings and brass fixtures. The showers are separate and very private, thank God.

I push open the door, and the spa-like music bounces off the walls. It sounds extra hollow, like there isn't a soul around. It's a little strange—usually there are a few people in here chatting about golfing or surfing or having dinner at one of the restaurants on the property.

And that's awkward, right? I mean, that's not just me? Bathrooms and locker rooms are so not the place for casual conversation. Get in, do your thing, and get out.

I catch myself in the mirror and walk over to the sinks. I pump some eucalyptus lotion on my hand—Mom says it's good for sunburns—rubbing it into my slightly red forearms.

I'm getting too much sun, and the dark circles under my eyes are really bad right now. My hair needs a wash, and I already need to shave again.

A strangely familiar voice calls out: "Hello?"

I stare into the mirror, trying to see behind me, but nobody's there. I turn to face the showers—none of them are running, and there isn't a pair of feet to be seen. This is the beginning of a Michael Myers movie, isn't it?

The voice from nowhere persists: "Hey, is someone there?"

I look the other way and begin to walk slowly. There are two rows of lockers, and I have no idea who's hiding between them. Ideally not an axe murderer or an escaped convict.

"Hello?" I say.

For a moment, my brain stops focusing on my mental to-do list and hops on the Anxiety Train. They sound similar, but one is far more severe. The Anxiety Train has charming stops like: What if it *is* an axe murderer? Or someone dangerous? I shouldn't be trying to talk to someone lurking in a locker room—what am I *thinking*?

"Hi," the voice says, definitely coming from the direction of the lockers. "Yeah, I'm... Um. Could you help me out?"

I slowly take one step forward, even as my brain screams at me to stop because if it is, in fact, a masked murderer with a hook, I'm walking closer and ensuring I'm a victim and not a Final Boy. If Final Boys are a thing.

"I'm sort of stuck in my locker," the voice says. "I just need, like, a towel and for someone to let me out..."

"A towel?"

"Locked in without my clothes." The voice laughs awkwardly, a little forced, but he doesn't sound sinister at all. "It's not a big deal, just some simple hazing, the usual stuff. Classic case of 'the guys being the guys.'"

There's a hint of sarcasm in his voice, understandably, and I grab a towel from the rack. "Uh, which locker are you in?"

The person raps on the metal. "1303."

"Okay," I say. Part of me is still a little hesitant. This is very weird. But as weird as it is, I'm not really getting *danger* vibes from this guy so I just go with it. I can hear my mom now: *You don't get* danger vibes *from serial killers most of the time, Harold. Come on!*

I chew on the inside of my cheek. "Okay, how should we do this? I'll crack the door and hand you the towel?"

"Yeah," the voice says, now a little less desperate. "Thank you *so* much."

He tells me the combination, and I unlock the door, letting it creak open ever so slowly.

"Thanks," he says, grabbing the towel and pulling it inside the locker.

I turn around instantly, suddenly unsure of what to do. Should I just go? Stick around to help him get his clothes? Maybe at least wait to see who it is.

"Okay," the voice says. "I have a towel on now, so."

I spin on my heel, eager to find out who got locked in a locker without his clothes, and see the boy from the pool earlier, pale with his hands clutching the towel like he's absolutely *not* going to let go. He has a little freckle on his collarbone.

Not that I really notice. Obviously. Because I *just* told myself guys only create more problems than they're worth.

Though I have to give him some credit because he's slim, but he's not completely without definition. He has the start of abs, and his flexing arm is impressive. Truthfully, he's not quite my type, but he *is* cute. He's the kind of guy with adorkable charm someone could find to be really…comforting.

"You're new here," I say slowly, trying to look away from his figure and feeling a little annoyed because I'm finding it hard to. *Focus*, Harry.

"Yeah." His face goes from a Nantucket Red to a deep Fell Asleep in the Sun Red and he bites his lip. "I'm Logan. I'm sorry that this… Sorry you had to deal with this. I know it's super unprofessional for me to ask a guest to—"

I wave him off. "It's really not a big deal. I'm sure weirder things have happened than…being stuffed in a locker naked…" I realize that *is* probably actually one of the weirdest things to happen in a while. "Well, in theory, weirder things have happened to someone out there."

"That's a cool T-shirt," he offers, obviously trying to change the subject.

I've forgotten what shirt I'm even wearing, so I glance down. It's blue, a little too big, with a dinosaur skeleton. Mom bought it for me in New York when we went to the Museum of Natural History in October of ninth grade. We both agreed it was better to get the large and grow into it, though I think it will always hang a little loose off my shoulders.

"Thanks, it's from a museum," I say, as if he can't read that on the shirt. This is the single geekiest item of clothing I own.

"Dinosaurs are cool," Logan says. His face says he's embarrassed he just said that, but I nod in agreement and rub the back of my neck.

We don't say anything for a second, and then my shoulders fall. "Um, okay, do you know where your clothes are?"

"Not sure," he says. "I'm guessing they're somewhere around here…"

He takes a step toward me, and I instinctively move back.

"I'm just going to look for them," he laughs.

"Okay," I say. I don't know what this is exactly, but I feel a little nervous around Logan. "I'll help."

We split up and look around the locker room. I don't see anything in the bathroom, but when I get to the showers I gasp.

"What?" Logan says, coming up behind me.

"I found your clothes," I say and frown, pointing at a pile of sopping wet clothes on the floor. "God, that is gnarly."

Logan's face falls, but then he looks at me and tries to smile and laugh, attempting to recover. "It's fine. It's not a big deal. I'll just put on my trunks and act like I was swimming."

"Who did this?" I say, watching him pick his clothes up. "Here, you can borrow a T-shirt from me. I have a couple in my bag."

He shakes his head. "No, it's okay, honestly."

"You're going to be cold," I tell him, with just enough of an eye roll to let him know I'm not taking no for an answer. "Come on."

I walk over to my locker and open it, reaching for a weekender I stowed a couple of things in. It's not my first rodeo, after all. Many years of coming to the club have taught me to have a few outfit options on hand in case something unexpected comes up.

"Do you have a preference?" I say, hauling the bag onto the wooden bench beside us. I start to pull out a couple of T-shirts, and his serious face finally breaks. He giggles and then corrects, trying to force his mouth into a straight line.

I look up at him. His laugh is kind of contagious, so I'm giggling a little, too, even if nothing's funny. "What?"

He points to the shirts. "You just have something for every occasion. I'm sorry. I'm not laughing *at* you, I promise. I just kind of thought you'd have, like, an old ratty T-shirt or something. Not that you look like you'd have ratty clothes. I mean. Well, you know what I mean."

I tap my chin. "You never know when you'll need a change of clothes. Clearly."

"Okay…" He raises a brow like people do when they want you to tell them something.

"Harry," I say.

He reaches for my hand, and we shake, though his other hand's knuckles go white as they clutch the towel closed over his waist.

"So. Right. Pick a shirt already."

Logan inhales and closes his eyes. He reaches out, and I grab his arm.

"What the hell are you doing?"

"Just grabbing one randomly," Logan says, opening one eye.

"What?" I realize I'm still holding his forearm, so I drop it.

Logan smirks. "It's more fun this way. Letting whatever happen. Statistically speaking, I have a good shot of liking whatever I pick. You have good taste."

I can't argue with that, so I just cross my arms and raise my brows.

Logan shuts his eyes and reaches, grabbing a green-and-white-striped T-shirt. He opens his eyes and shrugs. "See? Not bad."

"Not bad," I agree as he pulls it on. "You didn't answer me. Who did this?"

"Some of the lifeguards." He shrugs. "It's not a big deal at all. Just, like, hazing. You know? Initiation. But we're all friends."

Jesus, I've never had friends who took my clothes, left them soaking wet in the shower, and locked me, naked, in a locker. Is that normal?

"Are you sure?" I say, throwing things back into the bag.

"Yeah," Logan says, giving me an earnest smile. The shirt suits him—the green is nice with his pale eyes and dark hair. It's a little small on him but not too bad.

Logan disappears behind the lockers. When he comes back, he's wearing his soaking wet trunks. "Wow, feels great."

I laugh without meaning to.

"Do you mind doing me one last favor?" Logan rocks back on his heels. "Could you call my phone? I'm not sure where they put it."

I nod and hand him my phone. He dials his number, and I hear the ringing, so I step up onto the bench and reach atop the locker, my hand stopping on what feels like an iPhone. When I pull it down, I see my number disappear. There are several missed calls from Charlie and a bunch of texts from Annie ♥. I can only catch one clearly—That's normal after a breakup, it just takes time.

I hand him the phone, not showing any disappointment in the fact that he's getting so many texts from a girl with a heart emoji.

Because I'm not disappointed. Obviously.

"Well, if they keep this hazing up and it gets to be too much…"

"It won't," he says, handing me my phone. "It's not. It's cool. Really. I mean, this was funny. Right? I'm glad it was you who helped me. I don't know anyone here, yet, really. Just got to Citrus Harbor a few days ago."

And what am I supposed to say to that? I don't want to come off too strong, but I know if I were new in town, I'd definitely want the opportunity to make friends, and I'm guessing the guys at the club aren't banging down Logan's door to hang out with him.

"Well, do you have plans tomorrow night?" I say. "Because if you want, there's a party over in this neighborhood called Madre Cove. It'll probably get way out of hand and get busted, but it'll be fun for a while. The only thing to do at night around here is go to parties, basically. You can meet my friends. They're awesome. A ton of people will be there so, I mean. Just. If you wanted to meet people— Um."

Logan instantly brightens up so much at this, I don't feel as awkward or weird for inviting a stranger.

"I'm not really big into parties, if I'm honest," he says. "But it'd be fun to hang out and make some friends. My evening pretty much includes Netflix documentaries and leftovers of this meat loaf my uncle made last night."

"Yeah," I say, thinking a night in like that sounds weirdly comforting. "Well, you'll love my friends."

I let him know I'll text him the address, and his smile is so contagious, I wouldn't mind if I *had* to see it all summer.

Inviting Logan to the party was definitely the right move. Everyone deserves the chance to have some fun and nobody should have to spend the summer without friends. I'd guess getting stuffed into a locker naked isn't giving the best impression of the social scene in Citrus Harbor.

As I walk outside, it's still sunny, though there are some gray clouds and the air is wet and hot. No doubt the remnants of an afternoon shower—a regular occurrence we all learn to plan our summer days around. The pool is empty except for a few kids who are just getting back into the shallow end.

My phone buzzes.

MOM: Taking Lot to change—are you coming with us or going with Hailey?

And when I look up, I see a few guys talking over by the cabana. One, in particular, has his head thrown back laughing. He's got a backward baseball cap on and a white polo with his favorite Ralph Lauren swim trunks—the ones with the tropical pattern and RL teddy bears.

I know they're his favorite because it's him.

It's Grant Kennedy.

He's standing in the open-air hallway, and though the club lobby is busy behind him, time stops. I blink and wonder if I'm awake or hallucinating because I'm certainly not in Los Angeles, which means Grant Kennedy is *here*, in Citrus Harbor.

I spent months wondering what I'd say if I ever saw him again. If he ever came back or if we ran into each other out in LA once I went to college.

Eventually, I figured out the perfect thing to say. The thing that would wound him.

Seeing him, though, I'm more stunned than I thought I'd be. I could turn around right now and forget I even saw him. I could let this go—let the past be the past.

Or I could start walking toward him, just as he pats one of his friends on the arm and starts to walk away. I could fake confidence and say what I want to say.

Except when he sees me, everything goes out the window. When we're walking right up to each other in this familiar place, and it feels like we're entirely different people with a year of distance between us, something twists up inside me and begins to take on a life of its own.

Anger. It's that red mist people talk about, and it's descending. I'm suddenly *infuriated* with Grant Kennedy for breaking my heart and for having the nerve to show up here, all smiles and sunshine with that arrogant walk of his.

"Harry!" Grant grins and throws his hands up once we're within a foot of each other.

"What are you doing here?"

It's not what I planned to say, but the red mist is getting thicker.

"That's my 'welcome home'?" Grant furrows his brow, that grin slipping into a smirk.

"No, *this* is."

I don't know exactly what it is. Maybe it's the way Grant endlessly makes everything all about him. Maybe it's the memories of last summer flooding in, or the way he's so nonchalant about running into me.

Or maybe it's the fact that he was about six inches from the edge.

All I *do* know is it feels damn pretty nice to reach out and push Grant Kennedy—his arms flailing around as he grabs at the air in an attempt to catch himself—and watch him fall backward into the deep end of the pool.

You're My Hero

by Harry Kensington

OVER BLACK

Music begins.

EXT. A WARM JULY DAY, THE SUN BEGINS TO SET

NEW YORK CITY, THE GLASS BUILDINGS REFLECT THE ORANGE OF THE SKY.

The music intensifies.

We cut to THE METROPOLITAN MUSEUM OF ART.

EXT. ROOFTOP GARDEN

A black-tie affair put on by WOODS INDUSTRIES. Pure destruction and chaos. Screams, small explosions.

RORY WOODS—son of the CEO—is college-aged, cowering in a corner and wearing a tuxedo. He's carefully guarding a glowing blue canister. He stuffs it into his jacket.

RORY (V.O.)
The day it all started.

THE PYTHON crosses the roof toward Rory.

Enter THE STING: our hero in a yellow suit with blue rings.

Rory hurries across the roof—The Python grabs him and
leaps, crashing into a glass building across the avenue. The
Sting follows.

The Python yanks Rory up and scales the building, climbing
high above the city. He holds Rory over the edge, taking the
glowing canister from the boy's jacket.

In one hand, The Python holds out the canister and in the
other hand, Rory, indicating a choice for The Sting.

He drops Rory.

CLOSE-UP. The Sting's mask. Time seems to stop.

WIDE SHOT. The Python escapes. The Sting leaps off the
side of the building and catches Rory.

RORY (V.O.)
The day The Sting saved my life and everything
changed.

MEDIUM SHOT. The Sting holds Rory close and braces
for impact, landing perfectly on his feet. The pavement is
crushed from the landing, but The Sting is perfectly fine.

CLOSE-UP. Rory's terrified. He gasps, clutching to The Sting.

>   THE STING
> Are you all right?

>   RORY
> He got away with the antibody—

>   THE STING
> It's okay, don't worry. I'll take care of him.

>   RORY
> *(shaking)*
> You saved me.

>   THE STING
> Of course I did.

They stand there, breathless in each other's arms.

>   THE STING (CONT'D)
> Wow, your heart is beating so fast.

>   RORY
> Don't most people have elevated heart rates after
> dropping almost 100 stories?

>   THE STING
> Oh. Yeah, of course.

Another beat.

>   RORY
> Well, aren't you going to go after him?

>   THE STING
> Yes, yeah, I am.

He's still holding Rory.

>   RORY
> Good.

>   THE STING
> Okay. Going now.

He lets him go, taking a step back.

>   RORY
> Thank you for saving me.

>   THE STING
> Anytime.

He takes another step.

>   RORY
> Wait—

>   THE STING
> Yeah?

>   RORY
> (thinking of what to say)
> …be careful.

>   THE STING
> (saluting)
> Aye, aye, Cap'n.

The Sting turns, and he's off, speeding away.

We see a sense of wonder on Rory's face.

WIDE SHOT. Behind Rory—CAPTAIN WARP, another superhero in a black suit, approaches. He's out of breath.

>   CAPTAIN WARP
> Rory!

Rory looks surprised.

>   RORY
> You're—you're Captain Warp.

>   CAPTAIN WARP
> Are you okay? I saw what happened and—

>   RORY
> Wait, how do you know my name?

CLOSE-UP. The iridescent lens across Captain Warp's helmet slides up to reveal JENSON BRIGGS, a handsome young man—college-aged, same as Rory.

MEDIUM SHOT. Reporters swarm the scene, and we cut to:

CLOSE-UP. Rory realizes it's Jenson, and his eyes widen with shock before his face twists into pure disappointment.

>   RORY (V.O.)
> And the day I found out my ex was Captain Warp.

FADE INTO TITLE SCREEN: YOU'RE MY HERO

2

HOW TO BE SINGLE

I'm about to triumphantly walk away when Grant surfaces and splashes a little pool water my way, just shy of my feet.

"I expected worse," he says with a laugh and with that typical, slightly teasing intonation. The one that somehow plucks at just the right heartstring and reminds me of when we used to tease each other. It reminds me of the human being under Grant's bionic-prep exterior.

So I roll my eyes and turn around, and now I'm handing him another towel as he dries off at one of the tables. Deep down—like, *deeeeeep* down—I feel bad for pushing Grant and now I'm no longer the spot-free party in this scenario. What he did to me was way worse, but now I've fired back after keeping my cool all these months.

"I don't really know what came over me," I say, probably sounding too proud of myself.

Grant raises a brow. "It's okay, I probably deserved that."

I narrow my eyes, holding the towel tighter so he can't take it from me.

"Okay, I *definitely* deserved it." He sighs, all of the jokes falling away. I let him have the towel. "I wasn't expecting to see you yet. I've been trying to figure out what I was gonna say."

Leave it to Grant to turn my entire world upside down in less than five minutes.

Grant is supposed to be a memory—a lesson learned. He's not supposed to be here, in Citrus Harbor. He's definitely not supposed to be confusing me with those charming eyes and that smooth way he says just the right thing.

"You could push me in the pool again if it'd help," he offers.

"It's no fun if you're expecting it," I say, sitting in the chair next to his.

I have a lot of questions. Like, how? And why? If I'm an expert on anything, it's the rom-com. I know how all of this is supposed to go, and this isn't right. There's not a single Cameron Diaz movie that has the answers for this one. It doesn't make sense. But it turns out when Grant flashes his pearly whites and strides into Citrus Harbor like he's returned from a holiday, nothing makes sense.

"So… What's been up with you?" Grant says.

What has been *up* with me? The club is spinning. *Grant* is sitting across from me. Grant is *here.* Talking to me like we're just catching up.

"What's been up? Like, since you moved away and told me with a text? When you were already on your way to the airport?"

It's not like I needed to be Humphrey Bogart, putting Grant on the plane with a tearful but understanding—and devastatingly romantic—goodbye.

Though I could have, if he'd given me the chance.

I didn't even get the opportunity to pull a Sam from *Love Actually* and stop him at the airport, or run through the snow like Bridget Jones.

Nope. Grant just did what worked for him. He pretended it was no big deal—the summer, him moving away. *Us.* It made him feel better to minimize it all, I guess. To reduce the conflict to a series of texts. No face-to-face. No watching me cry.

Really, can you even *imagine* how *Notting Hill* would have ended if the concierge didn't tell Hugh Grant where to find Julia Roberts? If she just flew home? Roll credits. That's it?

It's just not how things are supposed to be. Last summer made it all clear: Grant is no rom-com lead, but neither am I. Because real life and romantic comedies are two very different things.

Grant frowns, his hair still dripping. He's got one of the white towels across his shoulders and he leans forward. "I know, shit. I clearly don't know how to do this."

"Do what?"

"Apologize," he says, his eyes softening. "I'm sorry. You know—" He catches me poking my tongue in my cheek and sighs. "Come on, you know I cared about you. I still do. I'm always gonna care about you."

We sit in silence for a moment and I don't know what to say. I definitely don't know what I'm feeling. My chest is like a lava lamp, all up and down and super inconsistent.

"Harry," Grant says. "You know I've never been good at, like, talking about feelings… I was an idiot."

"Yeah." I take a deep breath.

"I wish I could just go back and do stuff differently," he says.

This is so unfair. I haven't even been thinking about this lately. Grant hasn't been on my mind as much, because I've been working hard to do better—*be* better.

"Harry, I know I went about everything totally wrong." Grant looks at me, those piercing green eyes like raw, sharp jade. "It's just... The truth is I loved what we had. So much. I didn't want to ruin a single moment of our summer. And I was going to tell you, but then it was too late."

I know that shouldn't help, but hearing him say it...

"So stupid," he says. "I didn't want to let you down, and then what I did was even worse. I'm sorry."

It's like he took a big serrated hunter's knife and dug it into an old wound. A wound that was scabbing, maybe. A wound that doesn't even get the chance to be a scar now because it's gaping and bloody and searing.

"I don't know what to say," I tell him.

I look at him and think of everything he *was*. In a weird way, I remember valuing his affections like an achievement. If *Grant* liked me, there must be something special about me. When he left, that worth was rotten, and now it's like gold dripping from his lips—him wanting me is like nature's way of breathing life back into the shell he left. But I don't know if I want him back or just want him to want me.

"Wait." Grant stands up and holds up a finger. "One second."

I watch him go over to the cabana. He and the guys behind the counter joke about something, and he leans up against the wall, tapping his knuckles against one of the decorative surfboards while he waits, just like he always does. Always did.

Grant returns with two frozen pink drinks—frosé. He al-

ways orders the frosé during the summer, because his mom taught him that. Grant always wants to seem more grown-up than he is.

This was one of the perks of being with Grant. Because of who his dad is, he never got told no. We never got ID'd or anything. But now that perk is way less exciting because I just feel like I shouldn't be drinking frosé with Grant. It feels like a charade.

"This is a peace offering." Grant gives me one of the cups.

"Now he wants peace," I say, taking a sip.

"Still counting down to submit your USC app in the fall?" Grant says, ignoring my comment, and my heart goes *thwack*, like a bow plucked every string.

"Who knows if I'll even get in," I say without even meaning to. I'm suddenly extra aware of how the same guy sitting across from me broke my heart so badly I became a zombie for a semester.

"What do you mean? I know you will," he says with a soft smile. "You're super talented."

Ingrid Bergman didn't just get on the plane and pretend Humphrey Bogart didn't exist in Casablanca, *Harry.* The fact that I even have to remind myself of this is exactly why Grant's good looks and innate charm are so dangerous. That smile could make anyone forget anything.

I clear my throat and look down at the table.

"Well, I'm working on a new screenplay," I say.

Grant throws his hands up. "Awesome! Are you following that formula my dad was talking about?"

I shake my head. "I don't think so."

"But there's a literal formula for blockbusters, Harry," Grant says, his smile twisting into a frown. "You should do that—just to get in, at least. Just to get started."

"I just don't think it's the way," I say. "I want my characters and my writing to be something different. A success, still, sure…"

Grant shrugs. "There's a surefire way to success, Harry. Hit those beats, the hero's journey and all that."

"It's just been done before," I offer.

"And it keeps making millions."

"Well, I guess we'll see. Once I finish, I'm going to submit it to a contest to try and get a letter of recommendation," I say, again not meaning to say so much. It still comes naturally with Grant, despite my best efforts. "To stand out on my application."

Grant considers this for a second and tilts his head. "You shouldn't waste your time with some *contest*, Harry. My dad's doing all kinds of business at studios in LA. I *know* he could get you a kickass letter of rec. He's asked about you a few times."

It's so like Grant for something that monumental to come to him as an afterthought. My heart races—Grant's dad probably could get me an amazing letter of recommendation. I'm not giving up on the contest, because I need three, but this would make for a much stronger second than Mr. Yates.

"I can see the wheels turning." Grant smirks. "I'll text him later. I don't think it'd be a big deal. I mean, he got Mitch a part in a commercial without an audition or anything. You know Dad."

I do know Grant's dad. *Formidable* is the SAT word that comes to mind. Mom says people don't have to be like Grant's dad to be successful—he's that kind of hungry shark constantly on the search for blood. He spent a lot of Grant's childhood in New York and LA, working in entertainment and finance and building his company. I always wondered why he stayed in Citrus Harbor, but as soon as Grant graduated, they moved.

"You really think he'd do that?" I ask.

"I'll make sure of it, if that's what you want," he says.

"Of course it's what I want." I gesture around us. "I can't wait to get out of Citrus."

I wonder if it's a deal with the devil. What does Grant gain from this? Only, as hesitant as I am to believe it, he seems genuine. If anyone knows how much my dreams mean to me, it's Grant. Grant, who'd tell me everything he wasn't supposed to tell me about his dad's film industry deals. Grant, who listened to every imagined scenario I had and who would lie with me and trace the outlines of my daydreams, adding little sparks and details here and there.

I drink more of the frosé and feel like it's last summer all over. Wine is not the easiest thing to drink—much different from the fruity mixed "cocktails" we have at parties—but I'd gotten used to rosé with Grant and his mom. There are tricks, too. Same as drinks at parties in red plastic cups—don't smell it, just hold your breath.

"Do you ever, like, think about last summer?" Grant says, his eyes not meeting mine.

My chest sinks lower and lower until I swear there's nowhere else for it to go.

"I… Sometimes. Yeah, of course." And that felt too intimate. That felt too honest. But it's Grant and now… Now he's offering me the keys to what I've wanted for as long as I can remember.

I think about last summer way too much, probably. And I think about you way too much. I'd go back to you every time—whether I want to or not, I would.

"But not as much anymore," I quickly correct.

"I think about it all the time," Grant admits, tapping his fingers against the base of his cup. "But the past is the past, right?"

"Yeah," I say. "Okay, anyway, tell me about LA. I can't even explain to you how jealous I am that you got out. Did you have so much fun all the time?"

"You could come visit." Grant's eyes light up. "We could do whatever you want. Tour USC? Some outdoorsy stuff in Malibu? Maybe do one of those movies in the graveyard or whatever—remember when you wanted to do that?"

"Hollywood Forever Cemetery," I say, laughing into my fist.

"Whoa, I got a laugh out of you!"

"Don't get used to it," I tease, careful not to give in to the smile.

Grant claps his hands together and grins. "Well, I'm here for the whole summer."

"So, you're going to school in LA?"

"Somehow I got into UCLA," Grant laughs.

"You worked hard," I say, not even really meaning to. But Grant always did plan for his future. Taking over his dad's company, being an innovative entertainment industry mogul. He may want to play it cool, but his grades were all him.

"Thanks. So, we should—let's plan for something. How about tomorrow night?"

"I can't," I say, remembering I invited Logan to the South Harbor party. "I have plans with Hailey and Justin."

"Huh." Grant chews the inside of his cheek. "I'm surprised they're still— Well, okay, when—"

"You're surprised they're still *what*?" I set down my cup, feeling any trace of a smile disappearing.

"Nothing," Grant laughs. "I was going to say. Um, whenever you want—"

"No, what were you saying about Hailey and Justin?"

Grant sits up straight and leans closer to me, the orange-yellow glow from the sunset causing him to squint. "Look, Harry."

"Grant."

"It's just…"

"What?"

"I really need you to promise you're not going to go nuclear on me," Grant pleads.

"I can't promise anything," I say, remembering the red mist.

"Last summer…" Grant exhales and sits back bringing his fingers to his forehead, he furrows his brows and closes his eyes, as if this pains him. "When we went on that surf trip to Big Sur, Justin and this girl had a thing."

"A *thing*?" I fight to keep my voice level. "Grant. Are you telling me my best friend's boyfriend *cheated* on her last summer?"

Now the club is spinning, and my chest hurts. This can't be happening. Of all things to be compounded on Grant Kennedy's return, Justin cannot have cheated on Hailey.

"I think I will take you up on that offer to push you again," I say, feeling my cheeks go hot.

"Harry, *please*," Grant urges. "It was a long time ago, and I shouldn't have said anything. I just thought they'd have…"

"You thought they'd have broken up," I offer. "Because you thought she'd have found out by now."

"Harry, look, I know this is… Shit. I am such an idiot. But Hailey's happy, yeah?"

"She's blissfully ignorant," I argue.

"Aren't we all, in some way or another? We can't possibly solve every problem—confront every single *tiny* negative detail, we'd lose our minds." Grant reaches for my hand and I'm too shocked to pull away. He runs his thumb over my knuckles. "There might be a reason people are *blissfully* ignorant, Harry."

Good to know that hasn't changed. Grant's still not a fan of confronting negative details. Noted.

All Hailey wants is to win the Cutest Couple superlative with Justin and for them to go to college together and live happily ever after. This would devastate her. This would ruin her life.

"Harry." Grant looks me in the eye. "I mean I don't even know what happened for sure, right?"

"You don't?" I want to believe him, though I can tell he's backtracking.

"No." Grant shakes his head. "Look, let's just please forget I said anything. They're happy, right? So, in my opinion, the best way you can be a good friend is by supporting her happiness. And if Justin steps out of line or something happens, *then*…"

"Yeah," I say, slowly taking all this in. "I should let her be happy, right?"

"Her happiness is what is important," Grant agrees. "We've all done things in the past that don't define who we are."

Of course *he'd* say that. I finish my frosé in one sip. "Or *not* done things, right?"

Grant tilts his head.

"Like *not* shared major life changes? Or not properly considered how someone else felt about something?"

Grant closes his eyes. "I really—"

"But, anyway, I have to look out for Hailey first and foremost," I say, not letting him apologize again. "And do whatever will keep her happy."

Which means I'm going to keep my mouth shut. Right? She deserves to be happy. I don't want her to be miserable. And if they're good now, that's what matters.

The frosé brain freeze I'm feeling right now feels aptly timed.

"So we're going to just forget I said anything."

But how am I going to look Justin in the eye? And how am I going to just pretend nothing's wrong when Hailey talks about their future together?

"Yeah," I say. "Let's just talk about something else."

Grant launches into a funny story about some Housewives in LA and how they were at a party his dad hosted, which is totally ridiculous, and I just can't believe I'm even sitting here with him, not pushing him in the pool a second time.

And then, when we leave and we've killed another frosé each, I go to hug Grant good-night, but somehow we've fallen into an old routine and our lips nearly meet. For a moment, the way Grant remains so still and stares into my eyes, I wonder if he's hoping I won't pull away. When I do, he just smiles.

"Good night, Harry."

"Night, Grant."

EXT. CENTRAL PARK

We see Jenson and Rory walking together:

CLOSE-UP: Rory, eyes darting to and from Jenson.

Music plays: We hear MARINA's "You" playing...

SUPER: **LAST SUMMER**

MUSIC OVER

THE PARK. Rory and Jenson eat ice cream and bump shoulders, laughing.

JENSON'S APARTMENT. Jenson ignores a notification on a futuristic device—a call for Captain Warp—as Rory is in the other room.

UPPER WEST VILLAGE. Nighttime. It's raining, and Rory and Jenson are soaked. They take cover under a floral shop awning, and Jenson plucks a pink flower from the shop. He offers it to Rory, who laughs, and, for the first time, they kiss.

UPTOWN MARKET. Jenson holds two giant oranges at crotch level and pulls a face. Rory rolls his eyes—how is Jenson so immature yet so adorable?—and laughs.

THE WOODS'S TOWNHOUSE. Rory and his sisters make lemon cake in the kitchen. Jenson walks in, escorted by Ms. Woods. He's holding flowers, and Rory's younger sister beams, grabbing them. Everyone laughs.

JENSON'S APARTMENT. Jenson has to go. Rory is on the couch doing homework. The glamour and sunny feelings from the start of their relationship are seemingly gone.

PARKER'S DINER. Rory and Jenson argue over the table, and Jenson leaves.

RORY'S DORM. Rory's textbooks are open on the desk and all over his bed. We see on the TV screen: *Captain Warp saves the day.*

THE LAWN. Rory is crying.

FADE OUT.

EXT. BACK TO CENTRAL PARK, PRESENT

RORY
So that's why you were always MIA… But what happened? I thought you were in London—what are you doing here?

JENSON
The Champions Alliance finally gave me an assignment.

RORY
The Champions Alliance? You're gonna be one of them?

JENSON
Not without your help.

RORY
My help? How can *I* help *you*?

JENSON
Well, your mom's labs—The Champions Alliance seems to think The Vicious are after my genetic material so—

RORY
(can't help but laugh)
Of course. It always comes back to you.

3

CLUELESS

After walking home from Luna's last night, I sat on the beach and listened to the waves for as long as I could stay awake. I kept typing messages to Hailey and erasing them. Should I tell her? Is it worse if I do or if I don't?

I wonder how things would have been different if Grant had told me he was moving away last summer. If he'd have given me a chance to emotionally prepare for him leaving, instead of just pretending everything was fine until it was too late.

But this is different. And it's not about what I'd want or how I'd feel. Grant is right—*gee, that's a fun phrase*—I have to consider what Hailey would want.

Today, I tried my best not to think about Justin or Grant. I scrolled through social media and saw Summer Mancini's posts in LA—a USC student and vlogger I found on You-Tube, she's interning at a studio and making some top secret show with big name stars. I kept telling myself one day none of *this* will even be a big deal. That will be my life, and everything will just be better.

The rest of the day was spent watching Milly and Lottie as they smashed their video game controllers for hours on end. Lottie screamed *Hamilton* lyrics as we ate lunch, and later she gave Milly a terrifying makeover, which prompted a shouting match. Milly, with flames in her eyes and steam coming out of her ears, stomped upstairs and slammed the bathroom door. An hour later they were all giggles, lying on the couch together watching *The Baby-Sitters Club.*

All in all, a standard day in the Kensington house.

Once Mom got home from work, I stood in front of my closet and took so long to pick one silly shirt for the party, I think time might have actually gone in reverse.

Now I've just gone through the gate in Madre Cove, with Hailey in the passenger seat, and my mind is a battlefield of thoughts. Replaying that almost kiss. Panicking every so often when I remember the bombshell about Justin.

I have got to chill out. Maybe this isn't that huge of a deal. I just need some time to get over the shock. Anyway, these things are all teenage distractions I shouldn't be spending too much time on. My brain should be all screenplay, all the time.

I'm making an exception tonight since I have taken it upon myself to help the new guy find friends. After this, no parties. No drama that derails me from focusing.

One exception.

Hailey changes the song and looks to me expectantly. When I don't say anything, her jaw drops. "You *love* this song."

"Right," I say, forcing a smile. It feels like I'm lying to her.

"Hello? You know Tommy's house is on this street," Hailey says just before we miss the turn. My right tires might leave the ground for a second. "You're supposed to go *around* the curb."

"It's dark!" I shrug.

I wonder if Logan is here yet. He hasn't texted me in a couple of hours—I hope he hasn't bailed.

Justin is parking across the street as I open my door and remind myself to just relax. For the greater good. Nobody wants a Debbie Downer. All I have to do is pretend the end of my conversation with Grant didn't happen. Justin is still the same Justin he was a couple days ago when we last hung out.

"We've got your back—if we see Kennedy, we can ditch," Justin says to me, throwing his arm around Hailey. I give her a look like *you already told him?* "We can skedaddle and hit the bowling alley or something if you want."

"No way." It's hard to even be around Justin now, but I act normal. And I don't tell them I already saw on Grant's Instagram story that he has other plans. I don't want to look like I care too much. "We have to at least make an appearance. Everyone's going to be here."

Justin raises a brow at me. "Including Foster, by the way."

"I don't care if Foster is here," I tell him, and it's obvious I'm overselling it—I care a little.

"Okay, okay." He throws his hands up and lowers his voice to a whisper. "It was a one-time slipup, Harry."

My stomach lurches at the way Justin smirks. Like he's got my number or something. When it happened—when I hooked up with Justin's best friend, Foster Billings, over spring break—Justin was a safe space. So of course I didn't mind him knowing, as long as it was only him and Hailey.

There isn't anything seriously *wrong* with Foster, but he has a reputation for being a player and a class clown. We just couldn't be more different. And at least Foster agreed to keep spring break our secret. I don't even know if he's aware Justin and Hailey know. Sure, Justin is his best friend, but clearly Justin's better at keeping secrets than I would have guessed.

Now, though, knowing what Justin did? *It was a one-time slipup, Harry.* Like we bond over our impulses. We're similar because we've both had moments of weakness, and maybe that makes it all okay to him or something.

Wrong.

We're not the same.

"One time is all it takes." I roll my eyes.

We walk up to the party together, and as we do, the music gets louder until I can practically feel the bass in my skull.

"Dude, I still can't believe you pushed Grant in the pool," Justin laughs.

"I think I blacked out," I say, opening the front door.

Most of the incoming senior class showed up, plus a few groups from other schools. Tommy Stivender's house is modern, massive, and on the strip of oceanfront homes in Madre Cove that have private beaches and gates to the driveways. The wooden pool deck alone is swarming with dozens of couples dancing and girls holding their phones up to make duck faces at their selfie cameras. The way-too-green lawn sprawls out to the wooden beach access. It's like a scene from an over-the-top teen rom-com.

I shoot Logan a text, letting him know we just walked in.

I try and do a nonchalant scan of the living room, but he's nowhere to be found.

These parties used to be fun, but it's like we're stuck watching repeats. Where's the new stuff? The excitement? Small-town parties are all one and the same, really. Same people, same drama. Same, same, same. I can't wait to get out of here and just see what else there is—to go to real parties where things *happen*.

"I feel like there are some randos here tonight," Justin mumbles.

"Scary Mary came," Hailey says, pointing over to a group of girls from our school huddled over a glass bong. Scary Mary got her nickname because she went postal on our gym teacher freshman year when we had to practice running the mile. Mary felt like she shouldn't be "subjected to the chauvinistic tendencies of the patriarchy that involve gauging strength and athletic performance against a national standard." It was completely wild the way she totally flattened a soccer ball with her bare hands. Convinced me.

"I'm bored already," I say. I check my phone and see Logan has finally texted and he's almost here. "Come on, let's do a lap."

As we walk through the party—past the drug couch, the make-out cabanas, the beer pong tables, and the fire pit—before settling into a spot in the backyard, I notice the song playing. And my heart goes to putty. It's like all the oxygen is getting sucked out of my body.

This song always makes me think of Grant. During the good days, when we were just starting out and really getting to know each other. When everything was new and exciting. It's so quick and there's no warning—I'm just consumed by the memory of lying in bed while this song plays, running my hands through Grant's hair one afternoon, wearing his T-shirt after he threw me in the pool.

I'm not going to let a few unexpected hiccups ruin my summer. I can still enjoy myself at a party without thinking of Grant or obsessively wondering whether I'm a bad friend. I can pay attention to Hailey without watching Justin's eyes to see if they wander when girls walk by.

"You're not listening," Hailey says, turning from Justin to me.

"I am," I argue, shifting my focus back to Hailey. "You guys have Cutest Couple in the bag."

She and Justin *are* a cute couple. They're on the chaise across from me, and they're objectively stunning. Justin is a tan, dark-haired surf god with sharp eyes and perfect cheekbones.

"Not if Claire and Sam keep it up with their new vlogging YouTube." Hailey rolls her eyes. "I mean, it's bad enough all the girls have to take the same senior pictures with those ugly black dresses and pearls. And nobody stands out in the swim team photo. Our only chance to express ourselves is with our senior superlative."

And of *course*, to Hailey, expressing who she is involves Justin.

"You guys will get it," I repeat. "Nobody is going to vote for Claire and Sam over you."

As long as they don't know... I push away the thought quickly before it can fully form.

"I just don't want to blend in." Hailey blinks. Justin squeezes her shoulder. "The senior yearbook is *forever*."

"We have an entire summer before we vote, so don't worry about it," I suggest. I don't know why they care so much about a yearbook. Nobody looks at them after we graduate and move on to the real world.

"Maybe we need to take cute couple photos at Disney World," Hailey mumbles. "With, like, the Chipmunks?"

My phone beeps.

GRANT: Eric and I need a movie rec. You're the only one I trust

Grant's little brother, Eric, will only watch shooters and war dramas. Anyway, this is not our new normal—he doesn't offer up a letter of recommendation and instantly become my BFF.

Nice try, Grant. I frown and type back.

ME: You don't trust Google?

GRANT: Oh come on, you're the expert

ME: Since when are you texting me?

GRANT: Since we're friends now

GRANT: I thought?

ME: Friends?

I send the GIF of Winona Ryder making confused faces at the Screen Actors Guild Awards.

"Are you so stoked for summer?" I hear the voice behind me and almost jump.

Cue the *Jaws* theme song.

I should be used to this song and dance, but I still sigh—a long, deep sigh—as Foster and Justin bump fists and Hailey avoids eye contact, fighting a laugh. Traitors.

Foster always has to come bother me, and tonight he's soaking wet. He reaches up to run his hand through his long dirty blond hair, flexing his biceps and stretching so the waist of his swim shorts slides a little lower than the deep V beneath his abs.

"Smooth, Foster." I roll my eyes, pocketing my phone.

"Come on, Kensy," he says, flashing that crisp white smile that pops against his tan.

Ever since middle school, he's taken my last name—Kensington—and turned it into this weirdly flirtatious nickname that absolutely nobody uses except him. I half think he does it to see how I react, which is why I no longer even blink at it.

"I saw Neptune's is playing old movies," Foster says, smirking. "A dark theater, just us… You could get whatever you want from the concession stand or, you know, we could share—"

"How decent of you," I mock, though it never fails to make me blush when he does this in front of Justin and Hailey. "But I'm not really in a *Rebel Without a Cause* kinda mood."

"If you're insulting me by comparing me to James Dean…" Foster throws his hands up.

What does Foster really want, anyway? Does he just think a little pointless flirty banter is fun? It's like he *enjoys* wasting time.

"Does Tommy put nail polish in the punch?" I ask the group, trying to end this little routine.

Foster's eyes go wide. "Don't disrespect the punch, Tarantino."

"That's not even—" I'm obviously much more of an Ephron. Though Foster *does* give me an idea, so I roll my eyes and exhale.

ME: Eric would prob like Once Upon A Time in Hollywood

It's only a movie recommendation. And it's more for Eric, anyway. Grant might take it as something else—like the start of us being friends again—but it's only one subjective suggestion. It means nothing.

I put away my phone just as Penelope Thomas walks by us. She's honestly the last person I expected to see tonight. She's dressed in denim shorts and a flowy top—way different from her usual buttoned-up outfits—and her long braids bounce around her bare brown shoulders.

"Penny," I say, stopping her, grateful to see someone who I don't know a life-changing secret about and who isn't trying to flirt with me.

Penny did drama club in freshman and sophomore year as part of her plan to have enough extracurricular activities to get into Harvard. I wrote the plays, and she managed the stage. We both can't wait to move to bigger cities, do bigger things. She's a thousand times smarter than me and *way* more responsible, which is why I'm surprised she's here.

"I thought you didn't do parties?"

"My mom made me," Penny laughs. "One of her parenting books swears I need this."

"It can be fun," I say with a smile.

Penny awkwardly fiddles with the thin rose gold ring on her finger and shrugs. "Well, ever since Roger and I broke up, I've been meaning to become better at...'going out.'"

I still can't believe she and Roger broke up after Spring Fling. Just goes to show dating as teens is seriously not realistic, even if you're a mega genius and badass like Penny.

"Are you doing all right?" Foster says, and Hailey and I exchange looks. I almost think there's sincerity in his question.

"I'm doing great," Penny says. "I just want to find a nice guy, though. You know? Like, look at you two." She smiles at Justin and Hailey, and suddenly Penny is no longer distracting me from the secret I know but magnifying it.

"I'm sure Harvard guys are the best." I smile.

"I hope so, but that's a while away. I wouldn't mind having someone to watch documentaries with before then." Penny seems to drift with this thought.

If only I knew someone who liked watching documentaries.

Perfectly timed, out of the corner of my eye, I see Logan open the front door and peek in. The way he eyes everyone and walks so cautiously makes me instantly warm inside, which I don't understand at all. I wave him over, and he looks beyond relieved to see a familiar face. I don't blame him—I just saw a sophomore riding a hoverboard down the hallway.

When Logan reaches us, he shoves one hand into his pocket and waves with the other. "Hi."

"Logan," I say, patting his shoulder. "This is Hailey and her boyfriend, Justin, and Foster. And *this* is Penny."

Penny's eye twitches in my direction. Am I being too obvious?

"I met Logan earlier at the beach club," I explain.

"Nice to meet you guys," Logan says, smiling and rocking back on his heels. "This is quite the party. I can see I clearly was sheltered during high school."

Hailey raises a brow. "You're in college?"

"Well, I just graduated." Logan nods. "I'm starting college in the fall."

"Lucky," Foster says.

"What are you going to study?" Penny tilts her head and I stand up straighter because I realize my gut instinct was right. The second she said she wanted a guy to watch documentaries with, I knew. And they're hitting it off.

This is perfect. Something sort of exciting and an ideal distraction—I can take my mind off Justin and Hailey and focus on a worthy pursuit, helping Penny get her documentary buddy and helping Logan make a friend.

Technically, Penny won't be focusing on a high school guy either, since Logan is going to college. So I'm really not even betraying my own morals here by setting them up.

"I'm going to get everyone drinks," I say. "What do you want?"

"Oh, er—" Logan looks taken aback. Maybe I shouldn't have jumped in before he answered her. Did I kill their vibe?

Foster takes the opportunity to go play ring of fire, while Logan says he'll just have a beer and Justin does this weird bro thing in agreement with Logan, which means, I guess, that they've bonded. Hailey says she'll come with me and tells Penny she'll pick a very special drink for her.

While we walk away, I stop for a moment to admire how cute they are. Logan, in his little short-sleeve button-down, standing awkwardly with a solid three feet between him and Penny. Justin looms over them and leads the conversation, and nobody makes eye contact.

The beginning is always the sweetest.

The warm fuzzies don't last long, though. I'm unusually uncomfortable with Hailey. I felt it in the car, too. It's like any second I'm going to explode and drop this earth-shattering thing. Or I won't, and she'll never forgive me if she finds out.

"Do you think sparks are flying?" I say as we round the corner to the kitchen.

"Probably the gremlins outside sparking up doobies," Hailey says, grabbing a lollipop from a bowl on the counter.

"Not those sparks," I say, rolling my eyes and grabbing plastic cups. As I try to figure out the keg, I can't even hide my grin. "I mean sparks between Penny and Logan. I think she likes him already. I mean, he's only here for the summer, but he just broke up with some girl—"

"Whoa." Hailey's eyes are wide as she jams the lollipop into her mouth and pushes it against the inside of her cheek. "I wonder... Do you think she'll make the move, or will he?"

I fill the cups with beer and contemplate as Hailey begins to pour vodka and some kind of juice into three cups.

"We'll just see what happens between them," I say, grinning. "But we have to play it cool. You know Penny will bolt if she knows what we're up to."

"Now *we're* up to something?" Hailey frowns. "You know how I feel about being up to something."

"You love being up to something," I say, turning from the keg to Hailey. "And duh, you're, like, an accessory now. You know everything. And get this—Logan likes dinosaurs. You know how anti-extinction Penny is."

"Okay, so why are you being weird tonight?" Hailey deadpans.

I stand up straight and frown. "I'm not. Am I being weird? I started taking these multivitamin gummies, but maybe there are side effects."

Is this the moment? It can't be. This can't be the moment I'm forced to ruin Hailey's relationship and her summer and, frankly, her entire senior year. She'll be devastated. But I can't quite read her face, and she's my absolute best friend, so maybe I owe her—

"Oh, that could be it." Hailey wags her lollipop at me. "Is it about Grant?"

"Yes," I say quickly. I sigh emphatically. "I'm really shaken up about him being back and all."

"Don't worry." Hailey smiles. "He's in the past."

"Right," I say. "And the past should definitely stay in the past."

Hailey brightens. "One hundred percent. The past is the past for a reason. Remember that book we read for Walsh? Where he thinks he can repeat the past and then that lady got hit by a car?"

It's not the time to bring up the irrelevance of *The Great Gatsby*, so I just nod. Hailey's right—the past is the past, and she's clearly happy living in the present, so for now, I'll keep my mouth shut.

When we get back to the group, Penny is nowhere to be found. Logan and Justin are all buddy-buddy, looking through something on Logan's phone, which has a Pikachu sticker on the back of it.

"Where did Penny go?" I ask.

"Bathroom," Justin says, not even looking up.

"You can't let her go to the bathroom alone at a party like this," I say, looking around and setting our drinks down on the windowsill. "She could end up in the middle of a cocaine hit!"

Hailey assures me she'll go get Penny, and I thank her, wondering what Justin was thinking.

"So, Harry..." Logan looks to me and thanks me for the beer before offering a gentle smile. "Are all the parties this massive here?"

I remember how he said he doesn't go to parties much, so I quickly nod. "Yeah. But you know, Penny doesn't like parties. Guess you guys have that in common."

"I just wasn't exactly cool enough for parties," Logan muses, and Justin squeezes his shoulder. "It's okay! I didn't really want to go, anyway. I was a total nerd. I spent more nights reading Agatha Christie or playing *L.A. Noire*."

"I love Agatha Christie," I say, but I'm making it about me, so I try to redirect. "Hailey went with me to the new movie, though she was annoyed because Penny actually spoiled the ending for everyone in AP Lang—she's a genius."

"Penny is totally smart." Justin nods. "And Hailey was totally pissed."

"So pissed," I agree. This whole selling Penny thing would be a lot easier if Penny were here. I look back toward the bathroom but nothing.

Finally, the bathroom door opens, and there's a sliver of hope this conversation can be saved. Just as Penny and Hailey are making their way back to us, the dumbass sophomore on the hoverboard zips up the hallway, knocking his arm on a doorknob and flying off the board, his foot kicking it right into the wall so it rebounds up, directly into Hailey. It's like watching a train wreck in slow motion. Penny's mouth flies open as she reaches out just a little too late. Hailey hits the deck, and we're all rushing over to her.

The party was doomsday, but for Logan and Penny, there is lemonade to be made from these lemons yet—I hadn't even taken a sip of my drink, so I volunteered to drive us back up north toward civilization. Penny thought we could all take refuge at the Italian ice stand by Sun & Surf.

I don't know how he managed it, but Logan *skateboarded* to Madre Cove. It had to have taken him at least twenty minutes, and that's if he pushed really hard. I made him toss his board in the trunk and sit in the back with Penny.

Hailey hadn't had anything to drink either, so she drove Justin's truck. Now we're all regrouping in the parking lot, where it smells like fresh asphalt and palm trees filter the fluorescent street lights.

"How do you feel?" I say to Hailey.

"Much better now that my ears aren't ringing from that S&M music," she says.

Penny cocks her head. "I think it was EDM."

Justin kisses Hailey's forehead. I stop myself from questioning the authenticity of his gestures—that won't help me move on and leave the past behind us.

The stand is super busy at all hours, which is a blessing and a curse. It's nice that it's been open our whole lives and will likely never close, except for the off-season, but it takes forever to get to the window sometimes. Especially tonight, when practically the entire middle school is here.

"Penny, I think we should have a do-over night," I say. "That party was tragic."

"Eh," Penny resigns. "I feel like I got the full experience. I should honestly probably just go home."

"I told you she doesn't like parties either," I laugh to Logan, who seems a little out of it. Hailey and Justin are getting really handsy behind me, so I keep my eyes set forward as we slowly step up in the line.

Eventually, after a long and arduous wait in silence, we get to the window and place our orders. I go for the classic lemon flavor and add custard, while Logan gets cherry. Penny doesn't want any, and Justin and Hailey decide to share a giant chocolate and pineapple combination something or other. My chest tightens, and I remind myself they're *going* to share things. Nothing has actually changed, apart from my opinion of Justin, which I'm keeping to myself.

When we finally have our dessert, we sit at one of the picnic tables, and I search in the silence for a topic—anything at all—to make this more fun.

Of course, my ridiculous brain wants to think about how it felt to come here and share a spoon with Grant last summer.

"Foster texted that the party got a noise complaint," Justin laughs. "The guys are all watching some surf doc at Martin's house."

Logan points his spoon at Justin. "I'm learning how to surf. Maybe you can help me out. I suck so bad."

Oh no, I think, *please—talk about anything but surfing.*

"Totally, dude." Justin nods. "You can come out with us one morning. We'll get you all set up when it's nice and glassy."

Why do people say it's better the devil you know? Wouldn't anyone rather not know the devil at all?

"Do all of you guys surf?" Logan asks, looking right at me. "Harry? Do you?"

"No way," I say. "But Hailey used to be really into boogie boarding."

We all erupt into laughter, and Hailey flashes beet red, remembering the time she was boogie boarding in eighth grade and her bathing suit bottoms flew off and floated away, never to be found. It took until sophomore year for her to be able to laugh about it.

"Shut up," Hailey laughs into her hands.

"Inside joke," Penny assures Logan while patting Hailey on the shoulder.

"So, why don't you surf?" Logan says to me, and I find myself a little annoyed that he's trying to be so inclusive. I appreciate the gesture—he probably doesn't want to make me feel left out since I invited him—but I want him to try and talk to Penny more.

"I just suck at it," I say, standing up and grabbing my empty cup. "Okay, guys. You have fun. I'm going to detox after being around who-knows-what at that party."

Logan leaps up, too, grabbing his cup. "I'll actually just follow you to your car and get my board. I should probably be going, too."

"Why?" I ask. "You should stay here. Have fun! I'll go grab your board."

Logan surveys the table—everyone's eyes are darting between the two of us. "I have an early day tomorrow. I had a lot of fun, though." He says it to Justin, Hailey, and Penny. "Here, I'll grab that for you." He holds his hand out for my trash. When I give it to him, he stacks the cups and starts toward the garbage bin.

"Hey, guys, Roger and Ty are over there." Penny points to the line. "I'm going to go say hello."

"Are you sure you guys don't want to hang out longer?" I say.

"Yeah, maybe play *Super Smash Bros* at my place?" Justin grins toward Logan.

"As if." Hailey hangs her head. "Not *Super Smash Bros*."

As Penny gets up and says her goodbyes, Hailey and Justin exchange confused glances—it seems like she can't get away from our table fast enough to go talk to her ex-boyfriend. I guess I can't really blame her. Things have quickly turned awkward.

Logan smiles. "Thank you, but I'm honestly exhausted. I seriously appreciate the offer, though. And a *Super Smash Bros* showdown is in our future."

"Okay, I'll text you guys. I hope you feel better," I offer, reliving the moment Hailey got wrecked by a hoverboard.

Following me down the sidewalk to my car, I hear Logan's footsteps and feel the irritation crawling up the back of my neck like the prickly legs on a spider. He's cute, sure, but does he think he's better than Penny just because he's about to be a college guy or something?

I'm about to pop the trunk and then I set my hand on it, turning around. "Do you want a ride home?"

"Uh…" Logan scratches the back of his neck and shoves his phone into his pocket. "Nah, it's okay, I can skate home."

"It's going to take you forever," I say, pulling my hand off the trunk and clicking the car unlocked. "Come on, I'll just drop you off."

Logan squints. "What's wrong?"

"What do you mean?" I ask.

"I can tell you're, like, annoyed or something," Logan offers, feet firmly planted and both hands in his pockets now. "I honestly don't mind skating home; I don't want you to go out of your way."

"I don't care about dropping you off," I say.

"So what is it you care about?" Logan says.

Who knew he's so sensitive? I'm hardly even annoyed, and I can't be showing it that bad. After opening my car door, I slide in. Once the key is in the ignition, I notice myself pouting, so I straighten up and put on some music while I wait for Logan to give in and join me in the car.

"It's super obvious you're pissed," Logan says, sliding into the passenger seat and shutting the door. "Was it something I did?"

I don't feel like getting into it with him right now, but I turn to face him and shrug. "You know, it's not a huge deal. I'm tired, and I have a headache. It's just…"

"Just?"

"I mean, I invited you to come hang out with my friends and then you bail," I say. "You said your night was documentaries and meat loaf."

"Don't knock documentaries and meat loaf," Logan says. "And I'm not bailing. You're leaving, so I figured it was fine to leave? I didn't realize you guys used time cards—should I go clock back in?"

"You don't have to be such a jerk about it," I huff, turning to face the wheel. "You didn't have to lead poor Penny on all night just to skip out at the first chance. I'm sure you'd love to be ditched for leftover meat loaf."

Logan sighs. "Again with the meat loaf. And I was *not* leading Penny on. What are you even talking about?"

"Come on," I say, hands gripping the wheel. "It's obvious you two were vibing and now what? She's probably wondering what she did wrong."

"Harry," Logan says slowly. "I don't think there was any kind of *vibe* between Penny and me."

"Of course not," I say. "Because what? She wasn't fast enough for you? Unbelievable. You should know she's really sweet." I'm seriously selling this thing, considering I could count on my hand the number of times I've talked to Penny in the last year.

"You shouldn't treat people like that," I say, resolute as I put the car into Reverse and start to back out. "So yeah, I guess I'm a little annoyed, but it's whatever."

"I can guarantee you Penny and I were not *vibing* like that," Logan says, staring out the window. "You're getting awfully worked up over nothing right now."

I groan as we hit a red light and I tell Logan I need him to give me directions to his house. I hate when people tell me I'm getting worked up. He points right, and we turn. "How do you know you weren't vibing?"

Logan snorts at this. "She's not exactly my type."

"Oh, real nice, Logan," I say, slowing for a stop. "And what's *that* supposed to mean? You should probably take a sec to think of a real good response since this is, like, a really good friend of mine you're talking about."

I can't believe this guy. Only twelve hours ago I was sure

he was a total babe with Nerdy Nice Guy Syndrome, but now it turns out he's a total jerk.

"Well, it means she's not my type," Logan says, condescendingly slow.

"And what *is* your type?" I hiss.

"Um," Logan laughs. "A male, probably. First and foremost."

Oh my God. I almost hit a trash can because I take my eyes off the road to make awkward eye contact with Logan, my jaw completely dropped.

"Are you serious?" I focus on the road and wince—I wonder about the texts from Annie ♥ but know now isn't the time to bring it up. "Oh shit. I am so sorry, Logan. I can't believe I didn't even think…"

"Yeah," Logan says. "I sort of thought you'd have some kind of gaydar or something along those lines."

And it makes total sense now why Logan was so comfortable with Penny but didn't make any moves. He never intended to make any passes at her. Did that mean he wanted to make passes at me? I quickly glance in the rearview mirror to check my appearance.

"I'm right here." Logan points to a house on the right. He only lives a couple of houses down from me. How weird.

"Logan," I say, slowing to a stop by his driveway and hanging my head. "I really am sorry I kind of went ballistic. I just thought you were ditching Penny on purpose or something."

"Nope," Logan laughs and gets out. He grabs his skateboard from the trunk and comes back around to the passenger door. "I really do have plans early in the morning. But thank you for inviting me tonight. You were right—your friends are awesome."

He offers a tight-lipped smile and waves before closing the door and walking up to the house.

When I get home, I call Hailey, but I get sent to voicemail. My sisters are both at friends' houses, and Mom is at book club (i.e., wine club). Not only am I a total jerk on so many levels, I'm completely alone, which makes everything feel a hundred times worse.

I lie down in bed and scroll through the apps on my phone. There's not much new or exciting, and I definitely don't feel like looking through everyone's Instagram stories from the party.

Maybe I'll go downstairs and put on a scary movie. That'll distract me from tonight's unfortunate events for sure.

I do have messages from Grant lingering in my notifications. I feel like if I click on them, I'm putting my foot in quicksand, knowing how it'll suck me in. Still, I read them.

GRANT: This feels like such a Harry movie already

GRANT: Either you're ignoring me or you're at Stivender's...

GRANT: Let me know if you need a ride home?

GRANT: I only meant like if you drink. OK I'll let my quadruple text end here. The whole thread is blue.

GRANT: Blue on my end, obviously gray on yours. OK now I'm done

My cheeks burn, and I realize I'm smiling at my phone. I blink, batting away the notion that these texts are in any way cute or endearing or funny.

My fingers hover over the keyboard. Should I respond? I don't actually have anything else to say, and it'd just give him mixed signals but—

Somehow, my phone slips between my fingers. I catch it just before it hits me in the face, but along the way I've hit a couple random keys and, judging by the swoosh sound coming from the speaker, I've sent the key smash text.

ME: Us

Really? Of all the letters my fingers could accidentally hit. *Us?* The one word I wouldn't send to Grant, because it's the one thing that definitively doesn't exist.

GRANT: Are you drunk texting me?

ME: No, I didn't mean to send that

GRANT: Right

ME: I didn't. My phone slipped out of my hand when I was reading your messages

GRANT: Oh. Well what did you mean to say?

ME: I didn't mean to say anything

GRANT: You were going to leave me on read?

It's a good thing Grant is going to work for his dad in entertainment. It'd be a shame for him to waste his talent of cornering people with their own words.

GRANT: Were you at Stivender's?

ME: Yeah, we left early

GRANT: What are you going to do for the rest of the night?

GRANT: My money is on Meg Ryan

ME: I was thinking a scary movie, actually

GRANT: "You like scary movies?"

He follows up with a Ghostface GIF, as if I wouldn't get the reference.

ME: You're hilarious

GRANT: But really, what's wrong?

ME: What? Nothing

GRANT: You only watch scary movies when you need to be distracted

I exhale.

GRANT: If we were friends you could talk to me about it. Whatever it is

I don't really want to talk about it, but I guess a friend—
one who knows me—doesn't sound horrible right now. Just
this once.

Like muscle memory, I start a FaceTime.

Grant picks up almost instantly, wearing a gray hoodie
with his hair messy on top of his head. I recognize the plaid
pillows he's lying against.

"What's up?" he says, offering a huge smile.

I settle into my bed and feel my own grin. "Okay, so did
you guys watch the whole thing?"

"Absolutely, even though I'm not a huge fan of Leonardo,"
Grant says.

"What? Are you kidding me?"

"Overrated. Brad Pitt stole the show, come on," Grant
scoffs. "Though I am going to have to make sure Eric doesn't
get a flamethrower."

"Such a good part," I say and, just like that—with a genuine laugh and those welcoming green eyes that know me so
well—I'm able to put aside our history and wonder if this new
Grant Kennedy might be the real deal, after all.

INT. UNIVERSITY COFFEE SHOP

Rory is waiting by the window, tapping his foot and watching his phone like a hawk.

>   RORY
>   *(to himself)*
>   Come on, Jenson, where are you?

Rory's name is called, and he grabs his coffee from the counter and walks outside.

EXT. UNIVERSITY CAMPUS

SKIP STANLEY is sitting on the steps in front of the coffee shop. He's wearing an R2-D2 T-shirt and takes out his earbuds when he sees Rory.

Rory doesn't notice Skip and keeps walking.

CLOSE-UP. Rory glances down at his phone.

        SKIP
Rory!

CLOSE-UP. Rory stops.

WIDE SHOT. The university lawn. Rory turns around and
looks up at Skip on the steps.

        RORY
Skip?

        RORY (V.O.)
Skip Stanley. Graduated with me from Empire Tech
High School. Apart from being lab partners a couple
times a semester, we don't talk much.

        SKIP
Um. Listen, I need to talk to you. See, the thing is… I'm
a university-level agent with Future Defense and—

Skip is disheveled, with messy brunette hair and one of his
Converse untied.

        RORY
A "university-level agent" with Future Defense?

        SKIP
Okay, fine, I'm an intern. And—

Police sirens sound, and Rory looks over his shoulder—oh no…

WIDE SHOT. The lawn. Skip stands up.

MEDIUM SHOT. Rory looks down at his phone.

CLOSE-UP. TEXT FROM JENSON: *Change of plans. The Vicious are robbing a bank*

> RORY
> Sorry, Skip, I actually have to go.

CLOSE-UP. Skip looks concerned.

> SKIP
> Look, actually, Mr. Wilson wants me to make sure you don't—

> RORY
> Mr. Wilson? Like, Quick Circuit?

Rory's phone beeps again.
TEXT FROM JENSON: *Can you call me ASAP??*

> RORY
> I really have to go, I'm sorry.

> SKIP
> I still need to talk to you!

4

DEFINITELY, MAYBE

During summertime, the living's *supposed* to be easy. I keep reminding myself of this as I close my driver door and my flip-flops slap against the pavement of the high school parking lot.

I wouldn't be at the school over break if it weren't for Hailey, but the swim camp happens during weekday mornings and after the middle schoolers go home, the counselors get free lunch which means Hailey can give me food and we can work on our tans together.

I feel like a terrible, awful friend for keeping Justin's secret from Hailey, and I'm not exactly proud of the way things went with Logan. The most shocking development has to be my born-again friendship with Grant, though.

Sometimes I wonder what it'd be like if my life was a movie. Would the audience be rooting for me, or would they think I'm just the worst? Do I think I am?

I've gone over the Justin thing a thousand times in my head

this morning and read conflicting articles on *Teen Vogue* and *Seventeen* about friends' boyfriends cheating and moving on from infidelity. One thing I've learned is that it isn't my call if they can get past this. It's Hailey's.

So I'm going to tell her today. Probably in the car after we leave the pool, then we can hit a drive-through and get comfort snacks.

I exhale and approach the school—an "open concept" campus just a few blocks from the ocean that's lined with palm trees.

I make my way through the senior courtyard, which is bright and airy with decorative surfboards lining the walkway. Every year, the seniors all decorate and sign a board—it's like leaving a legacy.

My mind is on overdrive right now imagining Hailey's reaction. And what will senior year even look like after I tell her about Justin? Maybe this could be a good thing for us down the line—instead of going to school with Justin, she could move to LA with me like we used to dream about as middle schoolers.

Crap, I think, *I need to actually finish my screenplay or I might not even get in to USC or move to LA at all.*

My chest is tight, and I feel like I'm not able to catch my breath.

"Finally," Hailey shouts as I tug on the gate to the pool and toss my bag onto one of the chairs. She runs over to me, her hair soaking wet. "Sorry for missing your call last night."

"It's okay. To be honest, I ended up FaceTiming with Grant for like two hours," I admit. "We just caught up. It was purely innocent, and he honestly seems to be...better."

"Uh-huh." Hailey narrows her eyes, taking this in, but doesn't say anything else.

Hailey leads me over to the foldout table up against the wire fence. I wave to a couple of the other girls in our grade who are counselors this year with Hailey. They're all wrapped in towels, stringy chlorinated hair drying in the sun as they eat their sandwiches.

"Dude, Justin thinks Logan is going to be his new best friend," Hailey says, grabbing a sub and a bag of jalapeño chips. "But it was kind of weird at the end, right?"

I pull a Styrofoam cup from the stack and fill it with fruit punch. "You mean before or after I was a total jerk and went in on him for not falling head over heels in love with Penny?"

"You did?" Hailey frowns. "Um, yeah, after that…?"

"He proceeded to tell me he's gay."

"I *did* think he was more into you than Penny," Hailey says, seemingly unfazed.

I fix my plate, and we sit on the edge of the pool with our legs dangling in the water.

"I'm such a doofus," I finally say, taking a bite.

Hailey doesn't say anything, just continues eating as the sun beats down on us. The air smells like fruit juice, sunscreen, and chlorine, and some of the girls are throwing Swedish Fish at each other as they dance to a rap song under the pavilion. As Hailey brings her cup to her mouth, I notice she's drawn a sun on her wrist with a Sharpie. She's very into experimenting with possible tattoos for when she turns eighteen. Before I can comment on her newest idea, she gasps.

"So maybe you should find out if he is," Hailey says brightly, like she just realized an award-winning idea. "If he is into you, I mean. Should I check my horoscope app?"

"This does not call for a horoscope," I protest, setting my cup down on the cement.

"Everything does," Hailey says, incredibly matter-of-fact. "Don't tell me it has to do with Grant. There's a sweet new guy who is actually nice and seems caring and thoughtful and funny and—"

"Logan's hardly interested after last night." I hold up a hand, chewing on my sandwich. "And to be fair, Grant and I are only friends. Plus, his dad is going to get me an amazing letter of recommendation."

"Oh, now you're *friends*?" Hailey clearly isn't interested in hearing the possibilities regarding Grant's growth as a human being. "I just don't really want to see you hurt like before."

"I know," I say. "I remember."

Because nobody forgets their first heartbreak.

"I can't believe I was so stupid"—I quickly raise a finger—"about Logan."

Hailey laughs and pulls open her bag of chips. "I have to admit, when you first said you invited him to the party, I thought it was because you wanted to flirt with him."

"He was literally naked and stuffed into a locker," I say with an eye roll. "Do you think I'm so incapable of doing something selfless? Besides, I was trying to get him and Penny together for both of their sakes."

"I think you can be selfless!" Hailey counters. "Maybe just not when it comes to boys?"

"Fair enough," I agree. "Well, I think I need to try and

apologize to him, right? I thought I should text him but then again, maybe I should do it in person."

Hailey nods. "You know where to find him."

"Right."

Hailey swipes on her phone and reads her horoscope aloud. She skips the part for singles and jumps to the section for couples, scoffing when she finds it's about lovers going through a rocky transit. "Some days I'm convinced it's for someone else. I mean, things are going so well. Justin and I were looking into off-campus housing for college because—"

"You're moving in together?" I blink. Just when I thought it couldn't get more *Invasion of the Body Snatchers*...

Nobody tells you that once your best friend gets a boyfriend, she's no longer *your* best friend, she's *his* girlfriend. It's all Justin, all the time—every thought, every decision, every plan.

"Well, that makes it sound so official." Hailey sets her phone down and I can tell she's annoyed I'm not fully enthusiastic about this idea. "It's not that big of a deal."

I sit up. "Well, Hailey, it's just..."

The secret is bubbling up in my throat. I don't want to reveal it now. Not here, with Hailey's teammates just yards away. But it's coming up like word vomit.

"Harry, please," Hailey groans. "I know you have strong opinions about dating or teenage guys or whatever, but I really love Justin. A lot. And you know you're my person, but he's important to me, too. Can't you just support me? Please?"

I swallow hard and nod. *Yes, Hailey, I can support you.*

"Of course I support you," I say, still nodding. "So, what are the options like?"

"My favorite is this old house they remodeled and turned

into apartments." She smiles. "It actually kind of looks like Books by the Sea on the outside—like a cottage vibe."

Holy shit. Books by the Sea. I totally forgot about the summer job I'm starting soon.

My mom said I had to get a summer job to learn a better sense of responsibility. I had no argument there. Practically everyone else works or volunteers, and I'd be grateful to have the extra money and start building my résumé.

I wanted to work at Peach's with Hailey, but they didn't have any other spots. And as much as I'd love nothing more than to work the box office, Neptune's Theater has the worst hours for summer hires—all mega late shifts. The last thing I want is to become nocturnal or something.

Then I got lucky and happened to get a bookseller job at Books by the Sea. I've been going there since I can remember, and it's a small town, so we know the owner well.

At first I was way nervous about working in a bookstore. I mean, I don't read *a lot* for pleasure—I'd personally rather watch a movie or something. Though sometimes a book by the pool or at the beach is pretty nice.

Anyway, I basically talked myself into being stoked once I remembered Meg Ryan's cute little bookshop in *You've Got Mail*. Still, as excited as I am to have a job and learn new skills, it's just a few hours per week so I can focus on my script.

Though I guess the fact that I forgot about my summer job goes to show Mom might be right about the whole responsibility thing.

"Why do you look like that?"

"I completely spaced." I sigh, dropping my head into my hands.

"Grant really—"

"It's not Grant," I say and then catch myself.

"Well, then what is it?"

Shit. I should have agreed with her. Except the real thing that's going to ruin my summer is this new knowledge about Justin—I wish I never found out. Does *that* make me a bad friend?

"Logan," I scramble. "I was such an asshole."

"Well, you can say sorry next time you see him at the club if it's bothering you that much," Hailey notes, waving a chip toward me. "Horoscope?"

"I don't need a horoscope!" I insist, knowing whatever advice the stars have for me will probably not make me feel better. "And it's not bothering me *that* much. It's just that he's new and…"

"So cute," Hailey says with a suggestive eyebrow wiggle. "And you know what else?"

"What?"

"He's not Grant," Hailey says pointedly.

Right.

I turn my attention to my phone, and I'm mindlessly scrolling through my Instagram timeline when one post stops me in my tracks.

"Hailey, what the hell is this?"

I hold up my phone to show her Penny's Instagram stories. Not only is she with Roger—her *ex*-boyfriend—but she's planning a summer of college tours. Penny. Who has *always* been obsessed with going to Harvard.

"She's considering the West Coast? No, what happened to Harvard?"

Hailey lifts her shoulders. "She must be going for Roger." As she chews her cheek, her eyes suddenly go wide. "Are they back together? They won't win Cutest Couple, right? They had that gnarly breakup, after all."

"She's going to win Most Likely To Be President." I wave her worries away and blink at the story. "But she wants Harvard, she always has. She can't change her life for a guy."

"If she loves him…"

I don't know what I'm expecting and I don't even really know what I'm doing, but my fingers are practically on autopilot as I text Penny.

ME: Omg I just saw your IG stories, you're looking at schools in CA?!

PENNY: Yes!! Who knows, maybe we'll both be Trojans!

A slightly unfortunate mascot. But wait. This can't be happening. USC is so selective, they probably won't take two kids from Citrus Harbor High, and all my hard work would be for nothing—this entire summer is dedicated to winning this competition so I have a better shot at getting in.

ME: That would be awesome! I thought you were totally into Harvard tho?

Penny types and then stops. And then she types some more. The waiting feels unbearable—like a hundred years have passed, when really it's probably been ten seconds.

PENNY: Oh, nothing is set in stone. Harvard would still be my top pick, but I'm just going to widen my application pool and see what happens. ☺

ME: Nice! ☺

"Oh, my effing God," I say calmly, holding the phone up for Hailey.

Once she's done reading, she deadpans, "What's the big deal exactly? She just said nothing's set in stone."

"She's *applying*," I cry. "She's smarter than me by, like, a gazillion IQ points, she killed her SAT, and she has every extracurricular known to man. I'd pick Penny over me in a *heartbeat*. Penny is amazing in literally every way. If Penny applies to USC, she'll be the Citrus Harbor student who will get admitted, while the others"—I point to myself—"will be rejected."

"They could admit more than one," Hailey offers.

"They *could*," I say. "But they won't. USC was already a reach for me!"

"You still have all your creative stuff and your letters," she says. "That gives you an edge! Don't stress about it. Just do your thing, and trust it will work out."

Trust it will work out… Uh yeah, it'll work out if I can manage to kick some serious ass with my creative materials. But if I can't, no amount of "trust" is going to set me apart from Penny Thomas. If she gets in, it's because she worked hard and she didn't make dumb choices like me, which is an even tougher pill to swallow.

"I think you're being a *little* dramatic," Hailey says.

Me? Never.

"I'm gonna go lay out while Justin surfs." Hailey flips her hair over her shoulder. "Want to come?"

More time with Justin is the last thing I want right now. And Hailey means well, but she's dismissing how big of a deal this is, and I'm not loving this feeling.

I open a text from Grant. We're not texting 24-7 or anything, but we're on more normal terms. He'll send me something funny or ask me about a movie.

While this friendship with Grant is a fresh start and I am anything but certain about it, I can't deny it's much more appealing than being around Justin or love-obsessed Hailey. Plus, the fact that Penny might be applying means I seriously need that letter of recommendation from one of Mr. Kennedy's connections.

ME: What are you doing today?

GRANT: Just got done golfing and was gonna nap haha why wanna do something?

"I can't," I say to Hailey, my eyes on my phone as I quickly type back. "I'm— Um, I have to watch Lot today."

Hailey nods, and as I make plans with Grant I wonder when it became so easy to lie to her.

EXT. ROOFTOP—LOWER MANHATTAN

     NEWSCASTER (V.O.)
We have just gotten intel that Volt has struck again, this
time attempting to rob a bank in the Financial District.

We PAN to see Rory and Captain Warp, watching as the
authorities release the civilians.

     NEWSCASTER (V.O.)
Captain Warp was able to save all hostages, though
Volt did escape with a currently undetermined amount
of gold and cash.

     RORY
Volt has gotten a lot stronger.

Captain Warp nods, removing his helmet and dropping his
shield.

JENSON
Yeah, I know.

NEWSCASTER (V.O.)
Breaking news! Reports of a break-in at Woods
Industries—The Python was attempting to steal
confidential nanotechnology. The Champions Alliance
has captured The Python, who is now in high-security
lockdown.

Rory and Jenson exchange glances.

RORY
My mom's lab?

JENSON
God, what an amateur move. This was a diversion and I
totally fell for it.

RORY
You saved everyone, at least. And it looks like nobody
was hurt at Woods Industries.

JENSON
The question is—what are The Vicious trying to steal?
And why?

5

NO STRINGS ATTACHED

"Remember that time you tried to bake cupcakes?" Grant walks out and shuts the sliding door behind him. He's wearing summery striped swim shorts and a pair of black Wayfarers. He hands me a can of sparkling lemonade and lowers himself into the pool next to me, dying laughing. "It was like a crime scene."

I roll my eyes behind my sunglasses, but I can't help laughing with him, popping the top of my drink and sitting up on the giant flamingo floatie. "There was something wrong with the recipe!"

"Of course there was." Grant swims across the pool to grab a raft and pulls himself up to lie out. The sun beats down on us—on *him*, highlighting the pool water sliding down his abs and thighs. He shakes out his hair and holds his lemonade up. "Here's to store-bought cupcakes."

"I can bake!" I say, lifting my lemonade in a toast, anyway.

"Just like you can surf." He raises a brow.

"I told you I don't like it," I counter.

Grant's parents rented this house for the summer since they sold theirs when they moved to California. His dad's still back in LA, but Grant's mom brought him and Eric. I think she missed her friends as much as they missed theirs.

This is probably the nicest rental house I've ever seen. There's a gate just to get to the driveway, brown faux-aged shingles, and fresh landscaping with beach access, a giant pool, and balconies on two of the bedrooms facing the ocean. Clearly Grant's dad is doing incredibly well out in LA.

I'm waiting for the right moment to ask Grant about him, actually, and that letter of recommendation. I don't want it to seem like that's the only reason I'm here. Which… As much as I wish it were, it isn't. A main reason, sure, but not the *only* one. I can't lie, I'm enjoying Grant's company. It's comforting to have him as a friend again.

"Besides, I seem to remember someone pretending to be a grill master last summer," I say, taking a sip. "And burning everything he touched."

Grant shrugs. "I was going for well-done. And that was still, hands down, the best Fourth of July party Citrus Harbor has ever seen. Will ever see, even."

"You're not even going to try to outdo yourself this year, then?"

"A legend must admit when he has peaked." Grant paddles his raft closer so we're floating next to each other. He hooks his pinky into the handle of my float. "Though if I remember correctly you left early."

I think back. "Oh yeah, I had to watch Milly and Lot."

"How are they, by the way?"

"Good," I say. "Milly is going through some phase where she's essentially an emotional time bomb—like, everything sets her off—and Lottie is as chaotic as ever, but she's still sweet."

Grant laughs. "They're awesome. God, Lottie really was the smartest little kid I ever met. And Milly's temper isn't *entirely* surprising—remember how she would drum? Like, it was sorta violent."

I do remember the drum set. Thankfully Mom convinced Milly to take up other instruments, and we sold the drums. I would have found a way to get rid of them in the middle of the night otherwise.

"Aren't you going to miss them when you go to LA?"

I swallow. "Well, yeah. But that's not for—it's like a year away."

Leaving my mom and Milly and Lottie is the last thing I want to think about. Like, ever. I have locked that away and filed it under "cross that bridge when we get to it."

"I wish my family was like yours," Grant says, super casually like it's an afterthought.

"You and Eric are close," I offer. "And you're close to your parents."

"It's, like, conditional." He's still playing it cool, but this is clearly more than a casual, random thought that just occurred to him. "You and your mom and Milly and Lot—you're all just who you are. You do what you want to do, and you all love each other for it."

Well yeah, that's family, I want to say. But I realize maybe that's not family for everyone.

"Eric and I are constantly being told what to do, who to

be." He sighs. "Getting uprooted against our wills and moved to California. Away from all our friends and…"

He doesn't have to say it.

"I'm sorry," I offer. "I didn't really realize. It always seemed like—"

"It's all about how it seems." Grant smiles and points at me like I just figured it all out. "As long as it all seems great, like we're the perfect, all-American family. Anyway, I don't mean to whine about my family. Obviously things could be worse. And they have my best interest in mind, I guess. Financial stability and all that. I'm sure Dad is right. Plenty of people would kill to get a job with him."

I can't imagine feeling that way about my family. I knew Grant had a somewhat strained relationship with his dad—that was no secret. He'd always said he didn't really want to talk about it, though, and I eventually just accepted that as the truth. This feels bigger, like it affects his entire world.

"Wait, you don't want to work for your dad's company? You always made it seem like you did."

"It's a cliché." Grant pushes up his sunglasses. "Son always trying to live up to Dad's expectations, blah blah blah."

"So what do you want to do?" This is news to me. It always seemed like Grant was stoked to take over one day.

"See the world." Grant doesn't miss a beat. "There's so much out there. I just want to see it all."

I guess that isn't a total surprise. Grant has always liked traveling.

"Why didn't you tell me any of this last summer?"

"I wanted to impress you," he says. "What's impressive about having no real direction in life? You have big Hollywood dreams, and they're all yours. Meanwhile, deep down, I'm really not sure what I want at all if I'm not being told by my parents."

Splashing him, I scoff, "I didn't like you because you had goals."

"Good to know," Grant says, his typical smirk returning. "What *did* you like?"

"Can't remember," I say. "Though, speaking of my big Hollywood dreams—"

"I know, I know." Grant chuckles and pushes off, his raft floating across the pool away from me. "I'm going to talk to my dad."

I exhale. *He remembers.*

"Just don't want to do it too soon." He smiles and drinks some of his lemonade. "Since that's the only reason you're hanging out with me and all."

"That is not true!" I say, my voice going too high. "It is *so* not! It's just Penny Thomas has, like, a 4.5 GPA, and now she might be applying to USC as an 'option,' which means my chances of getting in are now *even* lower."

"You're destined for that school," he says. Somehow that makes me feel a lot better. "Come here." He stands up and walks over to the chaise lounges our towels are sprawled out over. "Your shoulders."

They definitely feel hot, so I get out of the pool and join him. He picks up a bottle of sunscreen and squeezes some into his palm.

"You never put on enough sunscreen," he says, stepping closer to me and rubbing his hands together.

Grant's hands find my skin. At first, it's cold, but then it warms up, and as he massages circles into my shoulders and back, I think there are probably worse feelings. Pool water drips onto the pool deck, and I feel aware of everything—the tips of Grant's fingers and the pressure from his palms.

He turns me around and lowers his head, maybe unconsciously, and his hair grazes my collarbone before he stands back up and our eyes lock. There isn't any point in trying to deny how hot he is, especially right now, soaking and tan and—

My lips find Grant's, and it's easy, instinctive, even. His hands fall down my back and pull me closer, and there's not an inch of space between us. I bite at his bottom lip, and he breathes into the kiss, one hand finding my hair and tugging slightly.

Okay, Harry, snap back to reality.

I pull away and take a step back. "Um."

Grant's brows rise, and he licks his lips. "Something wrong?"

I shake my head. There isn't anything wrong. Not really. But what am I doing? What's happening? A week ago I was cursing Grant's name, and now *I'm* the one who's FaceTiming him and asking him to make plans and kissing him.

"I just want another drink," I say, turning around and heading over to the bar next to the pool. I take a deep breath.

I kissed Grant. Why don't I ever think things through before I do them?

"Whoa, no way," I hear Grant cry out, and when I turn back around, he's rummaging through a box of toys on the other end of the pool. He pulls out a giant water gun. "Oh, it is *so* on."

"Don't even think about it!"

But that doesn't stop Grant, of course, and before I can even grab a can of cherry Coke, he's pumping the water gun like he's Rambo or something. I don't make it far, just onto the grass, and am properly super soaked as Grant closes in on me.

I reach for the water gun, and we end up tumbling onto the grass and into each other's arms. It doesn't take long for the water gun to land a few feet away from us, completely forgotten.

Grant kisses me this time, once we've stopped rolling around, and he's leaning over me, his hair on my forehead and the sun glowing behind him like some picturesque movie moment. His lips are sweet, and the feeling of our bodies practically merging into one is even sweeter, our thighs meeting and his chest lowering to mine. I can feel him through his wet board shorts and I know he can feel me, too, especially by the way he presses into me and his fingers crawl up my chest to my neck.

Somewhere past the gate, inconveniently timed, a car door closes.

Grant rolls onto the grass and fixes his hair. "Of course. Mom's home."

"Maybe it's good timing," I say, biting my lip.

Seriously, Harry. Like, what the hell is going on? One minute you hate Grant. Then he's back, and it's like nothing ever happened.

Only I can't help but feel comfortable with him. It's like two puzzle pieces that fit perfectly together. I don't have to try, and neither does he.

"We're *friends*," I say finally, when Grant gets up and tosses the water gun into the box.

"Right." Grant smirks, holding up his fingers to do air quotes. *"Friends."*

I stand up and walk over to him, "No, no. Not 'friends.' Friends."

"Friends."

What have I gotten myself into?

"Say it again, just so I know you understand."

"Friends." Grant winks, grabbing at my waist. "Come on, I'm gonna text my dad about this letter, and you know Mom's going to want to see you!"

INT. THE CHAMPIONS ALLIANCE CAMPUS

GOLD HONOR and QUICK CIRCUIT stand at the head of a
long conference table.

Rory and Jenson hang their heads.

QUICK CIRCUIT
So you're telling me you two geniuses had a plan, and
The Vicious still managed to break into the Woods
labs and nearly steal invaluable genetic material,
nanotechnology, and weaponry data?

JENSON
When you put it that way...

GOLD HONOR
Jenson, I'm sorry, but I expect that shield to be in my
office before you leave.

           JENSON
     But you have so many—

Gold Honor furrows his brow.

           QUICK CIRCUIT
     Your mission is terminated, Briggs. And Rory, come on.
     What were you thinking getting involved at all? Your
     mom would have a field day if she knew.

           RORY
     Mr. Wilson, I just want to help. I think with the right
     tech—

           QUICK CIRCUIT
     Are you gonna make a silicon suit that mimics
     chromatophore transformations? A copper piece of
     machinery that could withstand a nuclear blast? Modify
     elements to turn your reality-warping friend here into a
     fission reactor?

           RORY
     Wait what?

           QUICK CIRCUIT
     I did all that. So don't talk to me about tech, kid.

Rory and Jenson exchange glances.

           QUICK CIRCUIT
     You two stay out of trouble. I don't want your blood on
     my hands.

INT. TCA CAMPUS HALLWAY

JENSON
That didn't go too well.

RORY
I'm can't believe that's the first impression I made.

JENSON
But, look, he's wrong. You and I *can* do this.

RORY
I don't know. I don't think I want to go against The
Champions Alliance.

JENSON
You're the smartest person I know.

They're close now.

JENSON
I need you.

Will they kiss?

A door opens, and Rory takes a step back, snapped to
reality.

RORY
I gotta go.

6

ALONG CAME LOGAN

I wake up in a cold sweat from a nightmare where I got rejected from USC and then was chased by Justin, who was wearing a Ghostface mask and brandishing a knife because he knew I wanted to tell Hailey what he did last summer.

My brain mixed horror movies there, but it's only because I'm majorly haunted. I can't believe I haven't even told Hailey I went to Grant's, and she has no idea we kissed. Two times. Secrets were never our thing, and now they just won't stop piling up. Of course, Hailey seems to care less and less about anything that isn't Justin, so who can blame me?

God, we kissed twice. What does that mean? He hasn't brought it up over text, so maybe we really can just be friends. We've kissed, like, a million times, anyway. What's two more?

Trying to distract myself—and desperate for progress—I spend some time at my desk with my script open on my laptop, just in case something comes to me. Some spark of inspiration. I have exactly two weeks and three days to get this screenplay finished and submitted if I want to even have a chance to get into my dream college, and I'm just stuck in a spin cycle.

Seventeen days. It's plenty of time if I can just be productive. I don't mean to procrastinate, but I find myself doing everything but writing this script.

Well, I mean two more kisses are really no big deal at all in the grand scheme. So, potentially, if we did kiss more, it would be nothing major and definitely not worth overthinking.

I'm supposed to be in control. I'm supposed to be the storyteller. That's why I love screenwriting, anyway—the way you get to tell the story exactly how you want. Build the relationships and define the characters and the setting. It's all up to the writer.

Well, I am certainly not in control here, and don't know who the screenwriter is for my life's movie, but I feel like they're effing with me.

When it seems like the distractions are relentless, I stand, stretching and eyeing the empty palm tree–lined street from my window.

I walk down the hallway gingerly, though there's not a chance Milly or Lottie will wake up. I could bang pots and pans or blast music, and they'd sleep right through it. Some gene I didn't get, clearly.

My mom's light is on—she's getting ready for work. Though there's a definite chance it never went off and she's been up working. Somehow she always ends up looking like she slept ten hours and walks around all polished and in a cloud of Jo Malone.

The hallway upstairs is nice and cozy—there are big black-and-white photos of us in matted frames all over the walls. Pictures of me in a cowboy outfit when I was three and photos of Lottie smiling in her kiddie pool (right before she peed in it) and even a pudgy Milly with a sweet grin in her gingham dress before she turned into a little American Eagle model with an explosive temper.

I tiptoe down the stairs, rushing to the coffee maker. Once it's brewed, I fill a steel tumbler for Mom with just as much French vanilla creamer as she likes. I fill a cup for myself, adding some chocolate syrup for taste before I make my way past the living room to the French doors that overlook the ocean. It's still dark, though light is peeking up from the horizon. I sip my coffee and hear Mom hurrying down the stairs. Her heels clack like a hammer to nails.

"You know, some teenagers take the summer to sleep in," she says, smiling and grabbing her keys from the counter. Mom looks like she could rule the world in her pencil skirt and cream blouse.

She sees the coffee and claps before rushing over to hug me. "You are an angel, thank you."

I give a lazy hug back, and Mom tilts her head as she reaches for the tumbler.

"Is something wrong?"

I sigh. *Yes, Mom, everything is wrong.* Normally, I'd tell her. But I know she'll just give me the "let's explore other options just in case" speech, and I don't have it in me to listen to that right now.

"You know how Grant and I are…friends?" I say finally,

thinking we can address at least one thing on my mind. "That *is* good, isn't it? People can change. Right?"

Mom thinks for a second. "I do think people can change. Maya Angelou said when someone shows you who they are, believe them. Has Grant shown you who he is?"

"I don't know," I admit. Maybe?

"I can't tell you if he's changed or not," she says. "I guess it depends who he really *is*."

I nod, thanking her but instantly wondering less about Grant and more about Justin. Does Hailey know who he is? Shouldn't she?

"For what it's worth, you're kids. So, yes, you guys *will* change. I know you'll figure it all out." She pats my arm and smiles before standing up straight. "All right, please make sure your sister doesn't have an apocalyptic meltdown if you can." She checks aloud that she has her phone, purse, coffee, and keys, stopping for a moment to type an email before looking up at me. "Unload the dishwasher? And get started on your summer reading. Okay? Love you."

"Love you, too," I say. It's easy for her to list off all the things I need to get done because she's good at getting things done. I'm not as good at it as she is, clearly, but one day I will be. One day, I'll be as successful as she is.

She disappears, and I hear the front door open, close, and lock. I wish I could be like her—always moving and accomplishing things. She doesn't screw up her chances or end up kissing the guy who broke her heart when she should be focusing on a big project. I probably *should* be asking her for more advice.

Coffee in hand, I step outside and close the door behind

me. It'll only be remotely cool for another ten minutes or so, and then the Floridian summer heat will fill the air.

I make my way to the sand and inhale, trying to stop thinking about my future for a second to take in the way the ocean feels like it's all around me. The gulls seem to welcome me out, wish me a good morning. The sea oats on the dunes are waving hello. Nature is calm and still—I wonder what that's like.

I fell asleep brainstorming and listening to film scores, so now I'm humming some Hans Zimmer melody as I feel the cool sand against my toes and find my way down to where the shore is damp. I sit down and hold my mug with both hands, watching as the sun climbs the sky. Some surfers appear to the left, and a young couple are holding hands some ways down on the right.

The air is rich with coffee and saltwater and the pure joy of summer. As I sit here and watch the waves, I try to focus on my screenplay ideas. On Rory and Jenson and Skip. But what's the message? What makes the script special?

I remember on the BAFTA podcast, that Nancy Meyers said to write what you know—write what's *you*. What even is *me*?

What if I don't have anything special to say?

Surfers flood the beach now, and I stand up, walking to the small pier a few blocks down. There are sometimes little starfish in the tide pools. Once I even saw a baby seahorse.

Full disclosure: It may not have been a baby. It might have just been a very tiny seahorse. I'm not a marine biologist. *That* was only a short middle school phase.

As I walk down the beach, I smile to a few people who look vaguely familiar. Of course, that's part of living in a town like this one. You recognize people everywhere, even on the beach at the start of the day. I know it'll be so different in California, where I only know a handful of people. A good kind of different, though.

There aren't any starfish today, only a few hermit crabs scurrying around. I wonder if they see my presence as threatening. I lean against the old sturdy wood of the pier and watch them as they hurry around each other like a dance. They're calm and frantic at the same time. I understand, weirdly.

After a few moments, I decide to do a quick sweep for shark teeth before heading back into the house. I scout out a pile of shells, a spot where they're especially concentrated, and squat down to examine the area. With my free hand, I sweep the stack of shells and turn a few over before I spot the first shining point of black.

Finding a shark tooth is like finding gold. Sometimes I like to imagine the shark. Maybe a baby shark, maybe a grownup. I always imagine the shark doesn't even miss its tooth at all, doesn't even notice it's gone because there are hundreds of others that can still shred.

I hear a grunt and look up to see someone crouching over a surfboard on the sand.

It's Logan. He falls back, palms stopping his descent. Then he sees me.

I stand and wave, realizing there is no way out of this since I'll have to pass him to get to my house. "Hi," I say, walking closer. I stuff the shark tooth in my pocket.

"Hi." His eyes are still the same blue-gray, but they're somewhat livelier in the sunrise. The skin under his eyes is a bit puffy, like he hasn't slept much or something. Kind of

weird, since he says he likes staying in with leftovers and documentaries, but whatever. He's wearing a wet gray T-shirt
with some sort of wave design on it, along with dull green
board shorts, and there's a SpongeBob towel sprawled out on
the sand—an interesting addition to this picture.

"I have your T-shirt from the other day. I just was going
to wash it for you—I'll get it back to you, promise."

"It's no big deal," I say with a laugh. I straighten up and
clear my throat. "Logan, can I just say I'm sorry again? About
the other night? The entire thing. I was a douche."

"A total douche," Logan agrees with a huge smile and breaks
into laughter. "Don't sweat it, Harry. It's not that big of a deal.
And it was kind of nice how you were standing up for Penny."

"Well"—I nod—"still a douche canoe, but I appreciate
the free pass."

Logan smiles and points to the board, wiggling his toes in
the sand and biting his bottom lip. "My uncle thinks he can
teach me."

"Good luck," I say with a laugh. "I could never really get
the hang of it."

"Well, if you ever want to give it another shot, he has a
ton of boards."

I scoff, "You wouldn't want to see me on a surfboard. It's
embarrassing."

"I can't imagine you're any worse than me," Logan offers.

"I'll think about it," I say, though I certainly will *not* think
about it. I guess the possibility is enough to make him smile,
though, which I don't really mind. Catching myself, I exhale.
"So, backing up, are you just here for the summer?"

"Yeah," he says. "I'm staying with my aunt and uncle."

Which makes sense. Beach town. Tourists. Not exactly rocket science. I wonder if I know Logan's aunt and uncle, but I don't want to overdo it, so I just nod. "And you said you're going to college this fall?"

"Columbia," Logan says.

"That's really impressive," I say and keep rambling on without even thinking. "There's a girl who won this competition couple of years ago—it's for young screenwriters—and she went to Columbia and now she has, like, some major deal writing for Broadway."

"Is that your thing? Screenwriting?" Logan asks.

I pause. It's sort of strange to talk to someone who doesn't know about my lifelong dreams. "Yeah, I think so. I'm only going into senior year, but I want to go to USC. Southern California, not South Carolina. Because Hollywood."

Logan just grins. "Nice. Pretty far from here."

"Yeah, but my dad lives out in California, in Newport Beach, which helps. He's been out there for, well, it feels like forever now. Since he and my mom got divorced." I'm practically spilling my life story, so I attempt to recover. "But yeah, I love screenwriting. I'm going to submit a screenplay to that contest the Columbia girl won, hence me talking about it. Twice now."

"Well cool." Logan tilts his head, like he isn't sure what to take from my rambling. "What kind of stuff do you want to write?"

"It depends," I say. Realizing I hardly sound like a writer, I straighten up. "I mean, generally, contemporary stories. I like writing about relationships."

"That sounds awesome. I like writing, too. I mean, I'm no good at it, but I do like it."

I shake my head. "I'm sure you're great."

"I've dabbled in some *Star Wars* fan fiction, sure, but I'm not really one to write original characters or anything."

The mention of *Star Wars* almost makes me recoil. I don't have anything against *Star Wars* fans, except for the fact that a few of them totally ripped Hailey and me a new one, all because we didn't want to participate in a trivia game in the line at a premiere a couple of years ago. Come on, I don't even know all the moons in *our* solar system!

"George Lucas went to USC," I blurt like an idiot. "Um. I loved the *Star Wars* movies as a kid. Not that they're only for kids. I mean, I saw one a while ago, but I'm not caught up."

"They're not for everyone." He smiles, shrugging. "Though I can recommend some sci-fi books, if you want." He blushes. "I saw you had some books in your locker, so I um… I figured you like reading."

"Very observant. But, honestly, those are summer reading books. I haven't ever read sci-fi," I say, wondering when he even had the time to notice any of my stuff. "Are you super into science? Is that what you're studying at Columbia?"

"I'm studying mathematics," he says. "And I want to do, like, criminal justice? I know it probably sounds funny, but I'd love to do something with the FBI. Like, they have STEM special agents and engineers and stuff. But you know, still figuring it all out."

Logan seems so go-with-the-flow and calm, not at all like what I'd expect a STEM FBI agent to be, whatever that even really means. Not that I've ever considered it. But I guess I'd picture them being stuffier. Maybe more socially awkward and possibly more buff… Though this explains his knack for noticing stuff.

"An FBI STEM agent." I tap my chin, wondering what the hell they even do. "Sounds too easy."

Logan chuckles. "Growing up, I always wanted to be an FBI agent, but I had to be honest with myself at some point—my skill set is a little better suited for counterterrorism and, like, digital investigations. I'm more the guy in the chair."

I catch the Marvel reference and raise a brow. "That's exactly what a superhero would say to throw off the scent."

"I guess you'll never know." Logan wiggles his eyebrows.

"Either way, I'll definitely hang on to your number," I say. "Never know when you need that security clearance."

"I'm sure every FBI agent divulges national secrets to their friends in Hollywood." Logan shrugs.

"That would explain so much," I say, and we both laugh.

An older man with a surfboard approaches us from a walkway. I've seen him around before. Maybe on walks or while grocery shopping or something.

"Harry, this is my uncle, Ron."

"Hi," I say, shaking his hand. Things have officially progressed too far if I'm meeting Logan's family.

Ron must be at least fifty, though his eyes and smile are those of someone young. "It's nice to meet you, Harry."

"You as well," I say. I look to Logan. "I'll let you get back to your surfing."

Ron gestures back behind him: "Want me to grab you a board? You're more than welcome to join us."

"Oh, I can't, but thank you. I have to get back," I say. "Plus, I was just telling Logan I'm the town's worst surfer. Trust me."

Ron looks unconvinced, so I just laugh.

"I think they actually may have put out a warning—told the lifeguards to keep me out of the water." I fake a frown. "They don't want me to endanger everybody else."

"Well, if you ever want to try it out, feel free to drop by," Ron says, sounding so much like Logan I just smile down at the sand and thank him.

"See you around," Logan says.

"See you around," I agree, turning back toward the house.

I feel so relieved the weird guilt I felt for exploding at Logan has vanished. It was a classic, simple misunderstanding, obviously.

As I head up the beach, I might turn back and catch Logan smiling at me—I might even feel my cheeks go hot. But *whatever*, I might do a lot of things.

INT. UNIVERSITY LIBRARY

Rory ignores the books spread out before him in favor of his phone.

Skip walks up behind him.

> SKIP
> You ever get off that thing?

CLOSE-UP. Rory rolls his eyes and smiles.

WIDE SHOT. The library.

> RORY
> Are you stalking me now?

> SKIP
> I go here too, remember?

           RORY
Tell your attendance grades that.

           SKIP
Touché.

           RORY
I'm sorry for running off the other day I—

           SKIP
Oh I know. Mr. Wilson told me all about you and
Captain Warp.

           RORY
Maybe I should have listened to whatever you were
going to tell me that day. Which was?

           SKIP
Mr. Wilson wants you to stay away from Jenson. But I
feel a little awkward being the messenger. And I'm sure
he made that clear—

           RORY
He didn't make that clear actually. But we didn't talk in
private, so maybe that's why.

MEDIUM SHOT. Skip looks down at his phone.

           SKIP
Shoot—I forgot my… Can we pause this conversation?
Future Defense business!

CLOSE-UP. Rory just laughs.

>RORY
>Okay, Skip.

>SKIP
>Don't get into any trouble!

7

ABOUT A BOY

It's my first day of work, and now I am feeling especially grateful my mom made me get a job. I need this so badly—something new and fresh. Something not related to any of the things stressing me out. This will be a good distraction when my little pea brain decides it wants to FaceTime or make out with Grant.

As far as first jobs go, this one seems to be the jackpot. It's super chill, I can use my people skills, and the dress code is way relaxed. Plus, I get to manage the shop's Instagram, and we have pizza on Fridays. All around a total win.

It helps that I know Books by the Sea like the back of my hand. I know the spots where the baby blue paint is chipped and shows the original bright canary yellow coloring. I know where the planks of wood flooring creak and where they've been replaced. I know each of the little round topiaries outside under the wide white-framed windows. I know the four steps and the landing to the little porch, the white door with the glass looking in and giving you a glimpse of true happiness.

Here's the deal. I may not be Citrus Harbor's biggest bookworm, but who doesn't love a bookstore? They just have this cozy sort of comforting vibe. There's infinite possibility in the stories along the walls. While part of me does wish the movie theater gave daytime shifts to high-schoolers—or that I could time travel and work at, like, a Blockbuster—I think this is honestly just as good. Stories are stories, however they're told, after all.

When I walk in, the bell chimes.

"Hi there." I hear the familiar voice of the store owner, Jesse, and whip around to see her at the corner window. She's got a stack of books in her arms. "Harry!"

She drops the books on a nearby chair and runs over, arms wide before they're wrapped around me.

I hug her back, laughing. I'm not a big hugger, but Jesse's hugs are always welcome. And she smells like cookies and the ocean all the time. Can you imagine a better combination?

"So excited for this summer!" She grabs my shoulders. "You look great, kid."

"You look great, too!" I say.

Jesse is probably one of the sweetest people I've ever met. She inherited the bookstore from her parents, who passed away a few years ago. She's in her midthirties, which I know because she graduated the same year as my mom, and she's always so busy. No husband or kids, though she did have a boyfriend for a little bit when I was in middle school. She lives in a house just behind the cottage and spends almost all her time at the store.

She's glowing, like she always is. I think the books make her happy. Her face is full, with a long nose and bright green eyes, framed by wavy dark brown hair.

The feeling in the shop is as nice as ever. It smells like citrus and the ocean. Fresh orange juice and coffee are on the big oak table by the windows. Books are stacked in the chairs and around the drink trays.

New, I notice, since I came in for my interview, is a giant stuffed unicorn in the back by the children's books.

Jesse must notice me eyeing it.

"That's Olivia Sparkle," she tells me very seriously, crossing her arms as we walk past the toy, and she opens the door to the office. "One of the kids' club parents just donated her. She's a fan favorite already."

In the office there's another girl who I think must be a year or two older than me. I saw her working here last summer, but we never spoke.

"Agnes, this is Harry," Jesse says, gesturing for us to meet. "Harry, Agnes. Harry's mom and I did Senior Women together in high school." She laughs and squeezes my arm. "Time flies."

Remaining silent, Agnes gives me a curt smile.

"Great to meet you," I offer.

Agnes nods. "You too."

I sort of wish Jesse didn't mention that she and my mom have been friends since high school, because now Agnes is going to think that's the only reason I got the job. Which, honestly, maybe it is, considering I have no qualifications, but I'm not going to work any less hard.

"I'm going to get Harry set up out there, but why don't

you guys stock the new shipment together in a bit? Get to know each other?"

We close the door and get my employee information put into the computer next to the register. Jesse tells me that, having spent a week in London, Agnes much prefers the United Kingdom to the States. She's switched over to the British spellings and only uses their slang and vernacular, so I shouldn't be thrown off if she uses the *loo* or makes sticky notes of her *favourite* books for customers.

Every time Jesse sees me and smiles, her eyes sort of melt into her cheeks, and her face is warm and full of sunshine.

Eventually, Agnes comes out with two large cardboard boxes on a dolly. When she sees me, her eyes pinch up real tight, and her cheeks shoot up into razor-sharp boulders on her face. Her lips are tense and taut. When Agnes smiles at me, it's like she's trying her hardest not to drop a deuce.

"So are you from Citrus?" I say, opening up a box and pulling out some books.

Agnes nods.

Clearly that's all she's giving me, so I try to find another commonality.

"Did you go to Citrus Harbor High?"

"No, I went to Her Lady of the Sea," she says.

"No way!" I laugh. "My best friend's parents always threaten to send her—"

I realize making Agnes's all-girls school sound like a punishment might not be the icebreaker I was hoping for.

I clear my throat. "Are you in college?" She doesn't immediately respond, so I fill the silence to make it less awkward: "I'm going to be a senior this year, but I really want to go to USC in LA."

"I had several offers for colleges in California, but I'd rather stay in-state and pursue graduate studies in the UK," she says. "I'm saving *heaps* to move to London."

"Um, so do you like *The Crown*?"

She narrows her eyes and flicks her hair over her shoulder.

Basically Agnes is the worst, and I get the feeling she is going to make my work life a living hell.

Jesse runs me through using the register while Agnes watches the floor, and we do a couple of transactions together to make sure I don't royally screw up. Agnes and I switch again while Jesse takes a call in the office.

After a while of sorting books in the children's fantasy section, I sneak behind the counter and check my phone. Grant has sent a couple memes, and I respond with a laughing emoji and then open Hailey's text, which is accompanied by a photo of her latest Sharpie tattoo:

HAILEY: Justin said he'd get it matching with me!!

I almost hurl. Matching couple tattoos are bad enough, but with an *adulterer*? I catch myself—I am so screwed. What if they get married? How am I going to give a speech?

Let it go, Harry, I tell myself. *It's like Grant said. There's a reason people are blissfully ignorant. Hailey is happy.*

Agnes goes on break an hour before I do, and I see her rush outside to greet her boyfriend. He has equally wiry hair with long sideburns that nearly reach his jaw and big glasses. They practically swallow each other whole as they swap saliva on the sidewalk before rushing off.

I grab a pile of books from a cardboard box and begin scanning them into the inventory system. They're all new shiny hardcover titles, and I mentally note a bunch I want to read before summer is over.

If I ever wrote a book, I think it'd be cool to see it on display here. Plenty of screenwriters have novels published, too, so I wouldn't want to limit myself.

"How's everything going so far?" Jesse comes up and leans on the counter.

"All great so far," I say. Which is true. No signs of any difficulty yet apart from Agnes's general demeanor.

Jesse picks up one of the books and opens it. While she's looking at the synopsis inside the jacket, I scan the shop. A girl is browsing the adult fiction section, and I turn back to Jesse.

"I'm going to go see if she needs any help," I say. Jesse nods, and I hope she sees I'm trying to take initiative.

The girl is short, with red hair tied up into two buns. She pouts at the spines, like the titles are disappointing her.

"Are you finding everything okay?" I say. Which sounds right, doesn't it? I've heard people say that before.

The girl tilts her head and points to the shelf lazily. "I just don't know what to get my mom for her birthday. She reads Lily Tilbury's books, but I don't want to get one she already has."

I show her a comparable author, since I know Lily Tilbury very well. After all, Reese Witherspoon developed and starred in one of her adaptations. So, obviously, I know all about it.

The girl thanks me, and I grab a big stack of popular paperback books and turn toward the register, ready to take an Instagram photo for the store.

Of course, the moment I glance out the window, I see Logan skating by. He does a double take before he disappears, his board zooming down the sidewalk too quickly.

I exhale. I mean, I wouldn't mind seeing Logan in theory, but I *know* I need to limit our communication since he's a very cute guy who happens to also like guys, and I know exactly how something like that would end. Plus, the last thing I need is *another* distraction. Clearly I cannot be trusted—I already have kissed Grant, even though I know better. So, really, it's a good thing he's already gone.

Except he isn't.

I see his bright beach club polo whiz back into view, and he's opening the door, holding the skateboard to his chest. He's wearing his tattered Vans, white socks that stretch to the bottoms of his calves, and khaki shorts that hit right above his knees. Today he's got on glasses with thick black frames. I also might notice how big his hands are as they stretch across the deck of the skateboard. I blink, willing that thought away.

"Harry," Logan says very seriously. "If *you* were a book, I'd need glasses, because you'd definitely be fine print."

I poke my tongue in my cheek and scoff, fighting a smile as Logan goes bright red and laughs.

"Okay, that was—I just thought it'd be funny or something..."

"What's up, Logan?" I say, determined not to give in to his dorky charm for a single moment.

Of course, I'm now grinning like an idiot and feel my face go hot as hell because I can practically feel Jesse staring me down. And not staring me down like a normal boss would.

She's watching like that aunt who always asks if you have a boyfriend yet. She's totally going to make this a thing now.

I hear footsteps and notice the redhead is ready to check out, but before I can move, Jesse locks eyes with me and indicates she's got the register under control.

"Just got off work and I saw you," Logan says when I turn back to him. His mouth is stretched into a wide and goofy grin. He nods toward the pile of books I'm holding. "Thought you said you don't read much?"

"Oh, these aren't, uh." I hate how he makes me splutter. "No, I work here. Now. As in today I started. To work here." *Jesus Christ.*

Logan's eyes go wide, and he hugs the skateboard tighter to his chest, standing up straighter. "Oh, shit, I'm sorry. I didn't mean to come bug you with my lame jokes while you're working, I just thought you were..." I catch Logan looking over my shoulder toward Jesse. "I think I'm getting you in trouble."

"Not a big deal at all," I say, though the books in my hands are starting to get heavy.

I find myself resisting the urge to laugh, though, because Logan's big, ice blue eyes are concerned and adorable and his lips are kind of pursed and they look really pink and soft and—

"Um. I should get back to, you know." I offer a smile and take a step back.

"Right." Logan snaps to, nodding and rocking on his heels. He pushes his glasses up on his nose. "I'll see you around. Next time *you* can wow *me* with a literary pickup line. No Googling."

I wait for the door to close, to see him drop his board and

push off out of sight, before I turn around and catch Jesse with a raised brow and a huge smile as she hands the redhead her bag and receipt.

I shake my head, dropping the books on the counter. "Not a chance."

INT. A LAB AT WOODS INDUSTRIES

Rory is helping some young students with their microscopes.

RORY
There you go, you got it.

STUDENT
Whoa, I see it!

Skip enters from the elevator.

Rory quickly crosses the room to keep from causing a
distraction for the students.

RORY
Skip! What are you doing here?

SKIP
I'm, uh, interviewing for an internship with one of the
geneticists.

RORY
I thought you had an internship?

SKIP
I do? *(pauses)* Oh! Right, well. Future Defense is *super* part-time and doesn't count for class credit, so...

RORY
Well, you should have told me you were applying here.

SKIP
I didn't want to put you in an awkward—

RORY
Want me to text my mom?

SKIP
No, it's okay. I appreciate it, though.

RORY
It's really competitive. Not that I don't think you'll get it. I mean, honestly, you're the smartest...

RORY (CONT'D)
(catches himself rambling)
You'll totally get it.

SKIP
You think I'm smart?

RORY
Occasionally.

SKIP
(flattered and feeling bold)
Hey, you wanna get frozen yogurt?

RORY
What? Right now?

SKIP
Well, no, not right now. I have an interview, and you
have—

RORY
(flustered)
Right, duh, of course. Um. Yeah. I do. Want to.

SKIP
Yeah?

RORY
Sure.

SKIP
Okay.

Skip starts to walk toward the desk.

SKIP (CONT'D)
Well, I'm going to, uh...

RORY
Me too.

SKIP
Cool.

     RORY
Cool.

MEDIUM SHOT. NATALIE WOODS, Rory's mother, is dressed sharply in a dress and blazer. She rounds the corner of the office.

CLOSE-UP. Natalie's tablet reflection shows up in her glasses. The Vicious are on the news again.

     NATALIE
Rory, I need you in my office.

     SKIP
Oh uh—

Rory looks between them.

     NATALIE
It's important.

     RORY
(to Skip)
Sorry. Good luck on your interview!

8

THE HEARTBREAK KID

Peach's Ice Cream is an iconic landmark in Citrus Harbor. Technically, it's been around since the '70s, if you don't count the years it was shut down in the late '80s. There were rumors some of the girls who worked there got abducted by aliens, but it was all just a cover-up because they had bugs. Anyway, it's a huge stand right on the boardwalk that stands apart from the surf shops, souvenir traps, and other restaurants because it is shaped like a giant ice cream cone.

Every summer, the kids working the stand get to decorate the swirl on top of the cone. This year it's painted cobalt with bright yellow stars. It looks really cool with the sun-worn waffle cone texture of the actual stand.

Hailey gets me a scoop of banana ice cream with Reese's minis sprinkled across the top. She straddles the seat of the bench next to me and darts her spoon into her own cup, which is filled with magenta bubblegum.

She's wearing a white T-shirt with the Peach's logo on the
pocket and rolled sleeves, paired with cut-off denim shorts
and yellow slip-on Vans.

"I didn't think there would be anything better than free
books," Hailey says sarcastically, grinning as she takes a bite of
her ice cream. "But turns out free ice cream takes the cake."

"I don't get free books." I roll my eyes.

Hailey nods. "You can always come to the dark side."

"I actually really like it," I tell her. "And I *do* get a dis-
count. Plus, if I want, I can work there during the school
year. Who knows."

Peach's closes for a few months in the "winter." Technically, I don't think Florida should be allowed to even use that
word, but we do get occasional chills. It's my least favorite
thing ever.

My phone buzzes—Grant and I are discussing the UCLA/
USC rivalry. He's saying I should wear UCLA colors so I
can hang out with him at the games, to which I reply that he
obviously is going to need to wear USC colors to hang out
with *me*. Now that we're friends, I'm cool with entertaining
the idea of us hanging out together. Platonically.

"Who are you texting so much?" Hailey says, furrowing
her brow.

"Just Logan," I say. It's not worth starting the Grant conversation with Hailey right now. She's going to have a lot of
opinions, and I don't know if I can handle hearing her hold up
her relationship as some golden standard for how a guy should
be when she has no idea what her own boyfriend is doing.

"So he *is* into you then?"

"Who knows?" *Why did I have to say Logan's name and open*

up this conversation? Why couldn't I have just said Milly? "Ugh, Penny and Roger are going to California next week. If she applies to USC…"

"You'll get in either way," Hailey says.

"I *could* easily get rejected."

"I *could* shove my manager's head in the Mint Chocolate Chip," Hailey says. "Anything *could* happen."

"You already want to shove your manager's head in ice cream?" I look past Hailey at the stand, where a few college-aged girls with sandy thighs and wet hair are bent over the counter, flirting with the guy at the register.

Hailey rolls her eyes. It's her first day, but I'm not super surprised. "I'm not working the register yet. He just has me on constant scooping duty, which blows. *And* I got dress coded, which doesn't exactly set me up for a great end-of-summer bonus. The worst part is the boys get to wear whatever they want—tank tops, those shorts that are ridiculously short with the '90s patterns. But if *our* shorts are too short…"

"That's no fair," I say. "You should say something."

"I don't know," Hailey says. "My parents would kill me if I got fired."

"For the record, I think you should say something."

"Anyway, enough about my misogynistic manager. I texted Justin to come sit with us after he's done," she says, pointing to the ocean.

Of course she did.

The amount of time Hailey spends without Justin is lessening with each passing day.

As the waves crash on the sand out past the hordes of sunbathers and volleyball players, beyond the rainbow umbrellas and bocce ball games, a few of the Citrus Harbor High Surf Team guys *Baywatch* their way out of the ocean, muscles glistening and hair dripping salty water onto their lips and down their chiseled jaws.

Hailey smiles and tosses her spoon into her cup. She stands up and waves to the group.

I hang my head, and Hailey bounces, her hair whipping in the wind and her boobs loose in her T-shirt. She knows exactly what she's doing, and I laugh, turning away as Justin and Hailey greet each other.

"Kensy." Foster sticks the butt—I don't know exactly what it's called, obviously—of his board into the sand. His swimsuit falls under his abs, and his dirty blond hair falls under his chin. He dusts some sand off his forehead, biting his lip and leaving his hand over his brows to shield the sun. The electric blue of his eyes is saturated and burning hot.

"Hey, Foster." I sit up straight and force a smile.

"I heard you guys left Stivender's early," Foster says.

"It was a bust." I grab my lemonade from the table and sip on the straw.

Justin and Charles are talking to Hailey while she takes tiny bites of her bubblegum ice cream.

Foster points to mine. "You like banana?"

"You're ridiculous." But my faux-serious straight face cracks because it's a *little* funny.

I roll my eyes and set down my ice cream before turning to him. "I can look forward to another entire summer of you boring me to tears with your incessant flirting, I take it?"

"Another summer of you resisting my charm, I take it?"

I raise a brow. "Has it ever occurred to you that I might just not be interested?"

"You were definitely interested over spring break," Foster whispers.

"That was my evil twin." I shrug. "Your 'charm' would never work on me, obviously."

"Saving the summer for Kennedy?"

"No," I say too quickly. "No, I don't have time for guys this summer, Foster. You know, you could probably benefit from a more focused summer, too."

"I like it when you're mean to me," Foster says. I try not to look at the way his biceps bulge as he stretches to brush his hair from his eyes.

"Not mean." I shrug. "Just honest."

"Show me *mean*." Foster flashes that bright, confident grin and laughs.

"Whatever, Foster." I laugh along with him, because this is just how conversations with Foster go. But I'm not even trying to be mean to him. Doesn't Foster care about his future at all? He just spends all his time goofing off, hooking up, and surfing.

"So what are you guys up to tonight?" Charles says, pulling at the leg of his wetsuit.

I turn away from Foster. "I'm closing tonight. At the bookstore. I get off around ten."

"The bookstore?" Foster raises a brow.

"Yes," I bite, narrowing my eyes.

"Come to Turner's, he's having people over." Justin's eyes light up as he says it, and Hailey grins.

"I don't know. I should stay in and work on this project

I'm doing," I say as I imagine a marquee, all flashing bright lights and a letter board reading DUE IN TWO WEEKS.

Hailey frowns. "Harry is stressing over Penny Thomas applying to USC."

"I am *not*." I give her a look—not cool.

"Oh, she and Roger are going to Turner's," Charles says.

I guess it is a worthwhile use of my time to see if maybe I can remind Penny of how amazing Harvard is and see if she won't recommit. At the very least, we can talk. I know I won't change her mind, but if she really is only applying to USC for Roger, maybe I can tell her how much it means to me and explain that, since she's a total genius and badass, if she applies, I'll never get in. If she's only going for Roger, maybe she'll consider UCLA or something. It's at least worth a shot to see how she's feeling and if she genuinely wants to go to USC or if it's truly just because of him.

Foster cocks his head and points to my ice cream on the table. "Mind?"

"Whatever." The corner of my mouth turns up, so I quickly turn my attention back to Charles and Justin, not giving Foster the satisfaction of watching him lick the spoon.

Somehow, it's nighttime, and I'm sitting on a wooden stool in Turner's parents' house on Sand Dollar Avenue. I'm tracing my finger across the lip of a red plastic cup while The Chainsmokers play in the background. I watch the kids at the party and think of things for background characters in my script. Bits of dialogue or stuff for character development.

I take a sip of my drink.

Penny and Roger didn't show. What a colossal waste

of time. And in hindsight, of all my impulsive and poorly thought-out plans, this was one of my dumbest. There's no way I can talk Penny out of applying to USC, no matter what her reason for going might be. And even if I could, I shouldn't.

Get it together, Harry. If Penny wins it fair and square, then she does. All I can do is give it my all with the creative materials, which I'm currently sabotaging yet again.

"You look perturbed," Foster says, leaning onto his elbows across from me on the gray granite island. "Any reason?"

"Wow, big word." I shrug. "What? Studying for the SATs?"

Foster raises a brow, looking down at his cup with his tongue in his cheek. "Gee, thanks."

"Sorry." I sigh. "I don't know, honestly. I just don't feel like myself."

He studies me with those big oceanic eyes of his, and I find I'm trapped in them. He knocks his knuckles against the granite.

"I'm not trying to be a buzzkill," I tell him, glancing around. Hailey and Justin are on the porch out back, commentating on a very serious beer pong game. Everyone else is into their own conversations.

Normally I'd enjoy this party and the fun people and I'd drink this disgusting whipped-cream flavor vodka with mango juice. But I'm on a deadline, and I'm increasingly aware of my counterintuitive actions and the very likely outcome.

"You're not a buzzkill." Foster grins. "It's weird, though. I haven't seen you like this."

"And how do you usually see me, Foster?" And the question's loaded, obviously, but Foster doesn't seem fazed.

"Bright. And maybe fiery." Foster lifts his shoulders. "I just haven't ever seen you—"

"Depressed?" I say. Maybe a little dramatic.

Foster narrows his eyes on me. "Want me to leave you alone?"

"Not really." I don't want to look lonely on top of being awkwardly quiet. "How's your summer going?"

Pulling up a stool, Foster sits and takes a sip of his drink. He tells me about his plans for the summer, which pretty much include surfing, working at the surf store, and trying to get TikTok famous with his friends. I make sure to take big gulps of my drink as we talk and accept a refill from Jeanine when she notices the hollow noise my cup makes when it hits the countertop.

I keep telling myself I'm going to go home. I'm going to go work on my screenplay.

But then, somewhere between built-up, indirect conversation, and stolen glances, I've gotten closer to Foster. Our conversation has evolved into something new for us—something real.

"I bet you'll get in," Foster says, like he's clairvoyant or something. "Honestly? I'm right there with you. I never really pictured you anywhere other than USC."

"Foster, why are you nice to me?"

"I know you." Foster shrugs.

Across the room, Hailey is cozy with Justin. I look to Foster. "Did you go on that surf trip to Big Sur last summer?"

"No, I couldn't make it," Foster says, tilting his head. "Why?"

"Well, you and Justin are best friends, so I'm sure you know what happened?"

Foster shakes his head. "What happened?"

"He didn't tell you?" I bite my lip. Of course, if Justin is so great at keeping secrets, why wouldn't he keep them from his friends, too?

"This whole time I think I just assumed you knew and you decided to keep it to yourself," I say, realizing how it sounds. How I assumed Foster would react, without actually giving him a chance. "All right, you can't tell a *soul*."

I hear myself saying it before I even decide to, and suddenly I'm telling Foster about Justin. I'm spilling my guts to him about how awful I feel and how Grant is back and I basically just keep screwing things up.

He doesn't say anything, though I hardly give him a chance because I'm *still* talking somehow. I just feel so guilty, and I don't know what to do. I tell him about how Justin means everything to Hailey and either way I'm a bad friend, and now I've known this long and haven't said anything so I'm basically screwed.

"You want to know the truth, Kensy?" Foster presses his brows together. "Truth is, you care about Hailey a lot, but only you can figure out what to do here. Right and wrong aren't black-and-white all the time."

"I hate the gray area."

"Okay, come on," Foster says, standing up and holding out his hand. "Let's just have some *fun*. Get your mind off all this for now. Beer pong?"

Since when is Foster so nice? Am I just now waking up to this, or has he always been this way?

As he gives me a reassuring smile, and I take his hand, stare into those blue eyes—there might be four of them, thanks to the drinks—and take a deep breath.

"We can't repeat spring break," I blurt.

Foster just laughs and pulls me in, wrapping his arm around my shoulders. "First of all, you're drunk. But even if you weren't, I wouldn't want to 'repeat spring break'— it's not exactly a turn-on to feel like someone's dirty little secret."

"Oh God, I'm sorry, Foster," I say. "It wasn't like that. I just didn't want everyone talking and—"

"Hey." Foster pats me on the chest and grabs a beer pong ball. "It's all good. For real, no worries. Let's play."

I wake up and hear Hailey snoring. And I see my laptop is open on my desk next to an empty lunch-size bag of nacho cheese Doritos. I remember getting home and suddenly feeling panicked by the idea of only having two weeks to work on my screenplay, though I don't know what the hell I wrote. So, that's great. Some of my pillows are on the ground, and my head is pounding.

I can't believe I got so wasted. And Foster had to walk us home—

Oh my God. Wait. I *told* Foster.

Hailey sits up and stretches out, her hair matted to one side. "Jesus Christ, what a night."

"It was a good one," I say, laughing nervously. Where is Justin? I didn't tell Hailey, too, did I?

"Um, do you not remember...?" Hailey says pointedly. "What you told me?"

Last night is sort of blurry. I remember drinking too much gross beer with Foster, Jamal, and Aaron. Followed by a game of What Do You Meme with Hailey and some of the guys from the soccer team. Then Hailey was barefoot with her shorts unbuttoned by the time we got to my front porch and I'd been skipping down Palm Avenue singing Ariana Grande, all while Foster Billings tried to make sure we got home safely.

"I am so mad at you," Hailey says, her eyes still closed.

How is it possible for me to be such a bad friend when all I was trying to do was preserve her happiness?

"Why?" I say, my heart thumping faster.

"You know why," she says, getting up and walking to the bathroom, she closes the door.

This can't be it. This can't be the end of our friendship. After a random drunken night at Turner's? There's no way I told her. Unless Foster did.

I grab my phone and text Foster.

ME: Hey, thanks for walking us home. And I'm sorry for how annoying I was last night.

Foster has definitely seen worse than me after a few drinks since he's friends with all the guys who party the hardest. Charles sank a boat once, so I'm fairly certain I'm smooth sailing. Still, I need to play it cool.

FOSTER: Lol u weren't

ME: Really?? I feel like there's something to apologize for on my end

FOSTER: Not at all. No harm done.

FOSTER: But let me know if you ever want to hang out when you haven't pounded half a handle

He's not fessing up, and he's acting normal—would he remember telling her?

ME: Do you remember what we talked about last night?

FOSTER: You mean about J Dawg?

Crap.

ME: Yeah... You didn't tell anyone, did you?

Hailey emerges from the bathroom, brushing her teeth with her hair wrapped into a bun. She narrows her eyes on me.

I glance down at my phone. Come on, Foster... Come on.

Hailey doesn't say anything, just turns around, steps back into the bathroom, and spits. She flicks on the faucet, and I wait for my phone to light up.

He was *just* responding to my texts so quickly. What is he doing?

Then my phone buzzes:

FOSTER: Course not, Kensy

"I mean, seriously." Hailey turns off the bathroom light and folds her arms. "When were you going to tell me?"

"I was going to," I start. "I just didn't know if you'd be mad."

"What? I mean, I'm not *actually* mad at you." She furrows her brow. "I'm only giving you shit. Honestly, I'm not surprised you and Grant kissed again. But I do think it's mature you're staying friends."

I blink.

"Can you get us waters?"

"Yeah," I say, needing a second to let my heart recover. I get up and let my feet fall to the cream shag rug. "Be right back."

Downstairs, Milly is sitting at the counter eating cereal. She doesn't look up from her phone, engrossed in the front-facing camera and adjusting her hair to lie perfectly against her violet hoodie, taking selfies with the morning light beaming in from the French doors. She takes a sip of her orange juice and gives me the evil eye.

"You're an idiot," she says.

I grab two glasses and start to fill them with water from the refrigerator door. "Thanks, Mil."

"Whose party did you even go to last night?"

"Turner's," I say, already a little annoyed with her tone.

Milly groans, "Sierra's brother? Great. Did you act like a moron?"

"No," I say. "Aren't you supposed to, like, think I'm cool?"

Of course, Milly doesn't really think I'm cool. She hasn't exactly thought of me as cool since we were little and pushing each other on the tire swing or recording each other singing Disney songs on the camcorder. Now I'm Milly's embarrassing older brother. Which is actually bullshit because I *am* fun and cool and her friends all like me.

"Drinking underage isn't cool," she says, like none of her friends ever touch alcohol at the parties in their grade.

I open my mouth to say something but just close it and

smile. I take the water glasses and return to my room, where Hailey is back in bed and scrolling through her phone.

She glances my way. "Horoscope?"

And with that I groan and walk into my bathroom as she yells out that the stars are aligning for a very confusing transit.

No shit.

EXT. A MUSIC FESTIVAL IN THE PARK. THE CITY IS IN THE BACKGROUND.

NEWSCASTER (V.O.)
Once again the city is looking at major reconstruction costs as a group of armed assailants rob another laboratory. Captain Warp was on the scene assisting SWAT with threat containment, but a large blast has destroyed one of the most iconic landmarks in the city—the statue of the Flying Goddess.

WIDE SHOT. Skip and Rory walk along the perimeter of the festival with frozen yogurt in hand.

RORY
We can't even go one day without the city being attacked, and I'm not supposed to help?!

SKIP
I know. These supervillains are getting worse and worse. For what it's worth, I think you're capable of

helping. It's just dangerous. And Mr. Wilson doesn't want you getting hurt.

RORY
Maybe I need to find a way to get superpowers.

CLOSE-UP. Skip narrows his eyes.

SKIP
Don't say that.

MEDIUM SHOT. Rory laughs.

RORY
I'm only kidding. But, actually, would that be so bad? I hate feeling helpless. Like I needed The Sting to save me. Which—no offense to The Sting, because he's awesome.

SKIP
You're not helpless. And I'm sure the superheroes— even The Sting—wish they had someone to save them every once in a while.

9

SOMETHING BORROWED

A few days later, I kick off my bike and lock it around a palm tree, inhaling the scent of fresh coffee. Shelly's is one of my favorite places in the world. It's a block from the ocean, in a two-story white house with cute pastel wooden signs that say things like Gone to the Beach or Mermaids Welcome.

Inside is more modern than the aged beach cottage exterior. It has white marble countertops and dark wood floors with chalkboards listing the available coffees and pastries. I don't recognize either of the girls working the registers, probably because they're about Milly's age. I do recognize Billy and Trey, who are bussing tables and have been in my classes since elementary school.

I order an iced coffee with coconut and vanilla before heading outside to the courtyard, finding a table in the shade. Shrugging my backpack off and setting my laptop up on the table, I try to focus on my script.

The morning is relaxed—I hear the ocean and can practically feel it from my seat. My laptop heats up beneath my
fingers, which I stretch over my keyboard.

But nothing happens.

No words are magically appearing on the page, or in my
brain for that matter.

What is missing?

"Harry?"

I look up from the screen, and it's Logan, glowing in the
light of the climbing sun. He's wearing a loose blue tank top
and holding a huge porcelain cup of steaming coffee.

"Am I interrupting?" Logan furrows his brow and scratches
at the back of his neck. "Sorry, I—"

"Um." He is, but since I'm not even actually writing, he *really* isn't.

He's just so nice. I obviously can't turn him away. I'll be
friendly. They say you're supposed to treat others how you
want to be treated, after all.

"No," I say, closing my laptop. "You're not interrupting. Want
to sit?"

Logan is, objectively, really cute. He's got a sort of all-
American-guy vibe about him with a hint of something I just
can't put my finger on. He's casual and easygoing, but also
careful. Calm. Steady.

He sets down the coffee across from me and pulls a chair
out. "What are you working on?"

Logan's questions feel genuine, like he actually cares when
he asks. He's not one of those people who asks how you're
doing just because it's the right thing to do.

I lean forward, resting my chin in my palms. "I'm working on a screenplay." I figure the fewer details the better.

"I gotcha," Logan says. He grabs a sugar packet from the tray on the table and knocks it into his coffee. His lips do look really kissable. "What's it about?"

"Um, I don't really know, which is kind of the problem…" I trail off and then realize I'm being completely self-centered and kinda zoning out, staring at his mouth. "How about you? How's your summer going? Working on any new *Star Wars* fan fiction?"

"No," he says, laughing and flashing a deep red. "The summer is good. Honestly just happy to be by the beach."

A few beats of silence remind me I don't know Logan very well, though it's a strange feeling—it's like we've been friends forever. This is easy.

I know I should be stricter with myself right now—how many times will I socialize when I should be focusing? But it's impossible not to enjoy the smell of coffee roasting in Shelly's, the sound of people laughing and enjoying their morning at their tables, the sight of light filtering through palms onto the sidewalk. Logan sitting across from me, drinking his coffee and smiling.

"You know… I actually was hoping to get breakfast."

"Oh, yeah, Shelly's has amazing pastries." I nod toward the building.

Raising a brow, Logan purses his lips. "Any chance you know a spot around here where they have proper breakfast?"

I rap on my laptop, looking off. Shit. "I know a couple places…"

"Want to show me around?" Logan smiles. "Unless you need to get back to your script. Don't let me distract you."

We're just two friends. I can *think* he's cute, and we can even flirt as much as we want if I keep that line drawn between friendship and something else. Remember that if I get distracted, I'll lose USC for good. If I keep my ducks in a row, I'll be fine. I just need to remember to watch Logan's ducks, too. I have no idea what his ducks might do.

"Can I be completely honest with you about something?" I say.

Logan nods eagerly. "I think that'd be best."

"I don't do the whole dating thing," I say. "Just… As a rule."

"You are consistently presumptuous, aren't you, Harry?" Half of Logan's mouth curves into a smile as he stands. "Come on."

Cheeks going hot, I don't even try to justify my comment.

We down our coffee and start up the sidewalk. As I watch Logan look around, I think of our differing perspectives. How I see a crack in the pavement and remember the time Alex Duncan's flip-flop got caught in it and he busted his lip open. Or how I know what boutiques used to line this street. Logan doesn't know the history, just the present. And there's something kind of great about that.

"What's your favorite book?" Logan says. "Since you work in a bookstore, you must have a favorite? Even if it's not your favorite pastime?"

"Is this an interview?" I tease.

"Actually, I think…" Logan smiles, raising a brow and

narrowing his eyes. "I think this is how people get to know each other."

"I don't know," I say. "I feel like I need to think of a good answer, since you're so smart and everything."

Logan throws his head back laughing. "I'm not *that* smart. Okay, it's a no judgment zone. Doesn't have to be an impressive answer. What's a book you love?"

"I like short stories," I say. "Like, I have a Hans Christian Andersen collection. *The Little Mermaid*, *The Ugly Duckling*…"

"*The Little Match Girl*." Logan frowns.

"That one is so sad!" I wave away the thought. "I mean, I like full-length books, too. Jane Austen is way timeless. *Sense and Sensibility*, obviously—with the sisters and everything. What about you?"

Logan nods and then seems to think for a minute. "Can *I* be honest now?"

"Definitely," I say.

"I think my favorite book would be *Love That Dog*," Logan says. "I know it's, like, poems and it's for kids, but it's always stuck with me. I just love that book."

"That's a really good choice."

We reach a four-way intersection where there are cafés and restaurants with outdoor patios. I can smell the fish tacos from one corner, gumbo from another, and burgers from a little spot down a few yards.

"Let's go to Sucré," I say, nodding across the street at the corner spot. It's contemporary in its light blue aged wood and Parisian accents, but it somehow fits here with the seaside vibe.

We cross the street, and I see my grandmother, Nana, approaching the door from inside. She's carrying a huge paper bag full of peaches in one arm, and she's wearing a denim jacket over a bohemian maxi-dress that's tied up to her shin in the front.

"Hare!" She pulls me in for a hug.

"Hi," I say, peeking into the bag. "Oh, are you making your pie?"

"For the ladies in my evening class." She nods.

She looks Logan up and down and then glances at me expectantly.

"This is Logan," I say. "And this is my nana."

"Nice to meet you," she says, offering her free hand.

Logan shakes it and agrees it's nice to meet her.

"Well, I'm going to go and get started on this. You and your sisters need to come by the house soon to see my new plants." She pushes her glasses up on her nose and gives me another hug before saying she loves me.

Nana waves to Logan, and, as he steps away and reaches for the door, she whispers to me in a blink-and-you-miss-it moment, "He seems much better than Grant."

I roll my eyes and shake my head, but she's already erupting in laughter and hurrying away before I can say anything.

Holding the door open for me, Logan grins. "So you call her Nana? She seems cool."

I nod. "She is cool. She's an artist."

I watch his eyes light up as we walk into Sucré.

It's a French bakery with a little market they added a couple years ago. Two walls of windows brighten the place as light wood floors and snow-white marble counters bounce the sunshine like mirrors. There are hanging exposed bulbs and wire shelves abundant with ingredients. The entire place smells sweet and fresh, like angel food cake or a pear sponge dessert with whipped cream and powdered sugar.

The couple who owns it is the coolest. They always wear cozy sweaters and aprons with flour all over them. Odette is behind the counter, helping the long line of customers. I swear it's always busy here. Her hair's wiry and gray, but it's lively and beautiful, tossed up effortlessly.

"Harold!" she calls out as we reach the cases of pastries. She folds a paper bag and takes a woman's credit card, smiling from ear to ear and no doubt saying something lovely. This process repeats for a bit until we arrive at the register and she grabs a piece of chocolate from behind the counter, handing me a piece.

"Oh, thank you!" I say. I break it in half and offer a piece to Logan. "Odette, Logan. Logan, Odette."

The two exchange happy greetings, and Logan looks like his world has been forever changed as he chews on the chocolate. He eyes the inside of the display—macarons are neatly packed into a sugary rainbow beside cupcakes and beignets and tarts with every berry imaginable.

"Logan's new in town," I tell Odette. Then, realizing Odette probably knows his uncle, I smile. "He's working at the club and staying with his uncle Ron!"

Odette studies Logan and nods. "Oh, Ron Waters. And your aunt is Jane."

"That's right," Logan says, and I think there's something like pride in the way he stands up a little straighter and smiles a little wider.

"Good people." Odette hands us another piece of chocolate. "*Rarissime.* Tell them Odette says hello. What do you two want? It's on me."

"Odette," I say, eyes going wide as I cover my mouth and swallow the chocolate.

"For you? And Ron and Jane's nephew? Please, I'm happy to." She leans over the counter. "And seriously. We have a wedding coming up in a couple weeks and they bought enough macarons to pay rent for two months! *À volonté!*"

I gasp dramatically, and we laugh. "Well, thank you."

"Yes, ma'am, thank you very much." Logan raises a brow at the menu. "Could I get the… Gaufres au Poulet Frite?" Only it sounds like "gophers, aw, pull it Frito."

Odette giggles at his pronunciation, her eyes turning up at the corners. "Sure thing, dear. Harold, croque monsieur? And some pistachio macarons?"

"*Oui*, you know me so well." I drum my hands on the counter.

Odette nods. "I just saw your nana in here. She seems to be doing well."

"Same old Nana," I say, watching the total rise on the card reader. I can't believe she's giving us all this free. How much does she love Logan's aunt and uncle, anyway? Typically, she gives me some chocolate—she has since I was little—and sometimes a pastry.

"I'll bring coffee." Odette beams. *"Bon appétit!"*

"Merci," I say. I like to think my accent isn't half bad after all these years of Odette giving me mini lessons, but I probably sound ridiculous.

"Merci," Logan says. I'm sure he'll get the hang of it eventually.

We sit at one of the tables; they're wooden and round with

pristine white marble tops and small vases with fresh flowers. *Les fleurs sont la vie*, according to Odette. That is, flowers are life.

Odette brings our coffee over in two beautiful white-and-blue-painted mugs. Clinging to her side and tugging at her apron is her six-year-old grandson, Henrie.

"Harold, did you know I started to read *Percy Jackson* last week?" Henrie claps his hands together. "It's a chapter book. Like the ones you read! I'm getting faster at reading."

"Wow," I say. "That's amazing. You're so smart. I bet Lottie would love it if you'd read *Percy Jackson* to her."

Henrie blushes, because he definitely does *not* have a crush on Lottie. He studies Logan, as if a little unsure of him, then he grins at us both and hurries away. Odette laughs, and I thank her for the coffee as she chases after him.

I glance over to see Odette, still all smiles and warmth as she dons gloves and reaches in the pastry case. Her husband, Jean-Claude, walks out from the back room, door swinging in with all his gumption. They always have this zest for life, and they treat us all like we belong at their table.

"So… Am I allowed to ask who it is I seem better than?" Logan looks at me over his cup.

Shit. It's a welcomed interruption when Odette brings over our food.

"Yeah, I'm sorry. I was hoping you didn't hear that," I finally say. "My nana just says things. But um—"

"You don't have to get into it," Logan offers.

"Just the guy I was hanging out with last summer," I say. "She must have thought you and I…" I stop myself. "He and I weren't ever 'official,' but it didn't end very well."

"I get it," Logan says. "Ex-boyfriends—er, in your case *not*-ex-boyfriends—can be the worst."

I lean back in my chair and remember the text I saw on Logan's phone the day I helped him out of the locker. The one I thought was from his ex-girlfriend but, now I fully realize, was about his ex-boyfriend.

"Care to elaborate?" I say.

Silence floats between us before Logan takes a giant bite of his chicken and motions that he can't talk with his mouth full, which successfully elicits a laugh from me. If he doesn't want to share, I can respect that.

"What exactly are those?" Logan says, pointing to the little pale green macarons on my plate.

"Macarons?" I pick one up and hand it to him. "They're life changing. You have to try one."

Logan accepts it, taking a small bite and closing his eyes as he chews. "Wow."

"I know, right?"

"Yeah, that's—" Logan sets down the rest of the macaron, reaches into his pocket, and pulls out his phone. His expression is unreadable, but he leaps up.

"Uh—" He goes to say something but stops.

I blink. "Is everything okay?"

Logan just sort of freezes for a moment before looking back at his phone. "Yep, just need a second. Sorry."

"Okay..." Before I can say anything else, Logan is hurrying past the other tables and out the front door.

I'm reminded of last summer, of Grant disappearing to make mysterious phone calls. I knew at the time it must have been something top secret, but I kept hoping he was working on a cool surprise or something. But nope, he was talking to his parents and ironing out details for their move the whole time.

Through the window, I watch Logan as he holds the phone up to his ear with one hand and runs the other through his hair before it lands on the back of his neck and he appears to groan. Frustration? No, the way his eyes lower and his mouth goes still, it looks more like sadness. Disappointment.

He kicks his foot at the leg of a bench and nods, stuffing his hand in his pocket as he begins pacing back and forth. There are all of these emotions riddled across his face, but I don't know him well enough to decipher them just yet.

Finally, he hangs up and puts the phone in his pocket, sighing and taking a deep breath before turning toward the door.

I spin around in my chair, hoping he didn't notice me watching his call.

"Everything okay?" I say.

"Oh." Logan offers a smile that doesn't quite seem to stick and sits back down. "Yeah, it's all good."

I nod. And it's not that he owes me the truth or some insight into his personal life. It's just I've been here before, sitting across from someone who wants to keep certain things to himself, and there's part of me that can't help but wonder why.

"All right. You know what I'd really love?" Logan says, straightening up.

"What?"

"If you'd let me read your screenplay," he says. "Come on, I know you're working on something great."

I consider it for a moment. "I don't know if it's great, but it's special to me, even though it's really geeky."

"Well, now I need to know what it's about," Logan says. "I'm assuming it's not *Star Wars* related?"

I laugh and shake my head. "No, it's a superhero movie. But gay. And also kind of a romantic comedy."

"Shit, Harry. That sounds awesome."

"Thanks," I say, looking down at my fingers as I fiddle with the corner of my napkin.

"So, can I read some?"

It's not that I'm ashamed of my writing or anything, but it's super personal. Writing is personal. It's one of the things I do that's just real and *me*. No pretense or "shoulds." Just what I want it to be. So, normally, I'd need to think this over, but when I look at the light in Logan's eyes, it's like I don't need to think. In this moment, his mysterious phone call or whatever isn't important. What's important is how I feel comfortable enough to talk about the script with him at all.

Besides, I could honestly use an extra pair of eyes on it before I submit. And eventually, lots of people will be reading my screenplays. It's time I get comfortable with sharing.

"Yeah," I say. "Yeah, Logan, you can read some."

Logan shuffles excitedly in his seat. "I have a good feeling about this."

"What's your email?" I say, knowing if I don't send it to him right now when he's got me all buttered up, I'll change my mind later because I *never* share my writing with people. He tells me his email once I've pulled my laptop out of my bag, and I curse internally, wondering for a split moment why I'm sending him this. Still, with the tap of a button, I've sent Logan the working file.

"It's really personal," I say, leaving it at that.

"It's in good hands, promise," Logan says.

I nod, drinking some of my coffee. It's so weird, but I believe him.

"So, you get a croque monsieur for breakfast?" Logan finally says, as if he'd been holding it in.

"Says the guy who ordered chicken and waffles," I chuckle. "Well, *attempted* to order them."

He holds his hand to his chest, mouth wide and expression aghast. "Are you saying my French isn't *parfait*?"

"I'd never say such a thing." I take a sip of my coffee and find myself laughing harder than I have in a while.

After Logan has headed back to his aunt and uncle's, I'm walking toward Shelly's to get my bike. I'm trying not to get too caught up in my head, but I can't deny for a second there, Logan and I were flirting. And I liked it. Which is against my rules and made even worse by the fact that he clearly is keeping his own secrets. There seems to be so much about him I don't know.

Yet, I do know Logan is ridiculously cute, alarmingly sweet, and not like the boys I have known in the past.

But where does that leave me?

INT. WOODS INDUSTRIES CAFETERIA

Skip and Rory are both dressed professionally. Skip's badge is in a Star Wars lanyard.

They take their trays and find a seat. The escalators lead down to the lobby, where there are numerous armed guards.

>   RORY
> We didn't use to have a million men toting guns around the lobby.

>   SKIP
> Can't be too cautious right now.

Rory picks up his burger and nods.

>   RORY
> It freaks me out. My mom's here all the time, and just knowing what's going on...

SKIP
(shoving his hoagie in his mouth)
Yeah, but she's safe.

RORY
True. The Sting would save her if anything happened.

SKIP
Oh, you do love The Sting.

RORY
Like I said—he saved me once. I know it probably
sounds silly, but it was, like a scene in a movie. And for a
second I almost thought...

Skip marvels at him.

SKIP
Thought what?

RORY
Don't laugh.

SKIP
I won't!

RORY
Well, I thought we were going to kiss or something. It
was just this *moment*.

SKIP
You know some people think he terrorizes the city. Like
that journalist? Steve Thunder?

RORY
My mom thinks so, too. Even after he saved me. But he's not terrorizing the city. He's protecting us.

SKIP
Yeah…

RORY
How could anybody not realize he's the good guy?

10

JUST FRIENDS

The next day, Books by the Sea is vibrant and bursting with life. There are new vases with fresh flowers—ceramic and tall glass pieces showing off long green stems and white peonies, yellow tulips, and every color of hydrangea. The smell of piping hot coffee wafts through the store, and, to top it all off, Jesse brought in a dozen donuts. The smells must be drawing in customers because we've been busy all day.

At the moment, Jesse is dancing around to the All Out '60s playlist and dusting like she's the fairy godmother.

"Someone is in a good mood," I say, taping up a box and sticking a shipping label on it. I wipe at my mouth, making sure there are no remnants of chocolate icing.

Jesse nods, and Agnes peers over to us from the book club shelf she's stocking.

"My nephew is coming to town." Jesse beams. "He's getting married this month, and it was supposed to be this whole thing in the Bahamas, but there was an issue with passports or something. Either way, the beach club had a cancelation, and now we're going to have everybody come here!"

"That's so fun!"

"Yeah, and they're excited to extend their honeymoon using the money they saved by not having a destination wedding. I haven't seen them in forever, so it's a big deal for me." Jesse smiles. "And we get to plan it all together. His fiancée is beyond stressed, but I know it'll be great."

Even Agnes smiles at this before directing her attention back to the books.

"Oh, Harry, incoming." Jesse winks and looks to the door.

The bell chimes, and Logan walks in, wearing his uniform and holding his skateboard, as "Then He Kissed Me" plays over the speakers.

"I'm not stalking you," he jokes, cheeks going red as I walk over to greet him. "My aunt wants the new Bottle Beach Murder Club book. She's really into them."

I laugh, nodding and taking him over to the new release shelf, right next to Agnes and the book club picks. I glance over to the door like I'm on lookout—Grant will be here in about thirty minutes, and I'm just not ready for them to meet yet. Maybe they'll never even have to.

"You're not going to introduce us to your friend?" Jesse calls out, walking around the counter toward us.

"Right." My chest tightens. Jesse might as well be my actual aunt, because she definitely knows how to embarrass me in that way only family can. "Logan, this is Jesse, and this is Agnes."

Much to my surprise, Agnes stands up straight and smiles, extending her hand. "Nice to meet you."

Jesse shakes his hand next and eyes his polo. "You work at the beach club? We were just talking about it—my nephew is getting married there."

"Oh, yes, ma'am. I'm just on my break, but I work at the pool." Logan smiles.

"I'm old enough to be *ma'am*, now." Jesse nods slowly, holding her hand over her heart as if she's wounded. She points at Logan as she walks back to the counter. "Touché."

"Sorry." Logan blushes. "I wasn't—"

"I'm only messing with you." Jesse smiles. "Truthfully I am old enough to be your mom. Don't know how that happened."

We all laugh at this, and Agnes sidles over to pull a copy of the newest Bottle Beach Murder Club book off the shelf, handing it to Logan. "Fair warning, she'll totally see the twist coming."

"I didn't know you read those," I say to Agnes.

"Oh, religiously," Agnes says. "My grandma got my sister and me hooked on them."

Logan nods. "They are kinda grandma books, but I have to admit they're sort of awesome."

"They're about three women who knit their own cardigans and live in a quaint, rainy beach town solving murders," Agnes tells me.

"And they always solve it by tea time," Jesse adds.

Logan raises his brows. "Don't tell me you're not intrigued."

"Here, you have to try this other series, too, if you haven't already." Agnes takes Logan over to the opposite corner of the store, and they become engrossed in conversation around a paperback series with retro covers.

Eventually, Logan realizes he's been in the store far longer than he meant to be and hurries to pay so he won't be late to work. He thanks Agnes, his new mystery-loving best friend, and awkwardly says sorry to Jesse again for calling her ma'am, assuring her she's "not ma'am age at all."

I wave him off and notice the little book cart—the one with sale books we keep outside under the window—is looking a little disheveled. I try to tidy it up a little, but the paperbacks keep falling over and the $1 books are mixed in with the $3 books and it's all just a mess.

I catch myself looking down the sidewalk, watching Logan make his way to the club on his skateboard. I absentmindedly arrange the books by their price stickers, thinking about him and the weird sense of comfort I feel whenever he's around.

"Huh, you weren't kidding about working at the bookstore, Kensy." Foster stops to lean up against the door frame of the store. He's soaking wet, like he always is, wearing board shorts, a surf shop tee, and Vans with little hibiscus flowers and palm leaves on them.

"I was not kidding," I laugh. "Is it so unbelievable?"

"Not at all." Foster nods. "I just thought it was an excuse to get out of hanging out with me. After the whole thing—which I'm bringing up *again*. Sorry."

"Don't be sorry," I say. "I actually forgot to text you last night, but my mom mentioned she's looking for a freelancer to help with some TikTok content. She has an agency, but she said their TikToks were really bad and she needs a 'real Gen Z,' and I said I know someone and—"

"What?"

"I mean you for sure don't have to if you don't want to, since I'm sure a beauty brand isn't your first choice," I say. "But I remembered you talking about your TikToks." I lower my voice just in case Jesse and Agnes can hear from inside, though the music and chorus of customers chatting is pretty loud, even out here. "Plus, I want to make it up to you. The whole treating you like a secret thing. Not that this will magically make it better, but I feel really bad, and this is at least a start, right?"

"Kensy, that's *awesome*." Foster squeezes my shoulder. "Sick! My sister is going to flip. Maybe she can be in them or something. She'll be back in town soon. Whoa, thank you."

"Of course!"

"And you *really* don't have to make it up to me." Foster smiles. "I promise."

"Cool," I say, though I definitely still want to make it up to him. "So, what are you up to?"

"Going to work," Foster says. "Got in a sesh—the waves are pretty great. One day you have to come out with us."

I offer a tight-lipped smile. "I'm so not surfing. Ever."

Foster chuckles and then holds up his phone. "I'm looking forward to TikToking with your mom." He winces. "You know what I—okay, see you, Kensy."

I almost double over laughing, but I wave goodbye to Foster and instinctively look to the sidewalk as if I might still see Logan on his skateboard, though of course he's long gone by now.

A few minutes later, the loudspeaker, now playing "Where the Boys Are," is interrupted by the chime of the bell and one more familiar face.

"Grant!" Jesse cries. "Oh my goodness, look at you! You are even more grown up than I remember."

"Hi, Jesse." Grant meets her for a hug, his old boat shoes padding across the wood floor.

"I saw your mom at Publix, and she mentioned you guys were here for the summer," Jesse says, clearly beyond excited to see him. She has no clue about last summer. I don't even know if she realizes Grant and I are friends.

That is still so surreal to acknowledge. *Grant and I are friends*, I think to myself.

"We are!" he says, looking from Jesse to me. "Harry and I are getting pizza."

Grant texted me last night asking if I had plans for dinner today. I'd agreed to hang out with him—how could I *already* have forgotten? I watch Jesse's interest rise as she realizes we're hanging out. Thankfully, the phone rings just in time, and since Agnes seems to have disappeared, Jesse goes to answer it.

"Though I actually do need a good book while I'm here."

"You're a little early," I say.

"I am?" Grant looks at his watch. "I thought you said you're off at 5:00?"

"5:30," I say.

We browse the shelves for what feels like hours, though it's actually as long as it takes for four songs to play.

"You like working here?" Grant says, looking over a couple titles. "Last night was the first time you mentioned it."

I furrow my brow. "Really? I think I've just been so preoccupied with my script."

"Right," Grant says. "I'm a little surprised you picked Books by the Sea over, like, Neptune's Theater."

"They only give high-schoolers the late shifts," I say. "But I honestly do love it here. It's fun."

"How Kathleen Kelly," Grant teases. I ignore the reference, since it reminds me of when we were more than friends, and look at the clock. Grant's eyes follow mine, and he nods, holding up his new political thriller. "Well, since I'm early, I'll put this book in my car, get a pizza, and meet you by the pier."

"Sounds good."

"And we can talk shop. My dad said the letter shouldn't be a problem, but he brought up some other good points about helping you get into USC."

"Awesome," I say. Perfect—keeping it very friendly and casual. Plus, talking about college couldn't be time wasted.

After Grant pays, he and Jesse catch up for a couple more minutes before he's out the door.

It feels a little strange that in the span of thirty minutes I've seen Logan, Foster, and Grant. I'm just grateful they weren't all here at the same time. That would have been awkward. Or potentially awkward. Though I guess it shouldn't be, really. It's not like I'm dating or hooking up with any of them.

Not wanting to think about guys anymore, I decide to spend the last fifteen minutes of my shift finishing the restock. I thumb through some of the paperback adult romances—it's like love is on my brain whether I want it to be or not. Seriously ready to think of something else, I shift gears to restocking the magazine stand. I flip through the latest issue of *Entertainment Weekly* and fawn over the summer box office features.

Agnes comes to take over my abandoned box of romance books, even offering me a smile, which is definitely new for us.

"Do all those guys like you?" Agnes raises a brow, speaking quietly, like we're two friends and Jesse is the adult who we don't want to hear us.

I laugh, though my voice shakes a little. "No!"

"Sure. Well, I'm invested, and I need to know which one you're going to pick," Agnes says.

"It's really not like that," I insist.

"Logan has great taste in books." She smiles.

Since when is Agnes so nice to me?

"I have to be honest," I say, not sure how else to bring up this sudden change in our dynamic. "I thought you didn't like me?"

"No, not at all." Agnes sighs. "Things are just a little complicated."

I try to read her expression—it's not the original sort of cold exterior I got from Agnes, but it's still one of slight reservation. "How so?"

Tapping her fingers along the spine of a book, Agnes chews on the inside of her cheek and then turns to me. "Let me preface by saying nothing could come from this."

"Okay," I say, setting the stack of magazines back in the box and giving her my full, undivided attention.

"I'm applying to internships in London," she says quickly, still a bit hushed. "Again who knows if I'll get one, I feel like I'm jinxing it by even saying it…"

I grin. "That's amazing!"

"Thanks," she says, warming up a little bit more. "Well, I've been the only other permanent staff member besides Jesse for three years now. You know, seasonal hires tend to come and go, and some are better than others. But now that I'm leaving, I'm just a little more critical of the new hires. I'm hoping we can find someone to stay on year-round."

That definitely explains why she was so chilly at first.

"Wait, are there other new hires?" I say.

"Not yet," Agnes laughs. "Jesse has been letting me do the initial interviews."

Enough said.

After a moment, I look from the box of books to Agnes.

"You know, I understand why you want to go," I say.

"What?"

"Why you want to go to London," I tell her. "I can relate. I can't wait to get out of Citrus Harbor and experience other things."

Agnes smiles, though it seems slightly off. "I don't know everything about your life, but it definitely seems like you have it all here. Friends, your family. Cute boys left and right. I've never really fit in or felt like I belong here, you know? And ever since my big sister—my only real friend—moved to London, I've been trying to save and make it happen. It hasn't been easy, though."

I frown. "What about your boyfriend?"

Agnes shrugs. "We've just been together for three years. It's not bad, but it's not like a romance novel either. He'd be fine with me going. We've talked about it."

That doesn't sound super amazing.

"It's funny, you guys have a lot in common actually." Agnes beams. "You and my sister, I mean. She's outgoing and a big dreamer—that's probably obvious since she moved to London and everything. And she always has all these guys fawning over her."

"I do not have guys fawning over me," I laugh.

Agnes raises a brow. "Well, anyway, I'm only saying all of this because I wanted to tell you it seems like you have a lot going for you." She shrugs. "So don't wish it all away just yet."

Before I can even say anything, Jesse hollers over to us. "What are you guys talking about?"

"London," I call back.

Jesse raises a brow and grabs a donut.

"Okay, now tell me about Logan," Agnes says, even *giggling* a little. "How did you meet?"

EXT. UNIVERSITY LAWN

Rory and Skip eat frozen yogurt on a bench.

      RORY
All right, so what do you want to tell me?

      SKIP
You know how The Vicious are trying to get all of these
different genetic materials and technologies?

      RORY
Yeah?

      SKIP
And you know how last year there was all that stuff
with the multiverse...

      RORY
Yeah.

SKIP

Well, when all that went down, your mom's labs enhanced Captain Warp's DNA to *literally* be as powerful as a black hole. If not more powerful. Which was great, because he saved the world. But, now, we think The Vicious want to duplicate that, to create a soldier that can effectively wipe out our universe entirely.

RORY

Why would they do that?

SKIP

It's complicated. Basically, we think The Vicious are from an alternate dimension and the only true threat to their power is The Champions Alliance, since they can travel through space and time and all that. Wipe out this dimension—

RORY

And you wipe out The Champions Alliance... Well, what does Mr. Wilson think?

SKIP

That's the thing. He doesn't know. We have reason to believe The Champions Alliance finding out is what triggers the apocalypse.

Rory raises a brow.

RORY

So I'm just supposed to take your word for it and not tell Mr. Wilson? You're a Future Defense intern!

SKIP
The fate of the dimension depends on you taking my word for it.

RORY
(standing up)
I can't believe I'm saying this, but meet me at Westside Park? 6:30?

SKIP
(saluting)
Aye, aye, Cap'n.

CLOSE-UP. Rory's eyes narrow.

11

SAY ANYTHING...

After eating pizza at one of the tables on the boardwalk, Grant and I decide to walk down to the sand.

While I wanted to bring up USC, it didn't come up naturally, and I really don't want to make Grant think that's all our friendship is about. My moral compass isn't steady on this one—it *is* part of the reason I agreed to have dinner with him, but he was the one who brought it up, so is that really so wrong?

Though, I have to admit to myself I don't hate the new Grant's company. He's open and comforting, and it's nice to have a friend who isn't completely obsessed with their relationship...

Unlike someone I know.

Grant walks a few steps ahead and crouches down. The swelling ocean inches toward his bare feet, and the wind whips around his tousled chestnut bangs. He turns to look at me.

"Remember what you said about sand dollars?" His smile

is sincere, and he squints a little as the sun pokes through the clouds above us.

I stop just behind him and roll my eyes.

"Remember?"

"Of course," I say. "They're good luck."

"And?"

Which is so like Grant—there has to be a little bit more. He has to push as much as possible because it's his way. I can't only remember some of it, can't only feel that entire conversation from last summer rush to the front of my mind. I have to say it so he knows how much it all still means to me.

"I don't remember exactly," I say, trying to fake it, but he shakes his head and stands up, his hands behind his back.

"You said if it's broken, like most of them are, it's a little lucky. But…" He signals for me to continue.

"But if the ocean had an ATM, an entire sand dollar is worth the most luck," I finish, my cheeks going hot. Grant brings out a different side of me, one that repeats the things my grandpa said to me when I was little.

Grant's mouth curves up, and he chuckles, holding his hands out in front of him to show me an entire, fully intact sand dollar, only made imperfect by all the sand flaked over it.

"Wow," I say.

"Right?" Grant says. "This must be *really* lucky."

We're standing here, way past the pier, because we've walked for ages—first in a knowing silence, then blanketed in Grant's desperate need to fill the void with random things he's noticed have changed since he's been back. I want to tell him not much has changed at all. That feels like I'd be betraying myself, though.

When we'd dropped our shoes by the lifeguard stand on 4th Street as the sun was beginning to set, I'd wondered where this would go, but now I'm just caught up in it like old times, and I don't know where any of this starts or ends.

"You know," Grant says as he gestures for me to take the sand dollar. When I do, and we start to walk again, he exhales. "I *do* feel lucky to be here. Walking with you. And I know I owe you more apologies. An infinite number of them, even. But I'm glad we're friends again."

"Me too."

Grant's footsteps are the same as they always were—they're soft and slow, but they're also confident, like him. He knows I'll follow. I keep reminding myself this isn't the same thing as last time—he may still be next to me, between me and the ocean in the khakis he's rolled up to his calves, but this time he didn't need to do that because we're not going to chase each other, laughing, racing the tide.

We're just two friends on a platonic walk.

We *can* be friends.

We have to be.

The wind hits us hard after we pass under a small pier, and Grant's hair looks so ridiculous I can't help but reach over and fix it for him. His eyes go soft, and his cheeks flash red. Unsure if I should have done that, I smile down at my feet, bringing my hand back and tracing the lines of the sand dollar.

"You don't have to... You're not going to catch fire if you touch me."

I swallow—inhale, exhale, and then blink, looking over to Grant.

I realize I'm hopeless.

"Last summer, at the carnival, we got stuck on the Ferris wheel—do you remember?"

Grant laughs, a big, heartfelt, knock-his-head-back laugh. "Yeah, of course. That was a good night."

"I'll never forget when we got back to my house, you were laying on my bed with me, and I ended up putting on *You've Got Mail*—"

"For the millionth time." Grant smirks.

"Not the point," I say, ignoring the fact that he only watched *You've Got Mail* with me a handful of times. Which is *not* that bad. It's only two hours long, and he got plenty of kissing out of it. "I was upset about the Ferris wheel breaking down because it messed up our perfect moment. It was supposed to be so romantic, kissing when we got to the top, but instead we were stuck, dangling there for forty-five minutes. It just killed that whole idea. Even though we still got our kiss, it wasn't how I imagined it."

Grant studies me.

"And you said I was only setting myself up for failure. You said 'life is not like the movies.'"

Grant chews on the inside of his mouth.

"Don't remember that?"

"I don't," Grant says. "Sounds a little harsh."

"Well, I guess you were right," I say. "I have all these big dreams and ideas, but I'm not in some movie where things magically work out in the end. A cinematic happily ever after isn't inevitable, after all. Maybe, in real life, I'm destined to fail. I'm going to be stuck here in Citrus Harbor, regretting all these choices I made. Like being here *right now*."

Grant raises a brow.

"I don't mean like, here with you," I say, laughing. "I mean the fact that, once again, I am procrastinating. I feel like I have to accept failure at some point. It must just be part of me, otherwise I'd be at home working toward my dreams. I'm all talk."

"Harry, you're not going to fail. That's nuts. Where is all this coming from?" Grant says.

"Because of you and LA and… You said I wouldn't catch fire if I touch you," I say. "And that's not true. I will. It'll be wildfire, and I won't be able to put it out. You were my first love."

That stops Grant in his tracks, and he turns to me.

"What did you just—"

"I know," I say, turning to face him as I feel my breath hitch. "I never said it, but I think you were."

"I never thought you would…"

"But if I am going to fail," I say. "If I'm not going to end up in LA, after all, spending weekends with you and watching *our* dreams come true… I don't wanna risk falling for you again just to say goodbye, I guess."

The ocean is calm behind Grant, and a few kids throw sand at each other to our right, but other than that this moment feels totally still. Finally, Grant breaks the stillness and starts walking again, this time back the way we came.

"You know, if I could, I'd watch *You've Got Mail* with you every day."

"Shut up."

"I mean it," he says earnestly, almost offended by my response. "I would, even on FaceTime, if you needed to take a year before you transferred? That's an option, right? I'd even act it out with you. Say all the lines. I still remember some of it. Would you want me to be…"

"Oh, you're definitely Tom Hanks," I say with a sly grin. "Without a doubt, you would be Tom Hanks."

Grant throws his hands up. "So what does that mean? I'm the big bad Fox?"

"Or you could be Greg Kinnear," I say.

"Ouch." Grant slaps his chest like he's just been wounded.

"Anyway…" I admire the sand dollar in my palm and question the meaning of this entire conversation with Grant. "I think if you had your way you'd never have to watch *You've Got Mail* again, and you'd just play video games and go surfing all the time."

Unfazed, Grant scoffs. "Maybe my proposal was a little excessive."

"Oh, it was a *proposal*." I feign amusement.

"That was implied." Grant buries his hands in his pockets and sucks his teeth. "If I could—if you'd let me—I'd be with you every day. Today. Tomorrow. On FaceTime. In LA. In your Brentwood dream home. At the Oscars."

My heart skips hearing that. Of course it does, because it's Grant and it's not like anyone wouldn't swoon a little hearing that from someone else. Especially if that someone was Grant Kennedy.

"I know we're just *friends*," Grant says. "But will you give me one date?"

"What? No."

"Come on!"

"I don't think it's a good idea," I tell him as I remember how nice it felt just being with Logan this morning. With Grant, it's overwhelming and all-encompassing, but it's also heavy, kind of like rereading a book when you know you love all the parts except the ending. "We're doing so well as friends!"

Once again, Grant stops walking, and I mimic him. The space between us closes quickly, and he's standing in front of me now, almost chest to chest before I stagger back.

"I remember when you and I went to Lottie's ballet recital," Grant offers like it's supposed to make me forget everything. "The one where she rolled her eyes on stage and stomped off, saying she hated ballet loud enough for the entire theater to hear. You know the recital I'm talking about?"

Lottie threatened to rip her leotard off Hulk-style in the wings, which we all also heard. So, of course I know the recital he's talking about. I only nod, though I want to smile thinking about how Nana gave Lottie a high five when Mom wasn't looking.

"After the recital, Lottie was supremely pissed at your mom for making her do ballet," Grant says.

"She was trying to help her be well-rounded," I offer.

"And you told Lottie sometimes we just try things, just to see," Grant says with a devilishly slick smile. "Didn't you?"

I burst out laughing. "Yeah, I did."

With that, Grant steps forward and brings his hand to my jaw. He pauses, our eyes locked, as if to ask if it's all right. I give the slightest nod and he kisses me. His lips feel familiar and new at the same time. It's like swimming in the same ocean but being caught up in the riptide. And I'm not fighting the current, not even trying to keep my head above water, I'm allowing myself to be swept away in it, to submerge, sink, and drown.

Grant's fingers trace the tips of my ears and my chin and tug gently at my hair. I'm only pulled from the current of his kiss when he breaks to take a breath and looks down, his forehead resting on mine.

I inhale sharply, with Grant's hands still cradling my face and mine still between us, holding the delicate sand dollar.

"I wonder if I could work at a backlot café before I transfer? Like *La La Land*."

"*That's* what you're thinking about after that kiss?" Grant laughs.

"I can't help it!"

"I bet you could," Grant says. "But you're putting the cart before the horse. You still have time to make sure you get in as a freshman. You just need to put your mind to it."

Duh, Harry. Put your mind to it.

Transferring is my last resort. And I'm in control of my actions. No more wasting time. No more waiting for the perfect idea or being all "woe is me."

Getting it together, I smile and pat Grant's chest before side-stepping and starting back up the beach.

"So the date?"

I shrug.

"You're *really* going to make me work for it," Grant chuffs behind me, though I can hear his smile.

"Well," I call back. "If you don't have any more trips down memory lane planned for today, I'll agree to go on *one* date with you."

Grant hurries to catch up and bumps into me, stumbling forward. "That's all I want."

"Better make it good."

And I wonder if he will. For a moment, I'm lost in this new chapter for us. I don't know the ending, but it seems to be starting differently.

Then my phone buzzes as I'm walking back to my bike:

FOSTER: Sooo... More people know about Justin

EXT. THE CITY AT SUNSET. A PARK ON THE WATER. IT'S MODERN AND BREATHTAKING.

Rory, Skip, and Jenson stop along the railing.

    JENSON
There's no way.

    RORY
Future Defense can predict this stuff.

    JENSON
Yeah, I know. I just think… How can we trust this kid?

    SKIP
I'm right here.

    RORY
Come on, Jenson. It's all up to us.

JENSON
Fine. Then, Rory, you need to break into your mom's
lab and get my genetic material so they can't get their
hands on it to replicate it.

RORY
Why me?

JENSON
You have clearance.

RORY
You can warp reality. You do it!

CLOSE-UP. Jenson frowns.

JENSON
If I come too close to it, who knows what will happen.
So you need to get it, and then we'll have to find a safe
place to secure it. For now, let's just get it, and we'll go
from there.

RORY
Half-baked plan, once again. Got it.

CLOSE-UP. Skip blinks.

SKIP
Mr. Wilson is gonna kill me.

12

WHAT IF

Restless, I roll over and tap my phone. It's now 6:15 a.m.

I'm going to have to tell Hailey today. There's no more putting it aside. If other people know, I have to get ahead of it.

I read my texts with Foster again. He says some of the guys from that surf trip were talking shit at the skate park yesterday. I find it suspicious that I haven't heard about this for a year and then suddenly Foster hears about it completely "randomly." What are the odds, anyway?

This is part of why being in a small town is so annoying.

On top of the knots in my stomach over what I have to tell Hailey, I now only have about a week before the submission deadline for the contest, and since I agreed to take one of Agnes's shifts at the store, I'm down almost another entire day. I'm getting nervous, but I'm honestly not as far from being finished as I thought. I only have to write a little less than a third of the script, and then I'm finished.

Grant is right. I just have to focus.

I can do this. I will do this.

This summer is going to be the death of me.

My lips are still buzzing after that last kiss. My entire body feels like it's still enveloped in Grant and his annoyingly charming arms.

After our walk on the beach and all the talk of *You've Got Mail*, I got some solid writing done. It helps the romance writing process when your heart is doing somersaults in real life—reminding you of that feeling of euphoric tension and the tug in your chest because it's all about the other person.

But I can't get ahead of myself. I can acknowledge that the kiss was great and there is a chance our date will go well, but I absolutely need to keep my eye on the prize and remember why I'm keeping Grant at a distance in the first place. This isn't some whirlwind fairy-tale romance, after all, this is only a second chance—a maybe.

All of the best movies help us feel something. They wake something up inside us, asking questions and giving answers. But on the other side of it, you know those writers are on their own journey. They're solving things and sharing experiences and emotions.

It's empathy, a two-way street.

As a kid, movies were everything for me. An escape from my parents' divorce and my dad moving away or even just a bad day at school. And as I grew up, I guess they saw me through it all—failures and heartbreaks and all the good stuff, too.

It makes sense that my best writing comes from genuine emotion, I guess.

Needing sustenance to continue my heartfelt excavation onto the page, I slide into my robe and make my way down the stairs to the kitchen. I grab the orange juice from the fridge and pour a generous amount into a glass. I'll get something to drink and a small breakfast and then I'll get to work on my script.

"It's too early," Lottie says, emerging from the hallway and taking a seat at one of the wooden island stools.

"For you it definitely is," I say, leaning on the marble she's now resting her head on.

"Pancakes?"

I sigh and laugh, ruffling her messy hair. "Sure. Want to see the sunrise first?"

Lottie never really *wants* to do anything before 10:00 or 11:00 a.m. She and Milly are the late sleepers. Mom is upstairs getting ready for work.

Lottie takes my hand and practically drags me out once I've promised her pancakes after sunrise. She's a girl on a mission. We pad down the wooden walkway, and she wiggles around as the chilly sand touches her toes.

"Come on," I say, pinching her waist lightly. She erupts into a ball of giggles, falling onto the sand and then running off toward the water. I follow quickly, and we sit at the edge of the ocean. It rises, and every so often it kisses our toes.

"This is nice," Lottie says, looking up at me before leaning against my arm.

She's not typically one for affection, so I take it gladly and smile off at the horizon. "It is."

"Don't you think it looks like a root beer float?" She points to the foam sliding up and down the glistening beige silk.

"Yeah," I laugh. "That is quite the observation."

We sit like this for a bit, some gulls chasing each other around in circles.

"Who's that?" Lottie whispers, pulling away and looking past me toward the miniature pier.

Logan's trekking across the sand, in a gray T-shirt and swim trunks, one hand in his pocket and one held up in a wave.

"Oh, he works at the club," Lottie tells me very seriously, once he's gotten close enough for her to see his face. "He's really nice."

I wave back to Logan and look back to her. "Is that right?"

"Yes." She narrows her eyes on me. "Be nice. He gives me lots of sweets."

As Logan gets closer, Lottie and I stand, brushing sand off ourselves.

"So you give Lottie lots of sweets?" I raise a brow.

Logan laughs and gives Lottie a high five. "I didn't know this little genius is your sister."

"Don't call her that," I warn, holding my hand up to faux whisper. "She doesn't need to hear it anymore."

Lottie folds her arms. "I do know an awful lot about science for a girl my age. Like about the cosmos and geology and even chemistry."

Logan nods, impressed. "That's right, you do."

"What are you up to?" I say it to Logan, though I am watching Lottie blush and pull at her pajama top.

Logan shrugs. "I like the sunrise."

"We do too," Lottie says before I can reply. "I usually like to sleep through it, but Harold was stomping around the house this morning. I'm getting pancakes once it's over."

Logan covers his mouth, laughing.

"I was not stomping," I tell Logan earnestly.

"Do you like pancakes?" Lottie says. "Harold makes special Pippa Pancakes."

"Pippa Pancakes?" Logan furrows a brow and studies me carefully.

Lottie places a hand on her hip. "Yes, haven't you heard of them?"

"I don't think most people have heard of them," I tell her. She looks positively perturbed by this news.

"Aren't you going to invite Logan?" Lottie looks at me like I have no manners. She grabs Logan's hand. "Come on, you have to try Pippa Pancakes. You can't say no."

"Well, I don't want to intrude, Lot." He looks to me as if to apologize.

Lot. Something bubbles up in me—like this is no longer even nearly in my control. Logan and Lottie have their own friendship. Logan is part of the world I live in now.

"No, you should definitely come in for breakfast!" I finally offer as Lottie's eyes set on me expectantly. "And I can make you regular pancakes if you're not a Pippa Pancake kind of guy."

Lottie squeezes Logan's hand and looks up at him very knowingly. "You will be. They're chocolate chip and banana with whipped cream and syrup."

"That does sound delicious," Logan says to her. He then looks to me. "Are you sure?"

I roll my eyes and smile. "Of course, of course."

By now, the sun has cast an orange-and-pink hue on the sky around us. A small crab scurries out of a hole and climbs over Lottie's foot, eliciting a loud squeal and then she's off running toward the wooden stairs, pulling Logan with her up to the house.

We wash off our legs and feet at the small shower Mom had installed in the backyard. She clearly had experienced one too many sandy disasters. Still, even with clean feet, I feel like there is something chaotic about this.

"Your house is really cool." Logan looks up at it while he's rinsing the bottoms of his feet. He wobbles a little, and I offer my arm for him to stabilize.

"Thanks! My mom redid a lot of it two summers ago," I say.

"I'll show you my room after we eat. I have a LEGO table," Lottie assures him. She's standing at the French doors, tapping her foot impatiently. The girl does *not* like to wait for her breakfast.

Once inside, we guide Logan past the family room and into the kitchen. He and Lottie sit at the island, and she shows him her favorite games on her iPad. She has a childproof iPad case—a gigantic purple bumper that's seen many falls and spills but still resists damage like a champ.

I pour coffee for Logan and me, giving Lottie a glass of milk.

"Just how big is your mom's beauty company?" Logan says, looking around.

"She's been in *Vogue*," Lottie says.

"*She* hasn't, but her makeup and skincare products have," I clarify. "But yeah, her stuff is pretty popular."

"You know *Vogue*, Logan?" Lottie raises a brow and nods

approvingly when Logan confirms he's heard of it. "And Sel-
fridges. It's British."

Mom comes rushing into the kitchen as I'm heating up the
skillet and mixing the batter, all dressy and ready for work.

"Hi," she says, looking from Logan to me to Logan to Lottie to Logan.

"Mom, this is Logan."

"Hi, Ms. Kensington." Logan stands and walks over to her,
offering his hand.

Mom shakes his hand and then hurries over to the coffee pot, opening the cabinet above it and pulling out a silver
thermos. "I've met you before, haven't I?"

"I work at the club?"

Mom smiles and nods, though her phone beeps, and she's
suddenly immersed in it. "Right, the club!"

"Lottie and I were just watching the sunrise, and we
bumped into Logan." I realize it must sound like I'm explain-
ing away a crime or some sort of disaster. Like the time Lottie shattered an entire box of china. Only Logan is definitely
not glassware, so I decide against any further explanation.

"He's never heard of Pippa Pancakes," Lottie shouts as if
it's the most shocking thing.

Mom laughs and raises her finger to her lips. "You don't
want to wake your sister."

"No, we do not want that," I say, raising a brow.

Logan's eyes pop against the blue tile backsplash in the
kitchen—I notice as he laughs along with Lottie at some
video.

"Okay, have a good day," Mom says, tightening the lid on
her cup and tapping on her phone again. She gives Logan and

me one final glance over, which thankfully he doesn't notice, before pursing her lips into a tight smile and turning away.

"Love you guys," she calls as she flies through the foyer and grabs her keys from the trinket tray by the door. "Good to see you, Logan!"

"Good to see you," Logan calls out as Lottie and I yell that we love her.

Milly comes stumbling down the stairs in pajama bottoms and an oversize band T-shirt from Brandy Melville. When she sees Logan, she only runs her fingers through her hair and rubs at her eyes before grabbing a mug. She greets him, seemingly not even fazed by the fact that he's in our kitchen with us, and they naturally fall into a conversation about some music they both like.

I cock my head. "So everyone knows Logan, then?"

"I'm working on replacing you, obviously," he says, eyes giving away the smile hidden behind his coffee cup.

I watch how Lottie and Milly fawn over Logan, and I feel myself fight the urge to do the same. Eventually, Milly and Lottie migrate to the living room, and after a brief moment of quiet, they're arguing over the remote.

"So..." Logan leans in close, allowing me to hear him over the squeals of my sisters' argument. "I read the screenplay you sent me."

My entire body ices over. Or it gets so hot it feels like it's frozen. I don't say anything, just feel my lips part as if there's a flicker of a thought I'd like to communicate. Logan read my screenplay. He *read* it. What I wrote. Now that I think of it, I can't believe I even sent it to him.

"It's amazing," Logan says. "I love the characters, and the story is so cool. You're really good!"

I can't exactly process this, so for a moment I just blink. He's complimenting my screenplay. This guy, who I know is intelligent and going places in life and has nothing to gain from lying about his feelings, likes my writing.

"And I love the setting, the way you have this whole fictional New York City." Logan smiles. "I could see this—total blockbuster. Summer hit. Tons of gay teens would really be super into this. Honestly, all teens."

Blockbuster...

"It doesn't follow the traditional blockbuster formula," I offer.

"So what?"

"So all those movies—the successful ones—have this formula they follow."

Logan's smile only grows, though. "You're making your own formula. Anyway, who says what's successful? Critics? The studio? The audience? Box offices? I'd say if it's something you love, it's already a success. Plus I, subjectively, think it's going to be a success, so. Not that my opinion is—"

"No, your opinion means a lot," I say. "I wasn't expecting you to like it so much."

"Well, you're *really* talented," Logan says. "USC is going to admit you, like, the second they get your application."

We laugh, and I go to pour us some more coffee, though the thought of USC admissions has made my chest a little tight.

"When can I read some more?" Logan says. "And when are you submitting it to that competition?"

"I have to finish it in, like, a week," I say, trying to play it cool, though it hits me the deadline is in exactly a week and three days.

Nodding, Logan taps his hands against the marble countertop. "Well, I think it's a guaranteed winner."

Before I can say anything, Logan's phone sounds. He holds it in his hand and studies it for a moment.

"Well, I should get going," he finally says. "But thank you so much for the coffee."

I don't know how to respond, so I just nod. It's like he's got Tony Stark or S.H.I.E.L.D. on the other end of that phone or something—someone he clearly doesn't feel the need to tell me about. Unfortunately, though, I don't think Logan is an Avenger.

I don't want to think badly of him or feel suspicious, but it's hard to control. I remember how I tried not to feel suspicious of Grant last summer when I should have been. How Hailey trusts Justin...

Sketchville, population of *everyone*, apparently.

"And submit your screenplay!" Logan calls out as he ruffles Lottie's hair and makes his way to the front door.

EXT. MIDTOWN—NIGHT

CLOSE-UP. A text from Jenson to Rory:
They're already there! We might be too late. We have to get that DNA before they do.

The city is raining and lit up by neon lights, a sea of umbrellas. We hear cell phones ringing, people talking, cars honking, street vendors shouting.

>   NEWSCASTER (V.O.)
>   …and the newest development is that a member of
>   The Vicious is inside the building. Witnesses say he's
>   wearing a clown costume!

Rory is hurrying along the sidewalk. It's crowded, and he's soaking wet, his hands inside his trench coat.

>   RORY
>   *(whispering to himself)*

Okay, this is only my worst idea ever. But if I'm right, I'm safe...

Rory's phone beeps, but he ignores it. It beeps again.

>   RORY
> Hello?

>   SKIP
> Whatever you're doing—don't.

>   RORY
> Are you watching me?

>   SKIP
> Wilson tracks you. *This* was not part of the plan. You can't go in there when The Vicious—

Rory hangs up.

We see a huge flashing billboard in CITY SQUARE:

BREAK-IN AND REPORTED GUNFIRE AT WOODS INDUSTRIES IN MIDTOWN

>   RORY
> In and out...

WIDE SHOT. Woods Industries

MEDIUM SHOT. Police lights and people running away. Rory walks toward the crime scene. He slips down an alley and uses his badge to gain access to the building through a loading dock.

INT. WOODS INDUSTRIES HALLWAY

It's dark, but a red light flickers on and off every few seconds.

Rory tries the service elevator, but it's disabled. He exhales and starts up the stairs, which are pitch-black. A few flights up—

BANG. Something on the other side of the door. Rory hurries up the stairs, a few more floors to go. When he finally opens the door, he creeps out into the darkness. An emergency siren sounds, and Rory runs toward the vault.

We see Rory's face lit up by the screen.

A door closes.

>THE STING
>Hey! What are you *doing*? You can't be here!

>RORY
>I'm saving *you* this time. Give me a second.

>THE STING
>What? No way—

Rory types quickly and enters the vault, retrieving the DNA sample in a glass canister. He hands it to The Sting.

>THE STING
>Come on, we need to get you out of here—

Rory rushes over to a computer and begins to type.

RORY
I have to wipe the server before they get this data. My
mom has a backup, but they're—

The alarm escalates:

ROBOTIC WOMAN'S VOICE
This is a level 6. Intruder alert. This is a level 6. Zone
threatened by armed intruder. This is not a drill, follow
safety protocol immediately.

Rory looks to The Sting, and then we hear banging from
the opposite direction. It's a man in a clown costume with a
gunman on either side.

DR. DREADWORTHY
Aha!

The Sting clutches the glass canister and gestures for Rory to
hide behind the desk.

The siren sounds louder. Emergency lights STROBE. The
Sting goes invisible: Dr. Dreadworthy and the gunmen
look around for him, gunshots firing in every direction. The
glass windows shatter. A computer explodes, and sparks
fly. The Sting, still invisible, paralyzes the gunmen, and Dr.
Dreadworthy escapes.

THE STING
What were you thinking?

RORY
It worked, didn't it?

THE STING
You could've gotten killed.

RORY
Chromatophores...

. THE STING
Huh?

RORY
That's how you go invisible. It's actually just hyperactive camouflage. Walt Wilson designed the suit.

THE STING
Please, *please*, try not to do anything like that ever again.

RORY
No promises.

THE STING
Look, I might not always be there. There are more of these guys now and—

RORY
I get it.

The Sting starts to walk toward the computer.

RORY
Wait, Skip?

THE STING
Yeah?

Rory laughs, covering his mouth and The Sting shakes his head quickly, holding his hands up.

>   RORY
> I knew it.

>   THE STING
> (walking closer to him)
> No—what'd you say? I don't think I heard—

>   RORY
> It's really you.

>   THE STING
> Nope, I think you have the wrong guy.

>   RORY
> What other dork says "aye, aye, Cap'n?"

>   THE STING
> Plenty of... Hey! I'm not a dork.

>   RORY
> (they're almost toe-to-toe now)
> I won't tell anyone.

>   THE STING
> (whispering)
> Dammit, Rory.

>   RORY
> I can't believe it was you all along, and I didn't even realize.

13

I DON'T KNOW HOW SHE DOES IT

A few hours after Logan leaves, I order pizza for the girls, and we spend the day outside.

Cue the montage: Diving for toys; Lottie dancing around the backyard while Milly works on her tan; Lottie putting sunscreen on Milly's palm while she's asleep and then tickling her nose, followed by Lottie wailing because Milly stormed off; Lottie passed out on one of the wooden chairs with a melting popsicle running down her arms and legs; Milly and Lottie laughing as they play Marco Polo.

Now, they're lounging on the couch, faces and shoulders a bit red with stringy chlorine hair.

There's a knock on the door, and my stomach flips. Under any other circumstances, I'd be thrilled to see Hailey's smiling face and bouncy chocolate hair, with its new honey-gold streaks. She holds up four milkshakes and dances past me, laughing as Milly and Lottie fawn over her and grab at the cup holder.

"Do you like?" Hailey beams and flicks her hair over her shoulder as I walk into the kitchen. "Mimi told me I look like some movie star over in the Philippines, which is basically the highest compliment from her. But I needed something new. For senior pictures! Justin and I are doing a few together, too. His mom recommended the most amazing photographer, and she's going to shoot at *golden hour.*"

I tried to let her live in a little bubble—protected and blissfully unaware and in love. But if other people know? I have no choice.

"I have to tell you something."

Hailey helps herself to microwavable pizza bites, but I can't stomach anything right now.

"Wait, oh my God, look who it is!" Hailey points to my phone, lit up with a text from Grant. "How's your *friendship* with him going?"

It's only a detour, but I'll take it. I'm *going* to tell her. Maybe somehow it'll naturally come up. That way it won't be so awful.

I take Hailey by the arm and drag her out the French doors onto the back patio, away from Milly and Lottie. I'll tell them about what's going on with Grant, for sure, but I'm not ready for the interrogation. They have strong opinions about him.

"Actually... I told him I'd go on a date with him," I admit. "Tonight."

"I was waiting for that. And what about Logan?" Hailey raises her brows. "You can't act like you don't like him."

She's right. I can't.

"Well, if I'm being honest, I have no clue. And he has all these weird phone calls and had to leave all secretively... Plus he's going to Columbia. Though I guess Grant's going back to California. I don't *know*. I just said yes in the moment."

Hailey considers this, nodding slowly. "Well, you never know. I've had to really consider how Justin and I will survive if we have to go long distance. You know? If we don't both get into UF, or if one of us decides something else..."

"And?"

Taking a big sip of her milkshake, Hailey inhales sharply. "I know you'll think we're rushing it, but if we're going to do long distance, we need to seriously consider engagement." I don't think I'm making a face, but she gets defensive fast. "My mom was engaged at a young age. And he and I have discussed it. We want a future together."

Oh, I'm *really* going to be sick.

"Hailey, it's just—"

"I know you don't believe in relationships and marriage or whatever," Hailey says. "But I have to think about the future."

"It's not marriage, it's just—well, it's Justin," I say.

Here it comes. The moment I've wanted to avoid.

"Justin?" Hailey shakes her head. "What about him? Harry, I *know* you like Justin. Is this because I spend more time with him now or something? Listen, I'm not going to keep going around in circles with you. At some point you have to respect my life and be happy for me. If you can't, then..."

I blink. "Then what?"

"Well, I don't know," she says, but it's clear what she's trying to say. If I can't be happy for her, we won't be friends.

That can't happen. I can't imagine life without Hailey.

"Can you just *please* drop this whole thing? I know you were hurt, but you can't project your past onto me and my relationship," she says. "I get where you're coming from, even with your mom's divorces and Grant and all that, but *I* am happy. We're different people with different experiences."

I frown, unsure of what I should do. Part of me feels angry that she'd ever make it him versus me. That her whole world revolves around him. But that part of me is eclipsed by the fear of not having my best friend around. I can't lose Hailey. And this is the closest I've ever been to feeling what it'd be like to. Maybe Grant was right, after all.

At the very least, if Hailey does find out, it won't be from me. I won't let what Justin did ruin our friendship.

"You're my best friend," I say slowly. "I just don't want you to get hurt."

"I know," she says. "And I love you for that, but I just need my best friend to support me. You know?"

I give her a brief nod before we're interrupted by my name echoing through the house. Hailey and I walk back inside, closing the doors behind us.

"Harold?"

I hear the front door shut, followed by heels against the wood. Mom is home way early. She rushes into the kitchen and drops her purse on the island.

"I'm actually glad you're here, too," she says to Hailey. They exchange glances over the island and she leans in, whispering, "I have a third date tonight!"

Her voice is so hushed, I almost worry I haven't heard her correctly.

Third?

"You do?" I don't mean to sound surprised. Wait—my mom and I are going on dates on the same night? I can't tell if that's a good sign or a bad one.

Mom exhales deeply. "I know. I'm ancient. Am I too old? Can you be too old? It's just hard, you know? It is. I mean, I don't say that to whine, and I shouldn't be saying it to you guys. But running a company that's expanding internationally, it's… It's hard work. And I love it. But what's hard is the juggling." She throws up her hands. "Juggling, like, all these *balls*."

Hailey's eyes go wide.

"How many balls are too many balls?" Mom says.

"A question we've all asked ourselves." Hailey giggles, and I bark a laugh.

"It's doing everything all the time. And adding in dating? Forget it. It's already too stressful. And I'm too old. Almost forty… I should cancel right? Maybe I just need, like, a second."

She inhales, shutting her eyes and clutching the counter.

"I mean I wouldn't trade how things are," she says, looking to us very seriously. She ties her hair up. "I love our family and our life here and I love our house. And Hailey, you're pretty much family at this point. It's just…"

She fans herself, lifting her shirt collar and furrowing her brow. "Is it hot in here?"

Hailey's jaw drops, and I get why. It's not every day we see Mom drop the "I've got it under control" exterior.

"It's a lot," she says. "What am I thinking? CEO of a company, mom of three with two ex-husbands? I shouldn't go on this date."

"Mom," I say, pausing to help her stop and breathe. "You *never* go on the third date."

"I know." She bites her lip. "It's so strange. This is different. And you know what they say, once you stop looking for it…"

"Then what?" Hailey blinks.

"It finds you." Mom tilts her head.

If there's anyone I hope true love exists for, it's my mom. Regardless of what has happened to me or how her past marriages went, I just want to try and believe in love in this moment, if only to encourage her to find it. And if she can be a CEO and a mom and still have time to date, maybe there's a way for me to have it all too…

"Also, you're not too old at all," Hailey says. "You're, like, the youngest of all the moms in our friend group."

Mom squints at us.

"A third date is great," Hailey finally agrees, popping in a pizza bite. Mouth full, she shrugs. "He could be the one. We should check my horoscope app."

"What if I don't even know how to seriously date anymore?" Mom exhales. "All these first dates over the years—I'm not prepared for the next step. I think I may have actually regressed in the dating department. You guys have to give me tips."

"Who is it?" I say.

Mom looks over the counter to the living room where Milly and Lottie are utterly absorbed in the TV. "Come upstairs."

After Hailey grabs her plate of pizza bites, we follow Mom up the Spanish-tiled stairs to her bedroom. Hailey sits on the rattan bench at the foot of the bed while I fall dramatically onto the king-size linen cloud.

Mom shuts the door and kicks her heels off, frowning at

her reflection as she sits next to Hailey on the bench. "It's that Mark guy," Mom says. "Do you remember him? From the Publix parking lot? Turns out his daughter knows Milly from school."

"Aw," Hailey says before straightening up and furrowing her brow. "Wait, you met a guy in a Publix parking lot?"

"Wait, really?" I remember how this guy rushed out of the grocery store to give us a bag the cashier forgot to put in the cart. Thank God he did, too, because it had Lottie's sub, and she would have been *pissed* if we had forgotten it.

Mom's shoulders fall. "Don't sound so excited."

"No—no, it's not that."

"He doesn't seem like a serial killer or a sociopath in any way yet," Mom says. "I've been running into him everywhere. Last week, I was meeting with a local vendor at Chez, and guess who was at the table next to me? Mark!"

"I think it's great," I say. Weirdly, I really do believe it.

Hailey grins. "It's like fate. Y'all couldn't stay away from each other."

"Serendipity!" I clap.

"Except Milly might go ballistic and kill me in my sleep if I date one of the dads in her grade?" Mom's face falls, and she looks to us expectantly.

"She'll be fine," I say, though I don't know that I'm convincing. Mom stands up.

"Can you guys keep this between us?" Her eyes go wide. "Oh my God. I'm a horrible mother. What mother keeps a secret like this from her daughter? I read a study—"

"You're not a horrible mother!" Hailey says.

I nod. "It's not even a big deal. We'll just keep it between

us while you see how it goes. Once it gets super serious, we'll
tell Milly. Very casually. Maybe whispered—and while she's
asleep. It'll be fine."

"Okay, right." Mom walks over to her mirror and opens
the blinds to let in some light. "It's just not worth getting her
riled up yet, right? It could still all go horribly."

"Hopefully it won't," I say with a grin.

"What do I wear? Is a black dress okay?" Mom opens her
closet door and disappears into its depths.

Hailey follows and examines a dress, an off-the-shoulder.
Mom looks at it and then shakes her head, gesturing for Hailey to give it back.

"I'm too old for that," she says, putting the dress back on
the rack. "It's too boobie-licious."

I sigh. "You have to get over this complex. You're not old."

Mom frowns. "The other day Milly asked me if I would
feel comfortable going on a run with her because she didn't
want me to get hurt. Like, what am I to her? A hundred?"
She turns to the sweaters and cardigans and eyes us.

"No sweaters," Hailey and I say in solidarity.

Mom groans. "Fine."

"But Mom," I say, because I can't help but think about
how this all relates to what I'm going through. "I thought
you weren't dating?"

"Not really by choice," she says. "I don't know, I was too
busy. But the company is doing well and—"

"You chose success over dating," I clarify. "I mean, didn't
you?"

She stops to consider it. "I guess I kind of did. Yeah. But it
wasn't necessarily a conscious decision—one over the other. It

was more prioritizing. The company wasn't just for me. It's for you guys, too. Everything I do is for you guys. But, you know, life is not all about success. There's a reason one of the most famous quotes is 'success is not the key to happiness; happiness is the key to success.' My life with you guys is my success."

"So, now that you're successful you can date?"

"Oh, Harold." She exhales. "It's not always so black-and-white. I hadn't found the one before. Not that Mark's the one. You know what I'm saying. And anyway, what does 'successful' mean? I'm sure even you two have different ideas of success."

"We do," Hailey notes. "Okay, this is getting a little too deep. Um, you're not reaching for a top with sequins are you?"

"Of course not." Mom quickly pulls her hand back. "Shit, I have no idea what to wear."

Hailey holds her hands up. "First, where are you guys going?"

Mom lights up. "We're going to Pier 30."

"Oh, wow," I say. *I hope that's not where Grant wants to go.*

"That's, like, the fanciest restaurant possible. He must really like you," Hailey notes. She doesn't look up from the black dress she's tracing her fingers over in her lap.

"Okay," Mom says, taking the black dress from Hailey and inhaling and exhaling all the way to the connecting bathroom. "I'm good. I'm fine. I can totally do this! Thank you guys for the emotional support. What am I—a teenager? Go, be young, do something fun that young kids do. But not drugs or drunk driving. Or unsafe sex or anything risky. Obviously."

"Are you sure you're good?" I call, as we slowly stand and make our way out.

Mom pokes her head out the door. "Totally! All chill and Zen. I got this."

I can't believe my mom is going on a *third* date. She never lets it get this far.

I'm flashing back to Hailey's nervous gummy worm consumption in my bedroom as she did her makeup before the date with Justin when he asked her to be his girlfriend. We both knew it was coming. I remember her bright, eager eyes—all the hope for the future and no idea he'd ever hurt her.

It doesn't exactly spark excitement for my date with Grant tonight. Still, if I'm going, I may as well try to be optimistic. Our friendship has a new, more mature foundation.

I'm giving him the benefit of the doubt for one night.

One chance.

EXT. UPTOWN ALLEY

Rory leaves the canister behind a dumpster and texts Jenson.
I left it where you said.

WIDE SHOT. Rory running down the stairs into the subway.

We cut to Rory coming out of the subway in midtown.

MEDIUM SHOT. Skip runs up behind Rory.

      SKIP
Rory!

      RORY
Skip?

      SKIP
You know, Mr. Wilson *is* probably going to murder us.

RORY
I have to go, okay? We'll talk later.

WIDE SHOT. The crowd gasps as Quick Circuit appears.

QUICK CIRCUIT
Oh no you don't.

14

HERE WE GO AGAIN

"Donna and the Dynamos!" Lottie screams, wearing a magenta feather boa and running into my room with her favorite Bag of Tricks. It's really just a canvas L.L. Bean bag with pink handles and her initials stitched into the side, but she claims it's magical and can talk to her. Somehow, it wakes up in the middle of the night and fills itself with the snacks Mom buys for Milly and me.

Milly hurries in after her, wearing a pair of bedazzled sunglasses and a blue boa. They're both in old sequined tops from Mom's closet that fit them like dresses.

"I told you guys," I say, closing my laptop and letting them sit on my bed. "I'm hanging out with Grant tonight."

Lottie rolls her eyes and reaches into her bag, tossing a bedazzled baseball cap at me. She then pulls out her iPad and hands Milly a hairbrush—the two of them adjusting their looks in the mirror next to my desk.

"Guys," I try, but Lottie holds her iPad up and presses a button. Immediately, she and Milly are in performing mode. Milly flicks her hair over her shoulder and points to me as Lottie runs over and strikes a pose on my desk chair.

"'You can dance,'" Milly sings.

"'You can jive,'" Lottie howls. She used to sing "you can drive," but we taught her the right lyrics.

I bury my face in my hands, pull on the baseball cap, and reach into my nightstand for a pair of retro sunglasses I have for this special occasion. Hurrying to meet them halfway, I run to my closet and pull down the disco ball, then plug it in and flick the ceiling light off.

"'Friday night and the lights are low...'" We all jump onto my bed and proceed to make our way around my room, in well-choreographed matching kicks and '70s dance moves we've spent countless nights perfecting from YouTube. Lottie steals the show a few times, stepping in front of Milly and me to be closest to the imaginary audience, but at the end, we all hold hands and stand perfectly aligned for our bow.

"Good work," Lottie says to me when we're finished. She pulls out a Capri Sun from her Bag of Tricks, and, as she sucks it down, she raises a brow. "Do you think we should put this on YouTube next time?"

"No," Milly says.

"I think we need to keep practicing," I offer.

"Don't make me go solo," Lottie says with a grin, and Milly tickles her. "Speaking of going solo, Harold, you should try it."

"Jeez, Lot." I pull down the bill of my cap and avoid eye contact.

"I actually think you should go solo with Logan, though," Lottie decides, pursing her lips.

"Lottie means anyone with a brain can see you *should* be hanging out with Logan instead of Grant," Milly says. But then, when I don't bicker back, her face softens. "We just don't want a repeat of… Well, you know where we're coming from."

"I get it," I say. "But you know, it's just different when you get older."

That's totally bogus, and I know it.

"Fine," Lottie says. "But just be nice to Logan! He looooooooves you."

"Does not," I say, way too high-pitched. "Okay, you guys got your Donna and the Dynamos. Time for me to get ready for tonight."

"I hope you have time to do Donna and the Dynamos on FaceTime when you're gone," Lottie says softly, and my heart drops.

We *never* talk about what it'll be like when I go.

As they file out of my room, Milly offers me the nicest smile she's given me in a few months, and Lottie does a su-permodel strut down the hall to her bedroom.

Once I'm alone, I take off the cap and go into my bath-room, looking at myself in the mirror. I shake off Lottie's comment for now. I can't get sad about that yet—it's too far in the future. I need to live in the moment.

Oh God. In-the-moment me is going on a date with Grant tonight.

Am I doing the right thing? Milly has perfectly legitimate

reasons to be concerned. But she wasn't there with Grant on the beach. She didn't see this new side of him.

I text Grant, making sure we're still on for tonight, and while I wait for him to reply, I wash my face and brush my teeth.

After staring blankly at my closet and open dresser drawers and only seeing Hailey's name pop up on my phone, I open Pinterest and start scrolling, adding pins to my Screenplay Inspo board to kill some time. But Grant doesn't text back for a full hour, and I wonder if he's trying to be funny.

Either way, he's supposed to be here at 7:00, and I decide to just get dressed and drench myself in a spray that smells like summer in case he shows up at my door and tells me how his phone was broken or stolen or lost or can't hold a charge or grew wings and flew to outer space.

Only, as I move my laptop from my bed to my desk, I sit there and stare at my screenplay and realize history's repeating itself. My feelings are, at the very least. Not knowing where I stand or if *I've* done something wrong.

Suddenly, this feeling is the hollow hole in my stomach last summer when my mom had a big work event at the club and I told Hailey I was bringing Grant as my plus one and I stood there, watching the door all night and hoping my phone would light up with an update or, at the very least, an excuse.

All at once, this feeling is the day I was supposed to go to Disney with Grant and his friends at the beginning of the summer. It's the feeling I had when he was twenty minutes late and said he just felt like an out-of-town trip together was too big a step when we were only "hanging out." It's the way Milly looked way sorrier for me than a little sibling is supposed to look for her big brother, and the way I not only had to look at my duffel bag through tears, carry it upstairs, and drop it on my floor but also had to unpack every item, put it back where it came from, and pretend it didn't all mean too much to me.

It's the way I didn't let myself fall apart and told him it was okay because he shouldn't feel rushed, and the way my chest sank every time their group uploaded fun, goofy photos and Grant looked like he didn't even mind I wasn't there.

These awful memories are so much harder to bury now. I feel like I should know better and do better and be better, but I'm still sitting at my desk alone, waiting and wondering, and it's like it's all happening in slow motion.

I feel beyond stupid, and I lie on my bed, waiting for thirty more minutes.

Thirty turns to forty-five, and that becomes an hour and a half, and then it becomes overwhelmingly clear he's not going to show. Maybe I'm being dramatic, and maybe he has a good reason, but I'm reminded of everything from before. Only, this time I'm not going to lie in my bed crying, feeling sorry for myself and trying to ignore it all.

I grab the baseball cap from my nightstand and reach for the hairbrush on my counter. Bringing the disco ball under my arm, I walk to Lottie's room and see she and Milly are on the floor building a LEGO set in their Dynamo costumes.

I sit on the bed, slide on the baseball cap, and hold up the hairbrush, pressing Play on my phone. Lottie grabs for her Bag of Tricks while the light piano starts.

Milly pats my shoulder, and Lottie dims the lights, smiling but giving me a hug, and I feel better as they wait for me to start us off:

"'I was cheated by you, and I think you know when…'"

It takes me two hours to turn tearstained pages in my notebook into furiously metaphorical pages. I blitz my pain onto the page, and that's it.

I have my twist.

My script is finished.

INT. THE CHAMPIONS ALLIANCE CAMPUS—
CONFERENCE ROOM

All of The Champions Alliance members are pacing around
the room, with Skip and Rory seated at the table.

> QUICK CIRCUIT
> I can't believe you two weren't going to tell us this.

> SKIP
> Mr. Fate told us not to tell you. He was doing his
> magic futuristic prediction stuff with other realms or
> something, and he was working with Future Defense
> and—

> QUICK CIRCUIT
> Shit. And where is that canister, kid?

> RORY
> I left it where Jenson told me to.

GOLD HONOR
Damn it.

QUICK CIRCUIT
We've been tracking this situation. We knew this whole time, but now...

SKIP
We'll just tell Jenson you guys need it!

GOLD HONOR
That's not Jenson!

RORY
What?

SKIP
(whispering to himself as he realizes)
Multiverse...

RORY
Oh no.

15

HOW DO YOU KNOW

Before, I'd have been completely devastated over Grant standing me up. I'd probably be miserable, crying and questioning my self-worth for days. But I've been through this. Same song and dance—same Grant. I've become used to this sense of total disappointment.

As of right now, I'm way more pissed than sad. My self-worth is not defined by Grant. I hold back from rage texting, if not only to torture him—it's only 7:00 a.m. and he's sent me several texts apologizing and asking what I'm up to today.

Sometimes silence is golden.

I decide to go for an early morning walk on the beach, and I'm not surprised to see Logan sitting on his surfboard. I wouldn't say I went on a walk *expecting* to see him, obviously. It's just a coincidence. One that conveniently gets my mind off the major disappointment of last night. He's soaking wet, wearing a black T-shirt and digging into a croissant with bared teeth. His SpongeBob towel is balled up next to him.

"You missed a great wipeout," he says as I sit on the board next to him. Something about his smile is so inviting, like it warms everything up really quick. It's instant.

And he doesn't start off with *good morning*, which I love. Sometimes with people you're comfortable with, I don't think there's a need for a greeting or niceties. I think you can fall into the rhythm without them, like how my friends and I can immediately jump into life updates, boy drama, and funny stories without even saying hello. It makes it feel like no time has passed since we last saw each other.

"Want one?"

"You got more than one croissant?" I say.

Logan turns from the sunrise to me and tilts his head, eyebrows furrowed. "Actually, I got two *chocolate* croissants."

"Oh, you knew I'd be coming." I poke his arm.

"I can still eat both." He raises a brow.

I shake my head. "No, no, no. I will gladly accept a croissant. *Merci*." When he pulls the bag up to pull out the croissant, I notice it's from Sucré. "You went back!"

"It's the best," Logan gushes, handing me the croissant. "I think it's my new favorite spot. Like, ever."

"I can't disagree," I say, tearing the croissant and taking a bite. "Sucré and the sunrise on the beach. I think this is heaven."

Logan glances over at me, water dripping from his hair onto his nose, his eyes a perfect cast of the ocean and the sky. "Definitely."

"So, is Ron not teaching you anymore?" I say.

"He is." Logan covers his mouth, chewing. "He's just been busy. I'm getting the hang of it, though. I could probably teach you all by myself."

I laugh.

"If you wanted to learn," he says earnestly.

"I told you! I am the worst." I bump his elbow with mine. "I appreciate the offer, though."

Logan finishes his croissant, and hugs his knees, resting his chin on his hands. "Well, if you change your mind…"

"I know who to ask," I agree.

The sky is like a million thin stripes—oranges and yellows and reds. It's like a mix between a warm-toned cotton candy and these striped flannel sheets my mom bought me for Christmastime. That's where my brain goes, anyway—it's cozy.

"Think Sucré will deliver to the Upper West Side?" Logan laughs.

I hate the idea of him leaving.

"I really will miss it here," Logan says, a tinge of sadness hanging from his words.

"God, why?" I groan. "I can't *wait* to get out of here. It's the same old thing. The same parties, the same people everywhere you go."

Logan tilts his head. "But your family is here, at least."

"That's true," I say. "I wish I could pack them up and take them to LA with me."

"I hate to be the bearer of bad news, but Citrus Harbor is definitely not the worst place to be." He smiles.

"Right." I bump his elbow again. "Still, I just can't help but imagine how amazing life could be outside of this bubble. Know what I mean?"

Logan shrugs. "I guess. I don't spend too much time imagining what *could be*, though. I mean, we only really have what is."

Interesting.

"That sounds very wise," I say. "But you've planned out your future, too."

"I have goals," Logan agrees. "But they're not my life. I'm not, like, stalking my Google Maps to see what the destination is like. I'm just enjoying the road trip."

"Enjoying the road trip is good," I say. "But you are going to become a really badass FBI agent who knows, like, mathematical codes and engineering tricks, so you can't stay here surfing and chasing the sunrise and enjoying the road trip forever. You have big things to accomplish."

"Right, right," he says. "Speaking of accomplishing things. Any updates on the writing?"

"It's finally finished, but I now have to revise before the submission deadline," I say, my fingers tracing the delicate lines on the croissant. "I have something to ask you, though."

Logan nods. "Sure."

"I know it sounds weird," I say, squinting out at the horizon. "But do you believe in love?"

The question has been bugging me ever since Mom dropped the third date bomb, though I wish love could exist for me, too. If anything, it could have been real for a brief period there with Grant. When he listed off all the things he loved about me or joked about getting matching silver bands from Tiffany. When we were in each other's arms or when he'd cancel his plans just because he said he had to see me.

When we cooked horrible subscription box meals or played arcade games when it poured rain.

All those good times somehow aren't enough to outweigh the bad, and in retrospect they don't add up to definitive, undeniable proof that love could be real outside of fictional relationships. Or that it could last.

"Like," I continue, thinking about how happy my mom was this morning after her date. I think she was even humming. "My mom went on a third date last night, which is awesome. And I want to believe in love so badly, but I feel guilty because I just keep thinking it's going to end in her getting hurt."

I don't mention how I got stood up and mostly hate guys at the moment except for Logan.

"Wow." Logan sighs. "That's deep. Why do you think it'll end up like that?"

"I don't know," I admit. "I guess it always has for us. That's how it was for her and my dad—and Lottie's dad, too. And I've never had… I've never had the best luck either. I don't know why I'm asking you. I guess because you're, like, obviously a genius. So maybe from a purely academic perspective."

Logan contemplates this. "From an academic perspective, I'd say I believe in love, yeah. Since it's historically rooted and documented, research would suggest it's real, I think? But on the same note, there's historically noted stuff that's definitely not real. So maybe this one isn't academic. Either way, I'm really sorry you had bad experiences before."

"No." I laugh it off. "I'm sorry, I didn't mean for it to come off like that. I'm fine. I don't know… I want my mom to find love, but I'm not even sure if it exists."

"For what it's worth," Logan offers. "I believe positive thinking creates positive results."

"Positive thinking creates positive results," I echo. "Like how Cary Grant said he pretended to be somebody he wanted to be until he became that person."

"I guess there's a way to connect those dots," Logan laughs.

"No, I just mean—it's kind of like the whole 'fake it till you make it' thing," I say. "Believe it—then it'll eventually be true. That's what Cary Grant meant, I think."

"Yeah. Cary Grant was in *North by Northwest*? Such a good movie."

"Yes!" I nod way too enthusiastically—Logan is speaking my language. "I should have known you'd like that one. Cary Grant is amazing. *To Catch a Thief* is, like"—I mimic a chef's kiss—"the French Riviera is totally on my bucket list."

"I haven't seen that one," Logan admits.

"Well, we are obviously going to have to fix that," I say, catching how flirty it sounds. "Grace Kelly is an icon."

Logan grins. "Deal."

The waves crash and roll out in front of us, and the sun looks like a poked yolk from a sunny-side-up egg, oozing out across the top of the ocean.

"Also, just as an FYI, from a purely academic perspective, don't think you're fooling anyone." Logan smirks.

"What is that supposed to mean?" I blink.

"Rory's understanding of molecular biology and organic chemistry is clearly deeper than a few Google searches." He raises a brow.

I shrug. "I don't *hate* science. So what?"

"Just saying, I know USC is no joke academically. And I

think you're perfectly capable of forming your own hypotheses," he teases, eyes almost glazed and fixed on the pier.

"My grades are all right." I hesitate, embarrassed. "But not amazing. And my SATs—I didn't do so well. My guidance counselor basically thinks winning this competition is my only chance at getting in, but I..."

"What?" Logan says.

"I don't even know if my script is any good, really," I admit.

"I think it's great," Logan offers. "And, hey, the SATs suck. Don't be too hard on yourself. If it all really does depend on this screenplay, I say you're gonna get in."

I just smile. There's such sincerity in what Logan says that I can't help but believe he's right.

I nod and run my finger through the shell bed at my feet. I spot a shiny black tooth with sharp serrations and a thin point. The root is a lighter gray. I hold it up for Logan. "Here."

He holds his palm out, and I drop the tooth. He holds it up between his thumb and index finger, looking at it against the sunrise. "Holy shit, this is cool."

"I have some that are wild. You have to come see them sometime," I say, which I cringe at a little because I genuinely didn't mean it as a pickup line to get him to my room. I just meant... Well, I thought he'd think the teeth are cool.

"Definitely," Logan says, setting the tooth onto his board. We're sitting there, smiling at each other for a beat. The wind is slow and calm, and the waves are even more peaceful. There's hardly anyone on the beach, and even the gulls are silent. I like how Logan doesn't act any differently after I just brought up the totally deep topic of love.

I look at him, with the golden light shining against the

side of his face. Saltwater drips from the tips of his hair, and his lashes are wet, just like his cherry lips that almost look bitten. And my imagination gets the best of me. More than anything right now, I want Logan to lean over and kiss me.

When his phone buzzes, my little daydream is interrupted. I snap to just as Logan furrows his brow at the screen. I can only see for a moment, but the name on the screen is big: *Charlie*. That name was on his phone the day we met, too, but now the screen has changed, just shows a log full of missed calls.

"Um, I have to go," Logan says abruptly. He stands up and grabs his towel, slinging it over his shoulder. "I'm sorry."

"Is everything okay?"

"Yeah," he says, his mind obviously drifting. "Just forgot I have to go pick something up."

He grabs the shark tooth and then his board, and his mouth turns up into a curve that seems genuinely happy.

It baffles me. It seems like every time he picks up his phone, he's suddenly upset or twitchy or leaving. But he still smiles at me, like there's nothing weird going on.

"Oh, a bunch of the guys from work are going to some party Friday night, and I think, believe it or not, I'm joining," Logan says. "They're really warming up to me. Why do I feel like you know what party I'm talking about?"

"Brian Fisher's," I say, realizing we're not addressing why he's leaving. "I wasn't planning on going. I am surprised you are, Mr. Anti-Party."

"Well, maybe I'll see you there," he says, winking like a total dork.

I say goodbye to Logan, wondering about what secret other

life he's reminded of every time his phone rings, and dash toward my house.

When I get there, my smile fades instantly because there's Hailey, crying softly on the beach access in the quiet morning glow.

EXT. UNIVERSITY LAWN

Skip and Rory sit under a tree eating lunch.

    RORY
I can't believe they took your suit.

    SKIP
I should have figured out Jenson wasn't Jenson.

    RORY
And now that they know? Even though Mr. Fate said
they weren't supposed to find out?

    SKIP
I think it might be the end of our dimension.

16

THE SWEETEST THING

It has been three days since Hailey's breakup. I told her what my mom told me after everything went down with Grant last summer: "You actually live a way charmed life."

My mom didn't say it *exactly* like that, but it was the lesson she wanted me to learn. She said if I could focus on the good things, I'd feel better faster.

So, on the first day, between ignoring Grant's texts, I talked Hailey down from moving to her aunt's in the Philippines for senior year and helped her focus on the positives. She has me, of course, and her friends she swims with and the ones from the ice cream stand. She's funny and kind, and she makes good grades for the most part. Her hair is never flat, and she always matches her foundation. Those last two really resonated.

The second day, yesterday, she was hit pretty hard with the harsh reality of a breakup. He wouldn't be around anymore. Her senior superlative dreams? Dashed. And he was blowing

her phone up. Which led to us talking about it. On day one,
I didn't ask any questions, just tried to be supportive.

As we talked through it, she told me Carla found out from
Lainey who found out from Stephen. Stupid Stephen. One of
Grant and Justin's friends. If Grant hadn't stood me up and I
wasn't giving him an ice-cold silent treatment, I'd ask him
if *he* told Stephen. But there's no point now. All I can do is
focus on getting Hailey back to normal.

Today, Hailey and I both had to work in the morning, but
once we were off, we got burgers and fries and took her Jeep
to the lookout. We watched the waves and laughed at funny
videos while pigging out. I surprised her with an astrology
book from the store, just as a little pick-me-up.

Honestly, she's handling it really well. I'm somewhat
shocked. I almost feel like I'm taking the breakup harder
than she is. I keep expecting her to talk about him. It's weird
to not make any plans for the three of us. But somehow she's
handling it like a champ.

"If someone is going to cheat on me, he's not a man at all,"
she says, studying herself in my mirror. "He's a little boy."

It's *so* weird to hear her talk about Justin like this, but she's
not wrong.

"And you're sure you're up for this?" I scroll through Instagram. "Because if you want to just stay home—"

"No way." She shoots me a look like I'm nuts. "Then everyone will think I'm staying home and wallowing."

So, instead of having a night in and editing my screenplay
like I'd originally planned, it's 11:00 p.m. and I'm tagging
along with Hailey in Madre Cove yet again.

The party is like every other party we go to. It's all loud

bass and high-pitched squeals and dizzying clumps of people congregating with red plastic cups. Brian Fisher's house is basically the most Gatsby-esque mansion in Citrus Harbor, so it's not a surprise that there are kids from every grade *plus* some of the college kids who are home for the summer.

I wasn't joking about high school parties all being identical. The crowd is the same, the music is interchangeable, and the drinks are just as putrid and horribly made. It's like one of those slot machines—pull the lever for a combination of vodka, hip-hop, and fully-clothed teens jumping in the pool.

Because Brian's house backs up to the beach, I'm not at all surprised to notice sand and spilled beer on the marble floors when we walk into the foyer. Hailey winces and steps around the mess. She has her hair curled, and she's wearing a bright highlighter with silver eyeshadow because she has been watching a new beauty YouTuber and *had* to try this look. Getting sand and beer all over her wedges would not complete her look.

"It feels weird," Hailey says. She frowns and looks to me. "Going to a party without him."

I ignore a gaggle of sophomore girls screaming as a Jell-O shot splatters on the marble staircase and study the disappointment on Hailey's face.

Hailey shrugs, pretending to be casual. "It'll be okay."

I pat her shoulder and nod, leading her toward the kitchen to get us some drinks. We each fill a cup, gulp it down, and refill it. I do a quick scan of the room, hoping to see any sign of Logan or anybody he works with, but no luck.

Walking out back with Hailey, we stop on the patio, and I see a giant bonfire on the beach. Hailey is trying to act all smiley now, like she's not totally devastated over Justin. I feel guilty even thinking about Logan right now. I have to focus on Hailey.

Think of the damn devil.

I look back and see Logan inside, sitting on the couch and looking at a phone with a couple of kids I know from school but can't place. He looks *ridiculously* cute in a white polo with yellow-and-blue stripes across the chest and arms. It's one of those polos that's soft, not scratchy, I can tell. And he's wearing faded jeans and white Vans. He stands out a little from all these kids who care way too much about wearing the latest trends, and I kind of love it.

"For you lovely people." Foster slides up next to us, holding three shot glasses. He's wearing a ridiculous Hawaiian shirt with even more ridiculous Vans that are covered in donuts.

"Are you in costume?" I tease.

"I'm dressed as a ridiculously good-looking dude," Foster confirms, handing Hailey and me shot glasses. "Hailey, man, I'm sorry. I'm bummed."

Hailey's jaw tightens, but she smiles and taps her shot glass to Foster's and then to mine, bringing it to her lips and shooting it back. She then takes Foster's, tilting it toward him like a toast, and knocks that one back, too.

"Fair enough," Foster says as I hand him mine and pat Hailey on the back. "For what it's worth, you're way too good to be treated like that."

I catch myself smiling. Foster really can be sweet.

"Thanks," Hailey says.

"Yeah, for real." He takes his shot. "I was telling Harry, Justin's a real dick for—"

"You guys were, like, talking about it?" Hailey laughs awkwardly, looking between us.

"Not extensively." I narrow my eyes at Foster for a split second, hoping he gets the picture. "Honestly, nobody's talking about it much."

My heart does a flip. Now is not the time for this can of worms to get opened. Not even *one* worm should get out. In fact, the can shouldn't even have a hole for the worms to breathe. Sealed shut. Hailey's especially sensitive right now.

I wait with baited breath for Hailey's reply, to see if she buys it.

Foster bites his lip. "You want another shot, Hail?"

She shakes her head, which is probably for the best.

"Try not to let it get you down." Foster pats her shoulder, taking the empty glasses from her. "It's just the rain before the sun, you know?" He smiles, walking up to the house. "No rain, no flowers."

"Whoa, Foster is, like, existential," I say, wondering if Hailey is going to press the fact that I talked to Foster about her and Justin.

"No rain, no flowers." Hailey smiles to herself.

Wow, Foster, good one.

"Want to go inside? I think there are finger sandwiches."

Hailey shrugs. "Fine."

So, we head inside, and Logan looks up from the YouTube video they're all watching, smiles at me, and gives me a little nod. I can't even help how wide my smile is, but I don't care. Logan's just too cute.

We keep walking toward the food laid out on a huge table in the massive living room.

"I do kind of wonder what he's doing. Guys get to just move on to another girl instantly," Hailey says, looking around like she's expecting to see him. "And then girls? We're pathetic if we're sad, and we're clingy if we don't move on, but God forbid we move on as fast as the guy, because then we're a slut. We can't win."

"If only Penny were here, she'd totally rebut that," I say.

"She'd say something about the pear tree," Hailey suggests. "I always forget that damn word, but you know what I mean."

"Yes, the patriarchy, exactly," I say, and getting a smile out of her is a victory, at least. "You don't *have* to do anything, Hailey. Besides, everyone loves you, and nobody is going to judge you if you need more time to feel okay. Do you want to leave?"

I catch Logan peering over the back of the couch, but he looks away. He doesn't get up or anything, so I try and keep my focus on Hailey, make it seem like I'm not checking the couch every five seconds for a progress report.

Hailey shakes her head. "No, I don't wanna leave. I think I'm going to go talk to some of the girls from the team. And you should go talk to Logan instead of just staring at him like a creep."

Hailey walks away with a smirk, and I'm left next to the snacks. I catch Logan looking at me again. I don't want to go over and interrupt him when he's with his friends. That would seem desperate and annoying.

Maybe if I walk outside he'll come after me. If he wants to talk to me, that is. I decide to try it, making my way out back and down the steps onto the lawn where a bar is set up, complete with a bartender. How the hell Brian Fisher got a bartender to serve all these underage kids is a mystery, but I smile and ask for a margarita. I'm being completely nice to her, but she has a real off-putting attitude.

"Harry." Logan's voice tickles the back of my neck, and suddenly the party feels like it's really alive. I feel his voice in my chest and turn to look at him.

"What can I get you?" The bartender is *way* more into Logan. She actually has some spring in her step while she gets him a beer from the cooler behind her.

Honestly, the smile he gives her is flirtatious back, and it's the white of his teeth that helps me realize he's gotten much more tan. Almost golden, like now *he's* one of those Apollo demigod guys. He's also looking fit, with his muscular arms and chest. And those big hands.

The bartender finally puts my drink in front of me. It's on the rocks, and I wish I'd asked for it frozen, but right now, a drink is a drink. Being around Logan suddenly conjures up a whole lot of nerves.

We clink glasses and each take a sip.

My God. Is this woman trying to poison me? It's all tequila with a drop of lime.

Surveying the backyard, I notice Foster is *totally* macking on some guy in a hammock. I fight a laugh as he looks Logan up and down and offers an approving nod. I roll my eyes and turn my attention back to Logan. Sipping my margarita, I wince and feel my stomach lurch.

Nearly spitting out his beer, Logan bursts into a fit of laughter, covering his mouth with the back of his hand. "Is it that good?"

"You try it," I say, looking to the bartender. She's moved on to the next group on the other end of the bar, but she clearly was trying to kill me.

Logan takes a slight sip and shudders. "You're going to drink it?"

I shrug.

"Is everything okay?"

Everything's great, I want to say, except it isn't. There's still this feeling of guilt I can't ignore. I should have been the one to tell Hailey. Plus, for the zillionth time I forgot I have things to do this summer that I've put off—summer reading, revising my screenplay, SAT studying. And on top of that, thinking about all the things that are wrong has reminded me about Grant being a complete dick, even though I *just* pushed that out of my mind.

Awesome.

"I've been better," I offer, sipping the margarita.

"Did you know you're not supposed to use alcohol as a coping mechanism?" Logan says, clearly reading my expression well. I frown and drink more. "I'm sorry. Do you want to talk about it?"

Along with just the *thought* of talking about the big confusing, jumbled mess going on in my mind, I chug the entire margarita and then hold my hand up to my mouth, wincing.

Logan's eyes go wide, and he stops, beer midway to his mouth. His jaw's hovering open, and he watches me carefully like I'm a ticking bomb or a rabid animal inching closer to him. I'm feeling the margarita smooth over the doubts I have about the alcohol. The music bouncing from the speakers is thumping, and the ocean smells so good. Or is that Logan? I lean forward. Maybe it is him.

"Did you just smell me?"

I laugh and wave him off.

"Do you want another one?" The bartender, clearly out for blood, looks like she's been waiting a thousand years for me to answer her or something.

"Please," I say.

Logan puts his face in his palms. "Oh, Harry."

"Don't *oh, Harry* me!" I push him lightly. "Come on. Let's have drinks and just have a good, fun night. Yeah? Don't you ever just want to say 'screw it'?"

"Was that your first margarita?" Logan looks at me like I'm a joke.

I shake my head. "No, I think it was during spring break— there was a whole tequila bar at one of these parties."

"No, like," Logan chuckles, "tonight. Was that your first one tonight?"

"Oh, yes," I say.

"And you're already wobbling around and smelling me?" He gives me a look now that says I'm a wounded puppy on the side of the road. He can't decide if I might be rabid. Should he pick me up? Leave me to my own devices?

Indignant again, I take the drink from the bartender once she brings it over. "I can handle it."

Logan purses his lips.

"I'm a big boy," I assure him, sipping it and grimacing.

As it turns out, I may not be as capable of handling it as I thought. I'm hanging on to Logan as we walk down the beach to my house.

The sand is heavy, and my stomach feels like it's doing flips and flops and somersaults. I'm spinning—we're spinning— and then I clap my hand over my mouth.

"Come on," Logan's saying, and then I'm in front of one of the huge garbage tins up by the dunes. The black bag inside thuds as I hurl my weight into it. "Yep, yep," Logan says, hand smoothing circles on my back.

This is really something.

I keep puking, and the more I think about how much I want to stop puking, the more I think about puking, which keeps me puking. And when I finally think I'm done, I just imagine puking again, and then I'm doing it. Finally, I take a deep breath, facing the ocean, and I attempt to sit but Logan stops me midair.

"No, no," he says. "Come on, you need to go to sleep. And get water."

I should feel humiliated. And I will when I sleep this off and wake up with a headache and stomach that's inside out. But right now, I can hardly focus on a thought. How many drinks did I have?

"I tried to stop you," Logan mutters as our feet meet the wooden planks of our walkway. "I'll remind you of that, too, just in case you forget."

I'm too drunk to roll my eyes, so I just groan.

We sneak in the back door, and I thank God nobody is downstairs. Logan follows me up the stairs.

"Your room is nice," he says. I moan and collapse onto the bed. "Wait, what's your script's big twist?"

"How do you know there's even a big twist?" I groan.

Logan laughs into his fist, pointing to the notebook open next to my laptop. "I just saw the words *BIG TWIST* in huge bold letters, and I used my ultrarefined, future detective skills."

I hop up off my bed and wiggle the laptop's mousepad until it comes to life. I type my password in after a few attempts because the keys are definitely moving. Once it's pulled up, I tap the screen and grin up at Logan. "All yours."

Logan sits in the chair, and I walk over to my closet and undress. I grab a big T-shirt from a surf shop in Newport my dad bought me and throw on a pair of plaid pajama bottoms. I glance up to Logan, who quickly looks away. I laugh, collapsing onto my bed again as he scrolls through the document.

"How are you feeling?" he says.

"I feel so…" I can hardly figure out what I feel like. "Like, when you square stupid, what do you get? That's a math question."

Logan doesn't say anything; he just looks back to me and frowns.

"You get me," I tell him, just as that sinks in. "I mean, there's something here, right? We like each other? I don't know why people don't just say that."

"We like each other," Logan laughs.

"But… It always ends the same way, doesn't it? My parents. Grant. Justin. That's the problem with stuff like this. We think this is different, but it's never *actually* different. Do you think it ever is?"

What is wrong with me? What am I saying? I look up at Logan, who's frowning. Words are coming out—things about Justin and about how love isn't real, about how Grant was right about me never finishing anything and how I'll never get my screenplay in shape to submit it in time. I can't even make sense of all the shit I'm saying, the words are too heavy in my brain and in my stomach. I take a deep breath and sigh.

"Don't you see? People are variables."

Logan says something, but I don't know what because my eyes fall shut.

INT. RORY'S DORM ROOM

MEDIUM SHOT. Rory falls onto his bed.

>   RORY
> Mr. Wilson was right all along. I'm helpless.

>   SKIP
> You are not.

>   RORY
> I am, too.

We follow Skip's eyes to Rory's desk. We see what looks to be one of Mr. Fate's fortune-telling cards. He blinks and realizes it's only an index card.

CLOSE-UP.

>   RORY (CONT'D)
> But I guess nothing really matters if our universe is being destroyed, anyway.

17

LIFE AS WE KNOW IT

It's been two days since I was a drunken mess in front of Logan. Not my finest hour. We've all had sloppy moments, but *that* was bad. Still, I don't know if I said something terrible or if it's just a coincidence Logan hasn't texted me any funny memes and he's been "busy" anytime I try to make plans.

It's very possible I was full-on Hurricane Harry at some point during the night because things were pretty hazy toward the end.

And it is so ridiculous, because two days is nothing, but I just can't even believe how much I miss the curl of his mouth when he fights a laugh or that woody pine smell of whatever body spray he uses. I need to sit down with myself and address what it means that I can't go two days without seeing Logan, but I'm saving that for later.

Right now, I'm going to go see him.

I texted him to make plans today, but he said he had to

work. Determined, I leave my shift at Books by the Sea and head up the sidewalk toward the club.

Only, when I get there, Logan isn't anywhere in sight. He's not behind the counter of the cabana or walking around the pool or in the restaurant. I even call out for him in the locker room just in case.

Finally, I find someone who looks like a manager and ask if Logan is around, only to be told he's not scheduled at all today.

Logan lied.

Why does everybody lie?

I walk along the sidewalk, watching the palm trees and trying to figure out if I should be annoyed or worried or both, but I'm mostly confused.

I want to know why he lied. He just told me we like each other, that much I remember.

Adding this to the list of weird things—the texts and phone calls and the obvious secrets and *Charlie*—I am completely unsure of how to feel. What is he hiding?

I figure the best thing to do next is just go to his house, knock on the door, and see what he has to say for himself. He might find it easy to lie to me over text, but I won't let him do it to my face.

As I get closer to his house, I wonder what I'll say. Where to even start. And I wonder if I'm being irrational to think he's hiding something. After all, he started lifeguard training, according to Lottie. That must be a lot—physically and emotionally taxing, I'm sure. Plus, I don't know what one does the summer before their freshman year at Columbia, but I bet he's preoccupied with that.

But I *like* Logan, and I want to figure out what's going on

and why he'd lie to me, even if that means hearing he's annoyed with me and doesn't want to see me for some reason.
Even if he's a secret agent for a guy named Charlie in a speaker
box and he's just trying to hide his double life from me.

I'd started off with great intentions, but now I'm gross and
sweaty and nervous. My T-shirt is basically stuck to me.

Finally, I'm at Logan's. His aunt and uncle's home is breathtaking. I've always thought so, passing it every single day. It's
pale blue and shingled with a huge white porch and balcony
wrapping around the top of the house. I imagine the view is
amazing in the back, facing the ocean.

I picture Logan reading up there. It's probably his favorite spot, where he kicks his feet up on the balcony, sunglasses
on and catching a tan while reading something Logan-esque.
Maybe *Catcher in the Rye*? I haven't actually read it, but for
some reason that feels like a Logan kind of book.

"Hi there." I hear a voice coming from the garage, which
sits next to the house. There are three garage doors. Two are
closed, but one is lifted to reveal a ton of gardening supplies
and Ron covered in dirt and wearing a wide-brimmed hat.

I smile, probably looking like a deranged, sweaty lunatic at
this point. As I walk toward him, I suddenly feel like I'm in-
truding.

"Harry, right? Logan's inside," Ron says, holding a small
cardboard box, and I can't believe he remembered my name.
He gestures for me to walk up the steps to the towering front
door. "How have you been? Logan hasn't gotten you out surfing yet?"

"No surfing yet. And I've been good, thanks. How about
you?"

"Well, we've been better," Ron says solemnly, opening the door.

"Oh," I say, unsure of how to respond. "I'm sorry."

He thanks me automatically, leading me through a beautiful white foyer filled with blue and white vases stuffed with green hydrangeas. There are family photos everywhere in frames of all sizes and colors. I notice Logan in many of the photos, age varying.

We walk past the kitchen, where a woman is working over the stove. Logan is on the couch with another woman, who's fast asleep.

"Harry!" Logan's face lights up like he's happy to see me, and he rises from the couch slowly, walking around to meet me in his Columbia sweatshirt and gray joggers. His bare feet are soft against the dark wood floors while Ron crosses to the kitchen, setting the box on the counter before opening the refrigerator.

"Can I getcha anything, Harry?" Ron asks. "Charlie's making some lunch for Jane."

I manage to speak up. "No, thank you. I'm okay."

Charlie. I look to the kitchen and stare at the woman who is now chopping vegetables. She offers a smile, which I return, though I'm really confused. Charlie is not who I imagined at all, which means Logan must not be a spy or an angel.

"I've got to go head back outside and finish something up in the yard," Ron says as he walks by us. "I'll be back in a few."

We stand in silence until the door closes and seems to jolt us awake.

"Good to see you," Logan says, though he looks a little

tired—maybe even sad. It's a marked difference because he's normally so bright.

"Um," I say quietly. "I thought you were at work today, and I went to the club, but you weren't there. So I wanted to come see if you were sick or something."

Logan rubs the back of his neck and takes a step forward. "I must have mixed up my shifts or—"

"Did I do something?"

"What? No, let's go outside," he says, eyes drifting toward the door behind me.

"Tell me what's going on first," I insist.

"It's hard to explain," Logan says, face going red.

"Well try," I say.

"Harry—"

"Logan—"

"My aunt is sick."

I feel my chest tighten because there's a *way* he says it— it's not "my aunt has the flu"; it's definitive and heavy: "my aunt is sick."

"Oh my God," I say, looking over Logan's shoulder to the woman on the couch and noticing pill containers. "I am such an ass."

Frowning, Logan nods. "She, um. She has Alzheimer's."

I involuntarily bring my hand to my mouth and feel my chest go hollow. "I'm so sorry, Logan. I had no idea."

"I know. I just thought it'd be simpler…" Logan exhales, his eyes misty.

"What would be simpler?"

"Me and you," he says.

"I don't—I don't understand?"

Logan sighs. "I feel like an idiot, Harry. I'm sorry."

"Why would you think… What would be simpler, Logan?"

He looks back and then inches closer, whispering. "My ex made it pretty clear I talked about my family stuff too much, and I just didn't want to do that again. I didn't want to make you feel like you had to take this on, 'cause I like you."

"Jesus," I say. "Logan, that is terrible. You should never feel like that. Family is important and I would never, *ever* be upset with you for caring about your family."

Logan studies me for a moment, and then I hug him. I wrap my arms around him, letting my face fall into the crook of his neck, the fabric of his hoodie is soft and cool. And he hugs back, arms tight on my waist.

Poor Jane. I can't even imagine what that must be like. How she must feel. And Logan and Ron, too. And here I am, always complaining about things. I act like minor problems are the end of the world, but how small does everything else feel compared to this?

This entire summer, Logan's been here with her. I can't even begin to understand what it's like. What he must be going through. Does she always remember him? Does she ever look at him and wonder who he is?

The hug lasts forever, and I feel Logan's heartbeat. I want to help him keep it steady. I want to help him feel better, safer. My heart aches to think of Logan, so kind and caring, being treated like that by his ex. Being made to think he was a burden? It's horrible.

And the icing on top is how he was hazed by the guys at the club, and he just laughed it off. They have no idea how hard he has it. And if they do, that makes it even worse.

When we break away, I wipe at Logan's chest. "Sorry, I'm all sweaty."

He shakes his head and smiles. "No big deal. Anyway, of course I was going to tell you. Eventually, I was. I just liked how we had this little bubble—just us, none of the bad stuff."

Logan pulls out a chair at the massive wooden dining room table and then sits in the chair next to it.

"I really am so sorry," I say, joining him at the table.

"You said that," he says with a teasing smirk.

"But I am. Sorry. About your aunt and that your ex made you feel that way and just…" Where do I even begin? "I'm also sorry for being a jerk and for making you take care of me the other night and for whatever I said or did when I was drunk…"

"You're too hard on yourself," Logan tells me. "You weren't a jerk. Well, when you were wasted you said some interesting things…"

I wince.

"Not the worst, though." He smiles. "You have a lot of strong opinions about reality television, and we had a fun conversation about Leonardo DiCaprio."

"I'm such an idiot," I tell him, looking around. "I thought you were, like, avoiding me or something."

Logan buries his face in his hands. "Oh. I guess I can see how it would seem that way. No, Harry, sorry. I wasn't. I just… Ron's been busy, so when I can, I stay in with my aunt."

I reach across the table for Logan's hand, and I glance over to Jane on the couch, where she's resting. I feel so sorry for her—it's heavy and unmoving. I feel helpless, and I wish I could do something to help, or at least make her feel better.

He puts his other hand on mine and rubs his thumb over my wrist. "So, yeah. That's why I'm here, in Citrus Harbor." And now he's tearing up, and I might be, too. "It's probably our last summer together." He says it hushed, like if he whispers then maybe it won't come true.

"It isn't all bad, though," he says, frowning. "Not the worst, though there are definitely some…moments. Those are hard. But it's nice being with her. Sometimes I help out with picking up prescriptions or grabbing things from the store if Ron or Charlie need me to. Mostly I just try to spend time with her."

I don't know what to say, so we sit in silence, holding hands.

I notice envelopes piled on the counter, and on the other end of the table is a laptop with a Columbia sticker next to a coffee mug and a stack of papers. Folded glasses and a pen hold the sheets of ivory to the table. I wonder if Logan looks forward to college as much as he would if he didn't have this heartache. I imagine it makes him want to stay in this summer just a little longer.

After a while, we move over to the living room, sitting on the couch across the room from his aunt. I check in several times to ensure he doesn't mind. After all, the last thing I want to do is intrude on his time with her.

When Jane wakes up, she goes to reach for a glass, and Logan hands it to her. She sips the water gently and slowly, and then he takes it back.

She smiles at me, soft and kind. "Hi."

I smile back. "Hi."

"This is Harry," Logan says to her.

I feel fear hot in my chest and cheeks—what if something

goes wrong? What if she doesn't recognize him? I don't know much about this disease beyond the basics, and I don't know what I should do if it happens.

Her eyes brighten a little. "Oh. *This* is Harry?"

I look to Logan, and his face flashes red, while I exhale, relieved.

"He *is* handsome," she says to Logan and then winks at me.

Logan holds his hands up, still a shade of red reserved for apples and tomatoes. "Okay, okay."

"Well, thank you," I chuckle.

Logan just laughs along with me, rolling his eyes a little before leaning over to kiss his aunt's forehead. "This is my aunt, Jane."

"It's nice to meet you," I say.

Jane is lovely. She asks me a few questions about myself, and I tell her how beautiful her home is. She actually collected rugs and fabrics for pillows from places like Marrakech and Cusco.

Jane tells us all about a little silver shop she visited in Mexico and how she has these gorgeous spoons with engravings on them. She tells us about a dress she was given by a woman in Greece and a man who drew her in Rome. She says it's framed in the hallway and that I'm welcome to see it if I'd like to.

There's something so magical about her telling us these stories. It's like learning what little things make her heart beat and getting a sample of the music in her soul.

As it turns out, Logan hadn't been to Citrus Harbor until this summer because Jane and Ron frequently traveled to North Carolina to be with Logan's family up there. That's why Logan is so close to them.

We talk about Sucré and how she's great friends with Odette and Jean-Claude. That's when I realize why Odette was so insistent when she gave Logan and me the meals on the house.

I marvel at Jane. Knowing how sick she is… I can't imagine what it must feel like. Still, she doesn't seem limited by it, if not only physically. Her spirit is so strong, and she's lived a life of absolute wonder.

Eventually, we talk about careers and college majors. We talk about my dreams, and she says to go after them no matter what. She says Logan's always been a little boy genius mathematician and he's all flushed cheeks and glancing down again.

"You know, traveling and seeing the world, chasing my dreams…" Jane's eyes light up. "Those memories I wouldn't trade, but I think most of my best times were here, in Citrus. You can go off and see it all—whether you're running to or from something—but eventually you realize home is pretty special. Being with the people you love is what matters the most."

When I leave later, we hug goodbye. Logan's hug is strong and secure. I lay my head against his chest, and he runs his fingers through my hair. Though I can't quite believe it's happening to me—and though I should be comforting him and not the other way around—I don't want him to ever let me go.

Then, when I step onto the porch, I ask him to let me know if he needs anything at all. I look back and just offer a soft, quiet smile. It's a smile that says more than I could vocalize. It apologizes one last time and tells Logan I want to see him again. It's a smile that realizes how precious time is and how incredible and rare Logan is.

He nods, his grin enough to keep me smiling on the walk home.

That night, I sit down to edit my screenplay, but I can't think of anything except Logan and his family. I feel so sorry for him and for her, and there's no way I can write when my heart feels like this, so I decide to take comfort with a Lily Tilbury book under the stars, with the sound of the ocean in the background. We have a little area for sitting on the beach walkup—the wood is built into benches on either side.

It doesn't take long to feel settled with my book. The beach always makes me feel better about anything that's bothering me. The calm purple of the nearly dark sky and the crashing waves.

Then I see someone sitting with their arms around their legs on the beach a few houses down. Even from here, I know it's Logan. I can make out his shape without a second thought.

Setting my mug down and leaving my book open on top of my blanket, I head down to the sand. The waves seem soft and gentle, like they're only trying to kiss the shore and not ravage it. The air is dewy, familiar. I keep my eyes on Logan, and it occurs to me he might not want company.

I hesitate for a moment, nearly turning around, but he must have seen me by now. So I keep going, the balls of my feet sinking against the damp sand.

"Hi," I say when I reach him.

Maybe I was right to hesitate. He's wiping at his eyes, and he just laughs, half a sob and half forced greeting. He gestures for me to sit next to him, like he always does, so I do.

He pulls his knees in closer and knocks his head against them.

"Damn it," he says. "This is no way to impress you. A big snotty crybaby."

"You always impress me," I say, without even thinking about it.

I lock my arm in his and reach for his hand before resting my head on his shoulder. He leans into me, and then he cries. And that's how we sit, as the violet sunset turns to deep night.

INT. A FUTURE DEFENSE HIDEOUT IN BROOKLYN

Rory sits on a beanbag chair in front of a monitor.

>   RORY
> What's the plan again?

>   SKIP
> First thing's first. We need to get my suit, and then we
> need to break the *real* Jenson out of the Vicious hideout.
> This monitor is picking up ridiculously high gamma levels
> on the east side, which can only be Jenson.

>   RORY
> This is so weird. I still haven't actually seen Jenson—the
> real Jenson, who's my ex—since he moved to London.
> Which means this could be a little awkward.

CLOSE-UP. Skip's eyes go wide.

SKIP
We're talking about the collapse of our entire universe,
I'm sure you guys can get past it?

RORY
Yes. Absolutely, you're right. Of course.

18

ISN'T IT ROMANTIC

Over the past few days, I've become an expert at ignoring Grant's messages.

They come through when I'm working at the store and when I'm playing board games with Logan and Jane. He texts me when I'm drinking those plastic barrel juices with Hailey at the school pool. I ignore his DMs when Lottie needs help washing blue Sharpie off her face because she thought she could do her own makeup and when Mom is offering her commentary to the housewives on TV from the kitchen island.

None of the contents of Grant's messages matter, least of all his BS excuse for standing me up. He says he's changed and it's not like last summer, but I don't care.

When Grant asks me if I'll go to the summer carnival with him after some more apologies, I almost laugh out loud at my phone. I want to tell him he must have lost his mind, but I opt for no response.

Grant can attend tonight's carnival dateless if he wants, but it's going to be great for me. And I think the games and the flashing lights will really brighten up Logan's evening. I mean it's technically half-selfish because I'm getting a fun night with him out of it.

I stop by Hailey's on the way. She and the girls from the swim team are going to Orlando for some super sweet Nike swim camp where they get to go to Disney and Universal. She told me about it between classes when she'd paid, but I completely forgot. Honestly, this is the best thing for her now. She can be with a huge group of girls who all adore and support her and be far, far away from Justin. And she can work on her tan while eating Dole Whips.

As far as getting over Justin, Hailey seems to be doing *really* well. There was a brief foray into dark territory just after the party where I nearly puked on Logan. I should have known it was too soon for her to be truly okay. It was all sad songs and late-night Snapchats eating ice cream out of the carton. She made lists of all the songs, movies, and TV shows she'd have to forever avoid so she wasn't reminded of him. I wasn't going to be the one to tell her avoiding *How the Grinch Stole Christmas* would be pretty hard since it comes on, like, every day in December.

But recently, we talked through surviving Senior Week and prom and graduation. She experienced less sadness and more anger, though it vacillated. She wondered if she could find another boyfriend in time to win Cutest Couple and *really* stick it to Justin, which I assured her she wasn't ready for.

Now she's in a weird haze that's kind of hard to read—is she mad? Sad? Glad to be single? She says she can't be held responsible if she happens to post Instagram photos with the hot guys at swim camp, though she's hoping they know how to avoid a goggle tan.

I send her off, my little single vixen, and hope she is truthfully doing as well as she says. While I feel majorly relieved to not be harboring the secret of Justin's cheating, I still feel a little guilty for not telling her first. But Hailey's the one who always says the past is the past, and it's not like I *lied*—I just didn't share. So it's not that bad, after all.

When I arrive at Logan's, Ron is working on the yard again. I think he enjoys gardening because he's almost always doing something outside. He waves and shouts that Logan's inside with Jane. Of course, I have a box of treats from Odette and I usually would just bound into the foyer like I'm on my way to grandmother's house through the woods, but I dial it back in case Jane is sleeping or not feeling well.

"Knock, knock," I call out softly as I shut the door behind me as slowly as possible.

"In here," Logan says.

"Is that Harry?" Jane coos.

I grin when I see them, playing Scrabble on the coffee table and drinking iced teas. Logan gets up to hug me, and I go over to Jane, offering a gentle embrace.

Honestly, I still don't know a hundred percent how Alzheimer's works. I've been researching it, though. A lot. And so I understand it can manifest in different ways for different people. Still, I get a little bit nervous that one day she may not remember me. But more importantly, I hope she still remembers Logan every day.

I push those thoughts away, though, because she's in high spirits.

"What have we here?" she says, peering into the box. I place it next to her and allow her to go through it. "You're too kind, Harry. You don't have to bring over gifts every time, you know that?"

But there's a grateful kindness in her eyes and so I nod and tell her I know.

Logan thanks me, too.

"Want to get in on the Scrabble?" Logan says.

I shake my head. "No, I don't want to interrupt your game."

"Not much of a game," Logan informs me, a smile creeping across his mouth as he looks to Jane.

"I'm sure he'll win one of these days," Jane tells me with a light shrug. "It's a very casual game, so you can play if you'd like to."

I agree, and Logan sets up a little place for me on one side of the board. My tiles are almost all vowels.

"Okay," I begin, fiddling with my letters. I may be a writer, but suddenly words seem out of reach. "So, um, Logan… If you have plans tonight, that's totally fine, but the Summer Carnival is at seven, and I thought it could be fun if you were interested."

Jane claps her hands together. "He has no plans. Oh, the Summer Carnival!"

I absentmindedly move a G next to an O on my stand, but my attention immediately shifts to Jane's elation. Normally, I'd be competitive and take much more time to analyze my tiles, but now I'm more focused on enjoying the company. Plus, asking Logan on a date made me weirdly nervous.

"That carnival is just the best," Jane says, hugging her hands to her chest. "Ron and I had such wonderful dates there. What great memories."

"It sounds like I am going to the Summer Carnival," Logan says with a smile. His gaze drifts across the Scrabble board, and like a pro, he plays QUELL.

"Nice move," I say with a stifled laugh as I decide to up my game just a little and play SUITS.

Then, of course, Jane plays vertically, attaching to other lines of words and using a blank tile, and she's formed QUIZ-ZIFY.

Is *quizzify* even a word? I don't know, but who am I to question it?

Logan, however, raises a brow and fervently types on his phone. I know that he's found himself at a loss as he stares up, wide-eyed, to meet a very pleased Jane's grin.

When we leave, I feel like a Coke that's been shaken up. It sounds cliché, but it's just how it feels. This moment, I think—right now—is everything.

We walk together down to the beach, shoes in hand. Our steps in sync in the sand, I see the sunlight perfectly hugging Logan's profile.

My skin feels warm, tingling with the kiss of the summer sun, delicate and sensitive. The sand is gritty, and Logan smells like sunscreen. When he catches me looking at him, he furrows his brows and laughs, looking down at his feet. His smile is making my stomach flip, so I just let myself enjoy the moment.

For the first time in so long, I stop and feel the moment, without even consciously trying. I feel the happiness and the bubbles and sparks, like I'm made of Pop Rocks and Mountain Dew and the only things I'll ever smell are coconuts and vanilla and Logan.

He knocks his shoulder against mine, and I grin at him, giving in to a giggle.

Logan's like the solstice in June—the sign of all the good things to come.

"What are you looking at?"

My heart quickens—did he do that? "You have a little…" I reach over and brush my thumb across his cheek, and he chuckles. "There, got it."

Nice save.

We get to the carnival, and it's all bright lights, the smell of funnel cakes and kettle corn wafting down the beach. The entire pier gets transformed into an enchanting destination. There's a Ferris wheel, an endless row of desserts and treats, and a ride that rises up and spins high above the boardwalk. There's even a big top, filled with games where you toss rings onto bottles or throw darts at balloons. A smaller big top was added last year, filled with craft beer vendors—evolving with the times.

"After you," Logan offers in his gentlemanly way as we reach the steps to the boardwalk. He follows me up.

Even at seventeen, I'm bright and starry-eyed when I see the brilliance of the carnival. Every year, something magical happens during or right after the carnival. "Entry of the Gladiators" is playing loud and high pitched. I only know the name of the song because it used to drive Milly absolutely *nuts* if I played it on repeat when I babysat her.

We play a few games, and I see Milly with her friends. She's

pretty cozy with some boy in a blue Billabong tank top and
board shorts. I recognize him from around school and wonder if they're together, but she'd kill me if I joined her little
group without a warning, so I just steer Logan in the opposite direction.

Lottie is with Nana because she hates carnivals and Mom
had to jet off to Miami for an event last-minute. In the back
of my mind, I had this strange hope Mom and Mark would
go to the carnival together so I could discreetly spy on them
and make sure he is a good match for her. But since that's not
happening and I don't want to risk embarrassing Milly, I'm
completely focusing on Logan.

"What do you want to do?"

We play a few of the classic games like the water guns and
the super hard game where you throw darts at balloons and
somehow they magically never pop. Logan tries so hard to
win me a giant stuffed octopus at the basketball, but it turns
out he's totally not cut out for the NBA. We are both pretty
shocked.

After hitting the heavy hammer and not winning anything,
we opt for a ride on the gravity machine and both collapse
into dizzy laughter after we get off. We tour the hall of mirrors, and Logan attempts to scare me but only ends up running straight into a mirror. We even sit together on the Ferris
wheel, looking out at the water and all the people having the
time of their lives. It seems like such a good time to finally
kiss him, but I don't want to rush it—Logan's hand fits perfectly in mine, and it feels like paradise, even without kissing.

We stop at the photo booth, and Logan and I improvise
four goofy poses, including plenty of ridiculous duck lips and

pig noses and being caught midlaugh. We tear them down the middle, each getting to keep two of the photos, because I think I've seen that in a movie.

Eventually, we make our way down to the beach, where it's dark except for some neon glow from the carnival. We sit together and share a pastel cloud of cotton candy, and when Logan tells me this has been the perfect night, I blush like a big baby. The sky is open, a vast stadium of twinkling, glittering lights, and everything's just glowing and glistening. My heart swells a little bit. Actually, it swells a lot.

"Okay," Logan says after a moment, leaning back and taking a sip of his soda. "So tell me when you knew you wanted to be a screenwriter."

I think back. "I've always loved movies. My whole life. And I wanted to be an actor when I was a kid—be *in* them. But then as I grew up, I realized I wanted to tell the stories. Make the movies, instead."

Logan nods.

"Can you imagine?" I say. "Having an idea—just a thought—and then it's a script, and then there's a cast and a crew. Then movie trailers and posters and marketing and before you know it, it's on the big screen across the country or across the world, even. And it means something to someone. It's someone's favorite soundtrack or their rainy day comfort film. Your little idea. That little piece of you."

"Wow," he says.

"You expected some shallow answer about parties on Mulholland Drive?" I smirk.

"Not from you."

"What about you? You said you wanted to be in the FBI since you were a kid?" I say.

"Oh yeah, I've just kind of always liked that stuff. Psychology and problem-solving and all that. Plus, as you know, movies kinda make everything seem so cool. Like, *Catch Me If You Can*."

"You really love DiCaprio, don't you?"

"Can you blame me?" Logan says.

"Fair enough. But why did you say you're more 'guy in the chair?'"

"Dunno." Logan looks off like he's thinking. "My dad says I get my math skills from my mom, and I definitely want to use those. And I guess, also, I like being more behind the scenes?"

"We have that in common," I say. "Now that I'm older, I can't imagine being an actor—I'll stick to writing."

"Exactly. So, tell me more about your dreams. I wanna know it all."

"This summer," I say in the best movie trailer voice I can muster. "A future FBI agent attempts to gain intel from the elusive and mysterious screenwriter."

Looking at me expectantly, Logan grins. "Exactly! And the mysterious screenwriter's favorite movie is...?"

"*When Harry Met Sally*," I say without missing a beat. "Because I was so self-involved as a kid I immediately gravitated toward anything with my name in it. And because it's one of my mom's favorites, too. The fake orgasm scene? Pure gold. There are a lot of reasons—how much time do you have?"

"I know this is a big surprise, but I haven't seen that one," Logan laughs, covering his face with his hands.

"We're going to have to watch it together," I say. "What's your favorite movie?"

He straightens up. "Mine is definitely *Titanic*."

I throw a piece of cotton candy at him. "Do you run a Leo fan club or what?"

Logan catches the cotton candy and tosses it into his mouth. "No, I'm kidding. I do love that movie, though. I have strong opinions on the ending, and we talked about this when you clung to my arm and said 'I'll never let go.' But I'm guessing you don't remember because you were drunk."

My cheeks go hot. "Oh, God." But he just laughs.

"It was cute," he says. "My favorite is actually *The Goonies*."

"Both of our favorite movies are from the '80s."

"We're really cultured," Logan laughs and rubs his chin. "What else should I know about you?"

"Are you building a file for me? Is there an ongoing investigation I should know about?"

"Always good to know the important stuff," he says. "Like your favorite season?"

I watch the lights bouncing in his eyes.

"True, you can't leave that one blank," I say. "Summer."

"Spring is mine. But I like summer, too," Logan says.

"All the best things happen during summer," I say, biting my lip.

"They do."

A beat passes.

"Okay." Logan claps his hands together. "What about music?"

"Love it," I say. "Film scores, pop, Broadway."

"What about, like, a favorite song?"

"Nobody has *one* favorite song," I say. "You have different favorite songs for different moods and periods of your life."

"I don't know," Logan muses. "I feel there's *a* song that stands out. Didn't one come to mind for you? Do you have a go-to karaoke song?"

"Um, I don't do karaoke," I say. "Trust me, it's my way of sparing society. But there is this one song from when I was young." I'm already dying laughing. "My mom had this '80s playlist on her iPod when I was little. I used my toy microphone in the car to sing along to 'I Drove All Night.' There are videos of my performances. I got in trouble for singing it at school because of the line about making love—I had no idea what it meant. It's pretty hilarious. Now that song always reminds me of fun times, dancing around with my mom."

Logan laughs, wiping tears from his eyes. "I am absolutely going to need not only a viewing of these videos, but a live performance. I need this in my life. And, you know, I respect this choice. Cyndi Lauper did do 'The Goonies "R" Good Enough.' It's pretty much a classic." Logan grins, and we laugh more while I throw another piece of cotton candy at him.

I tell him to share *his* favorite song now. Our eyes catch each other, and he sits up, nodding. "I don't really have a great story like that. But my favorite song is probably this, like, folk-rock song called 'Man on Fire.'"

"Sounds dangerous," I say as I feel myself turning to putty all over again. Like I'm watching myself from afar, I feel my eyes go starry as he blushes.

"Can I play it for you?" He holds his phone up. I nod, eager to get a glimpse into his world, and he chuckles. "On my phone, not, like, on an instrument."

As the song starts, as it feels like everything starts, I hear the strings and the humming, and I feel like I'm *lucky*. Logan's looking down at his phone, watching the cursor move slowly with the time changing second by second.

In this moment, I want to admire him. I want to remember every single thing about him and this and us. The sound of the waves crashing behind us, the soft glow of the carnival lights on his cheekbones, and the soft shadows of his eyelashes. His lips are barely touching, and he taps his finger against his knee.

He puts his arm around me, and I feel like I could float up and touch the stars—like I could slow dance with them and learn their names and tell them stories that light up the night brighter than ever.

And just as we're about to kiss, Logan's phone goes off, interrupting the song—a text from Ron. He says everything is fine, but I can tell he's worried about something. So, I just spring up and grab Logan's hand, saying we should go back to his place and binge HGTV with Jane, and, somehow, it feels like enough.

INT. INSIDE RORY'S DORM ROOM AT NIGHT

Rory sits at his desk in his pajamas, typing and flipping through the pages in his biochemistry textbook.

CLOSE-UP. Rory's phone screen. It's a news alert about Quick Circuit saving a gala from an attack.

CLOSE-UP. Rory's face looks somber.

There's a knock on Rory's door.

Rory looks up.

MEDIUM SHOT. Skip opens the door.

    SKIP
  Knock, knock, hope you're decent.

Skip rushes in, grinning.

SKIP
I figured it out.

RORY
Skip, you scared me! A little heads-up next time?

SKIP
Sorry, right. You should lock your door.

RORY
Skip.

SKIP
Okay, well, really *you* figured it out. Your idea—shrinking
the suit to fit in a water molecule since it's supposed to
completely adhere to my hydrological powers?

Rory nods.

SKIP
It's brilliant. So from there, I sort of used Future Defense
technology to hack into The Champions Alliance
Campus and figured out the nearest pipe. All we have to
do is flood the chamber and The Sting is back.

RORY
Mr. Wilson is gonna kill us.

SKIP
We make a good team, huh?

RORY
(blushing)
Yeah, we do.

19

SOMETHING'S GOTTA GIVE

I've never felt more like a fish out of water. Pun very much intended.

My swim shorts aren't even "baggies" or board shorts like Logan's. They're Ralph Lauren and hit at the thigh—they're more The Beverly Hills Hotel—and I'm pretty certain they were not designed with surfing in mind.

Still, I'm next to Logan, and he's wearing proper surfing shorts, bent over a board. We scrub the boards with what he describes as wax to keep our feet from slipping off.

Already, I know I am screwed. At least we don't have reefs for me to majorly injure myself on.

Though I told myself I wouldn't try surfing ever again after attempting once with Grant last summer—and basically being made fun of for failing, which is, like, my kryptonite—I'm doing this for multiple reasons. Jane is inspiring me to live my best, most adventurous life. She has experienced so much, and she's treasuring the time she has left. So who am I to take for granted however much life I have?

I may look stupid, but I'm going to try some new things. Broaden my horizons.

Also, I want to do something nice and selfless for Logan. Off the top of my head, this is a good start. A kind gesture. Considering he's mentioned teaching me to surf multiple times and I definitely can't, like, help him with anything math or criminal justice related.

"I'm not exactly an expert," Logan had said as we carried the boards down to the shore. "Obviously."

"Obviously," I said, laughing. "But you're confident you can teach me and I won't die?"

Logan had just looked at me and raised a brow.

Now, we're getting ready to begin. It's past sunrise, and the sticky heat is starting to cling to us. I blink, and Logan's looking at me like I missed something.

Maybe I did miss something?

"So, first..." Logan is tapping his finger to his chin. "Yeah, first, you learn how to paddle."

He lies down on the board and gestures for me to do the same.

The board must be nearly seven feet long. It seems excessive to me, but Logan says the longer boards are better for learning. I lie down on it and face the water. I mimic the way he fake paddles. Our arms are in sync, and when he catches me holding in a little giggle, we both end up falling into a fit of laughter.

Logan pretends to push off the board, hunching and holding both arms out like he's riding a massive wave. He sways and then falls to land beside me.

"You're a natural," I say.

"You too," he tells me. "Great paddling."

I nod and show off a little.

"So you have to learn how to mount it," Logan says. He looks at me, flustered for a moment by his choice of words then he just shakes it off, looking back at the board. "It's a pop up. You just…"

And he's showing me. He's quick, popping up and having his feet land at just the right angle.

I nod, pretending like I am capable of doing what he's doing. I sputter as he does it again and this time kicks some sand up to my face.

"Oops," he says with a laugh, brushing it off my shoulder. "Sorry."

It's my turn then. I'm not exactly a surf prodigy. We can leave it at that. No improvements from the last time I tried. I think my form could use some fine-tuning to say the least. He tells me we're best off just doing a few little exercises in the water to get my feet wet. He pauses for me to react to the pun, so I do—a full on sarcastic belly laugh. I then pat him on the back as we take our boards to the water.

When we're walking down, I catch a glimpse of him and feel my heart wipeout in a barrel. He's just so…something. He's like this place. He's become comfortable, and he's safe. The way the sun hits his profile and his skin seems to glow golden like something too good for me.

I haven't been able to stop thinking about how he won't be here forever, though. And that's how he's not like this place. He won't be here for much longer. He's got bigger things to do—theorems to solve, probably lives to change.

With his head down, Logan says something that makes him laugh, but I don't hear because I'm too busy admiring his jaw line and the crinkles at the corners of his eyes and his dimples and—

"What?"

"You'll see," he says, chuckling.

We stand next to the boards, and he slides onto his and instructs me to do the same. When I do, I can't quite get my balance, and I wobble a bit as I slide right across it and end up under water. I regain my composure, swimming up, and Logan's laughing again when I take a deep breath and open my eyes. I splash at him, and he only laughs harder.

We sit on the boards, and he shows me that we're going to paddle from point A to point B. And we do. Over and over and over. He says it's important to feel comfortable paddling. And after fifteen minutes or so, I do. My arm and thigh muscles are fully accustomed to paddling.

He shows me this move where he goes against the waves, pushing his board down and going under with it before resurfacing nose first. When I try it, I look like a massive idiot and nearly smack myself in the face with my board.

Eventually, after many tries and much instruction, I get it.

"I don't think I should even try to actually jump up on the board," I say as we paddle out a little. I'm already exhausted, and this is clearly not my sport. "The pop on or whatever."

Logan presses his forehead to his board and laughs. "Pop up. You don't have to do anything you're not comfortable with. I mean, if you want to just give it a shot for shits and giggles, be my guest. It's okay if you don't ride a wave on your first day, though."

Logan turns and begins to paddle with the current before nearly being consumed by the white rapids of the tide. He pops up onto the board, and he looks damn cool as he rides the wave in to the shore. He falls off his board dramatically and then looks back at me to see what I'll do.

Okay. I can at least try. I can do this. I can try to do this. It could be my compulsive need to try everything—the only thing worse than failing is never making an effort at all. I can hear my mom giving me a business-oriented motivational speech.

So I press my chest to the board and make sure the little line down the middle is aligned with the center of my chest, just like Logan said to. I paddle, hands cupped and chest and thighs tight. I can do this.

When I feel the wave surrounding me, I pop up like a bat out of hell. I'm standing on the surfboard! Eyes wide and wind hitting my face, water spraying my ankles, I open my mouth to yell out to Logan, and the moment is gone. I'm on my ass in less than a second—full on, legs in the air and embarrassing squeal as I slip and bust it.

When I wash up, Logan is standing there to comfort me, though we're both just totally consumed with laughter. He glances from me to the waves—as if to ask if I want to try again—and to answer, I just smile, take his hand, and start walking back up the beach.

"You were epic," Logan tells me when we make it to where our stuff is lying on the sand.

We unhook our leashes and fall onto our backs.

"Majestic, actually."

"Well, I can't be good at everything," I tease, turning my

face to him. He has his eyes closed, and his chest is rising as he catches his breath.

"That significantly reduces my interest in you." Logan sighs.

And I like the way his lips look when he smiles.

"You're interested in me?"

"You're ridiculous…"

I roll over, my hand stopping on his chest, and as his eyes meet mine, I lean down and press my lips to his. First slow, just gentle and soft, and then he's got his hand on my cheek and he's kissing me back.

It feels—to butcher my French lessons with Odette—like a *raison d'être*.

It's better than any kiss I've ever had, and I don't know how because I panic when our lips meet. My eyes don't even fall closed. I just sort of exhale when he pulls away and looks up at me under those damn lashes.

"Um," he breathes, still less than an inch from my face.

I hold my fingers up to my lip and lightly lick at the salt-water. "Sorry," I say. Maybe I'm not being rational right now, but it's not Just A Kiss. And I need to know why that felt so… "Can you… Can we do that again?"

"Yeah," Logan huffs with a smile, bringing his hand up to my neck and leaning in to kiss me. My eyes shut, and I'm breathless. This time he's deliberate, and there's something hungry in the way his lips part and he lightly tugs at my bottom lip. His nose grazes mine, and all of his skin is so soft. He runs his hand through my hair.

When we stop, I open my eyes, and he's looking at me again, this time with his mouth pursed as if to see if he did it right. If he can do it again, maybe?

"Wow," I say. Which is so not romantic, or well thought-out or impressive. But it's what I'm feeling.

So, I kiss Logan next. He puts his hand on my thigh, but it's delicate and gentle and respectful and almost *innocent*. His palm rests against my leg while his other hand traces the side of my face.

Kissing Logan is next-level. Kissing Logan isn't like anything else. It's fire and ice. It's crystal clear and burning hot.

I smile into the kiss. It's warm and delicate and all saltwater and sunshine.

"What?" He smiles back, and I just shake my head, water drops shaking out everywhere.

"I just like you," I say, unapologetically, and then kiss him again.

Logan's thumb runs across my cheek, and he grins. "I like you, too."

I rest my head on his chest and listen to his heart—it's fast and somehow it sounds like a promise. And the echoes of the feelings are like a reverb, growing louder and stronger as we sit together. We're lost in each other.

And I don't know when it all started. I don't know when he became this person to me. All I know is that he's sunshine and walks home through the palm trees and soft whispers in the middle of the night. All of this is familiar, I think. This ocean, this lifeguard stand, this beach access, and the sailboat that is always leaning against the dunes. The way the sun eventually creeps behind the pier and the buildings.

And suddenly, he's familiar, too. Like the surf. And the sun. And the sand. He and I are caught in the swell—roaring, yet calm at the same damn time.

★ ★ ★

Logan and I decide to go for brunch, this time opting for a new spot. One even I haven't tried before. This new modern-looking building has popped up across from an old closed bowling alley. It's usually busy, though we must arrive just in time.

It's called Stoke and, judging by the shaka image on the door, they're capitalizing on the surf vibe.

"Hey guys," a young girl calls out lazily from behind the counter.

The place is gorgeous. It's all light wood floors and hanging Edison bulbs with subtle yellow details: their logo, the salt and pepper shakers. On the far wall, there's a rack of surfboards in a creative ombre—orange to yellow from the top. I could get lost in the colors.

"This place is cool," Logan mutters as he pulls a menu from a wooden crate set up on a barrel.

I agree, peering over his shoulder and looking over the options. He always smells good. Which I don't hate. He smells like the beach, of course, but also like a very manly deodorant. I don't know, I think he smells like Old Spice or something.

Does Old Spice smell good?

Logan's finger lands on some burger with guacamole and applewood-smoked bacon. "I think I found a winner."

"Sounds good," I say. "I think I want the mac 'n' cheese."

"Adventurous," he notes. "Can I steal a bite?"

He puts the menu back in the crate, and I nod, all dreamy eyes. *Dreamy eyes?* Who am I?

We walk up to the counter, and the employees are all super young. Like, Milly's age.

"What's up?" the girl says. She's wearing a black T-shirt that says "stoke" in cool, hipster lowercase letters. Her hair is braided, dirty blond with sparkles and bits of pink.

"I'll do the Goofy Guac," Logan says, and I watch the trace of a smile on his lips. I actually have to stop myself from cracking up.

The girl asks him a few final questions—how he wants it cooked, does he want fries, what to drink—before turning to me and offering something resembling a smile. She's too cool for school.

Obviously.

"Could I please have the Macking Mac?" I say, feeling as if I'm pronouncing it wrong. She presses at her screen, and I raise a brow. "Why is it called that?"

The girl, who isn't wearing a nametag like the rest of the staff is, purses her lips.

And it's at this point that I realize I've made a mistake. This young girl, who I'm going to call Brit because she kind of just seems like a Brit, has no interest in talking to me *at all*. Probably, there are about a hundred other things Brit would rather be doing than taking orders at a restaurant and answering questions about the menu vocabulary. She gives me such an irritated and astonished look, I almost take a step back.

"You know..." She mocks thinking. "I'm not really sure but if you, like, really want to know, I'll get my manager."

And now Logan's snorting because I'm trying to tell her I don't actually want to know anymore, and now I see there are a few people behind us in line, but she's gone to the back, a revolving door swinging shut.

"I didn't need to know that bad," I tell Logan, who's laughing into the back of his hand.

The woman behind me has two kids who are both tugging at her shirt and complaining about how long this is taking. She doesn't disagree.

Finally, Brit comes back out with her manager, who seems really irritated and proceeds to explain that every item on the menu is inspired by surf lingo. She makes a point to show me her phone screen—a Google search—and deadpans, asking if there's anything else she can help me with.

So that's cool.

Logan squeezes my waist as we get our fountain drinks. "That was fun," he says.

My cheeks are still burning as I get some sweet tea from the giant metal container. "Fun?"

"Fun-ny," Logan corrects, topping off his Sprite. "I think the final straw for her was when the card reader did that little *erk*, *erk*, *erk* noise. Also, um. Harry?"

"Logan?"

"Do you know what day it is?" He pops a lid onto his soda.

"Yes?"

"It's officially less than one week before the competition closes submissions?" Logan raises a brow. I've mentioned it so many times, and now I almost wish I hadn't.

"Oh my God," I mutter to myself.

"What?"

I give a huge, overenthusiastic grin. "I'm working on it."

Logan opens his mouth, but I stop him. "It's just not ready yet. I need to think about…stuff." I've barely made a dent in editing it, but now that I'm so happy with Logan, I hardly want to revisit the story that has Grant so clearly in its DNA.

What a tangled web I consistently weave.

"I'll figure it out."

We sit down, and then I see my mom's name pop up on my phone. She doesn't typically call me when she's at work, and seeing as she's in Miami right now, I have to make sure nothing is wrong. I tell Logan I'll be right back, and then I run outside.

"Hello?"

Mom sighs. "Hi, Hare. I need a favor."

"What is it? Is everything okay?"

"Everything is fine," Mom says. "It's just your sister is not answering her phone, and your grandmother has to go teach a class—I really need you to watch Lottie if you can."

"Of course," I say. "Yeah, of course. She's at the house?"

"Yes, thank you so much! Order some lunch and rent a movie," she says. "Thank you, thank you! Love you!"

I run inside and frown as I reach the table. Logan looks up at me.

"Everything okay?"

I nod. "Please don't hate me."

"I could never hate you," he says, which kind of makes me melt.

"My mom needs me to go watch Lottie," I tell him. And I do feel bad, ending the day like this, but I have to go. "I'm sorry, I can get our food to go…" I throw my hands up. "Unless you still want to eat here—then I can just get my food to go! Totally your call. Are you mad?"

Logan laughs. "Okay, slow down. I'm not mad at all. Why don't I just come with you? I can help with Lottie. If you want."

"Well." I smile. "Yeah, I want. I mean if *you* want. Are you sure? You don't mind?"

"I don't mind," Logan says.

The line has sort of died down.

"Wish me luck," I say.

I rush over to Brit. "Hi, Brit, I'm *so* sorry but I need to make that order to-go and add a children's meal to it." She blinks.

"Wait," she says. "What did you just call me?"

Lottie runs up and bear-hugs Logan, locking her arms around him with such furor I'm afraid she'll pop him like she did with her blow-up narwhal last summer.

"I'm very glad you're here," she says seriously, taking the bag from Stoke from him and smelling it. "This smells wonderful."

Sometimes Lottie gets in these moods where she only talks as grown-up as possible.

Don't get me wrong—she never goes *full* five-year-old, but she does have moments where she'll just say the most ridiculous, out-of-this-world thing only a five-year-old could think of.

For example, we're at a relatively quiet restaurant for dinner. Lottie drops her iPad, silverware clatters, and she looks to Mom, disturbed. "They keep dinosaur poop, you know. I don't want a scientist to put my poop in a museum."

Cut to shocked patrons around us.

"Please tell me my poop won't be in a museum," Lottie pleads.

She's not in five-year-old mode right now, though. She's five going on twenty-five, even in her Elsa costume.

"I have started writing a book." She places the food on the coffee table and brings us over to where she's set up shop in the corner between the entertainment center and the couch. In an appalling development, Lottie has pages of scribbled words on the floor surrounded by colored pencils, empty applesauce packets, and cookie crumbs.

"It's a little messy," Lottie says. "Writers can be a bit messy."

Logan looks to me expectantly, and I throw my hands up. "I'm not *that* messy."

"What's your book about?" Logan says, peering over her shoulder at the pages.

Lottie frowns, throwing her arms up. "Don't look at these pages! This is the middle of the story. Don't you know about *spoilers*?"

I sit down and open my food. "I'm just going to…"

Lottie pulls Logan's arm over to the coffee table and sits him down on the floor. "First, we'll eat. Then we'll go over the book." She gives him a pointed look. "Starting from the beginning."

Logan laughs and nods.

"Listen to this," Lottie says, pulling her iPad off the couch and playing a song. "It's a song about ponies who dance and sing and poop magic sprinkles and rainbows."

And Lottie is back to being five.

Logan and I are both unable to contain our laughter, and Lottie loves it. She dances around, making unicorn pooping noises (which are very delicate, wistful pooping noises) and twirling along with the song.

When the song is over, she sits down next to Logan and sips her drink. "How is your aunt Jane?"

"Lot," I mumble.

"It's okay," Logan says. He gives her a big smile. "She's doing well, thank you for asking."

Lottie leans her head on his shoulder and nods, wrapping her arm over his chest.

When Milly gets home, I don't even *attempt* to say anything about her not answering her phone earlier and having to rush Logan out of Stoke. It's just not worth it. At her age, it's zero to ten thousand in a matter of seconds if I say the wrong thing.

I'll let Mom have that one.

Milly and Lottie settle on the couch and watch crappy reality TV. Lottie's probably not *actually* allowed to watch it, but, again, picking my battles.

Logan and I walk up the stairs to my room, and we pass Lottie's chaotic whirlwind of Pottery Barn Kids. It's all pastels and white wood furniture—a huge LEGO table with a full-on cityscape and a pink wicker basket of stuffed animals. Milly's door is cracked, too, but I can only see clothes spilled out all over the floor and the Fleetwood Mac poster hanging over her perfume-covered dresser.

"I love how your rooms are all so *you*," Logan says.

I open the door to my room, and we walk into my bedroom. It's pretty standard—ocean-colored striped comforter, blue walls, and a TV hung up across from my bed.

There are pops of color from the assorted spines on my bookcase and the giant yellow *Roman Holiday* poster framed on one wall, which features Audrey Hepburn and Gregory Peck on a scooter with the Colosseum behind them. On another wall, there are pages from magazines and surf stickers—

a collage that Hailey and I did one day when we were trying to copy TikTok trends.

Logan walks to my desk and leans over to take a closer look at the little corkboard I have plastered with photos, various movie tickets, and other stickers I never stuck to things in case I changed my mind about their placement.

"Very cool desk setup," he says, pulling out the chair and sitting down. "Is this what you do?"

I rest my chin on my hands. "What I do?"

"When you write," he says, grinning. He straightens up and fakes typing. He sips an imaginary cup of coffee with his pinky up and squints at the black screen. "Oh, yes. Right, yes. I've been struck with genius! Aha! Rory, do this. Skip, say that!"

His British accent isn't actually horrible. Thinking of Rory and Skip reminds me I *need* to finish editing my script in the next five days if I don't want to totally screw up my chances at getting into college, but I still laugh nonetheless.

"Just like that," I tell him, clapping. "It's the only way to write. But don't forget—wearing my monocle and smoking a pipe."

"Obviously," he jeers. He points to one of the photos on my bulletin board. I can't quite see it from my bed, but I recognize the outline and remember the day really well. "Is that you and Hailey?"

"That's the day we became friends," I say. In the photo, we're six and both have red eyes from crying and goggles on top of our heads. The picture was texted to our parents, unironically, by the teenaged counselor. "We got in a massive argument over who could wear the mermaid fin at summer camp, and then when we were fighting over it, we broke the strap so neither of us could."

"And that led to you guys becoming friends?" Logan squints.

"Justin Bieber's *Never Say Never* movie had just come out on Blu-ray, and we bonded over it in the rec room while we were supposed to be writing apologies to each other." I shrug. "The rest is history."

Nodding, Logan points to a poster on the side of my bookshelf. "Did you guys bond over TSwift too?"

"Hey, don't judge TSwift," I say, sitting up and raising my brows. I gesture to the *Lover* poster. "That album is, like, my favorite. If my life was a movie, I'd want it to be the soundtrack for sure."

I don't tell him I've been listening to "Daylight" and daydreaming about him. Because *ew, Harry, for real?*

Logan throws his hands up. "Noted."

He gets up from the chair and comes to lie next to me. He falls onto his back, folds his hands on his chest, and stares up at the ceiling.

"Your room smells nice," he says. "What is that?"

"My mom got me this candle." I shrug, rolling over to mimic him. "Huckleberry. She put, like, three plug-ins in Lottie's room."

He laughs and looks to me. "You smell good, too."

"I was just thinking *you* smell good earlier," I say.

"You smell like coconuts," he says.

"You smell like Old Spice," I say. Then I furrow my brow. "I think. I don't actually know what Old Spice smells like. But you smell clean and fresh. Nice."

"Not Old Spice, but thanks." Logan smiles.

"Logan?" I say, turning to face him.

He looks at me and raises his eyebrows. "Yeah?"

"I'm sorry if I don't ask you about Jane enough or if I'm not there for you in the *right* way," I tell him. "I want to be. I'm not great about saying the right thing, like, ever, but I want to comfort you."

Logan takes my hand and sits up. "Harry, no way. You're perfect how you are."

"Not perfect," I say.

"Not *perfect*," he agrees. "A little too worried and a lot too cute."

I roll my eyes. "The Columbia boy now says things like 'a lot too cute.'"

His lips curve up. "That's what you do to me, I guess."

I don't say anything.

"Please don't worry about me," he says. "I promise you don't have to."

"We haven't really talked about it," I whisper.

Logan nods. "It's hard to talk about. Like you said."

"You don't have to," I say. "I just mean if you want to, you can."

Logan frowns. "Well, she's okay most of the time, but it's getting worse kind of slowly," he says. "Early on, she would forget simple things. She wouldn't remember things like which fruit she liked in her yogurt. And she stopped keeping track of her checkbook."

I stay quiet, my thumb tracing his palm. He looks down at our hands.

"Sometimes she thinks she's somewhere she isn't," he says. "But a lot of the time she knows what's going on, you know?"

I nod, and I see a sparkle of hope in his eyes.

"But." He looks down again. "At best she'll be in assisted living next summer. At worst she might not make it that long. And the thing is, summer is our thing, you know? Like, they'd come up to visit us every summer, and we'd play Scrabble, and Ron and my dad would surf and sail. We'd always go running in the rain, we'd look for butterflies in the bushes, and every summer Jane and I would plant seeds and watch them sprout."

Logan sighs.

"And, um," he says. "Well, it's just Dad and me up in North Carolina. My mom died when I was really young. Jane and Ron lived with us for a few years when I was in elementary school. Dad's actually coming down here in a couple weeks once he can get the time off. I don't know, I guess it's just..."

I don't say anything, just keep my hand in his.

"I remember being little, and when anything would go wrong, I always knew Aunt Jane would fix it," he says, sniffing. "When kids at school made fun of me or if I felt really alone, she said the sun would always come up and things would always get better.

"And I remember this one time, we had a Mother's Day luncheon and every kid was sitting with their mom in the cafeteria... I was nine and sitting alone, just thinking about how lucky all these kids were to have their moms with them. I was remembering how Mom would always do three sprays of her perfume and how pretty she always looked and how she'd sing when she cooked. I was just starting to cry, and I felt so embarrassed about it. Then Aunt Jane saved the day—she showed up and sat with me, and I didn't feel alone anymore.

"So, um, now this is going to be the last summer we have

together." His shoulders drop, and he chokes on the words. "It's honestly hard to even comprehend it, if that makes sense."

I squeeze his hand, and he wipes a tear away with his other one.

"God, I'm sorry," he says. "See? Way more fun to just not talk about it."

"I want to be here for you," I say, pulling him in for a hug. He cries on my shoulder, and I let my hand circle his back. "I'm sorry about your mom and that this is happening to Jane. She doesn't deserve this. You don't deserve this."

After a few moments, he sniffs and pulls away, laughing as he wipes away the signs of his sadness. "Okay," he says. "Okay, okay."

I blink.

"Come on, shake it off," he says. "Smile. Let's be happy about the moment, the right now."

So I smile. Because I am happy about the right now. Very happy.

That night, I make sure to give my mom a big hug.

EXT. ROCKEFELLER CENTER

Rory and Skip are both wearing sunglasses and hats.

> RORY
> I can't believe we got it.

> SKIP
> Now we need to get Jenson. The real Jenson. And we
> need to hurry because if Mr. Fate's right, we have three
> hours to save the world.

We cut to Skip going into Rockefeller Center. A revolving
door swings.

We cut to Rory being tugged toward 5th Avenue by The
Sting, who is invisible.

WIDE SHOT. The Sting carries Rory to the top of a nearby
building, and we see The Champions Alliance Tower.

MEDIUM SHOT: They look over the streets.

THE STING
Are we ready for a Warp face-off? Maybe there's a
reason they haven't let him go. I mean, their powers
against each other could literally rip our reality apart.
We don't even know what Other Universe Jenson can
do.

RORY
It's the only shot we have.

20

YOU'VE GOT MAIL

No customers have come in for a while. We had a few at the start of business, before the rain began to pour down and everyone was running up from the beach with their towels tented up over them like makeshift umbrellas. For a couple of hours now, it's just been Agnes and me. She's been working on organizing the children's section, and I've been slowly dusting and sweeping and mostly daydreaming about Logan like a big sap.

It's just one of those days—when Agnes and I have the *Little Women* movie score playing over the speakers and we're both wearing cozy hoodies and the candle and antique lamps in the store feel warm and inviting.

Agnes and I have really been bonding lately, and she demonstrated just how badass she can be yesterday. Sadly, I wasn't there to witness it, but she said Justin came in, and when he went over to the table with coffee and juice and all that, she *accidentally* spilled the juice all over his crotch so it looked like he peed himself.

All hail Agnes!

As the rain gets heavier outside, I remind myself today is a good day, regardless of any bad weather, because Hailey gets back from camp this afternoon. She won't be able to hang for long since she's going to some wedding with her teammate, but I am dying to hear about the cute boys she had on her Instagram. I'm going to take the night to focus on my script anyway, since I have three days left to submit it, and I'm nearly there with my edits.

My lunch break is soon, and I wonder if I should try and run to the pizzeria a couple stores down without getting too soaked. I imagine they're not too busy either. As I'm plotting my lunch break strategy, the door swings open and disrupts the chill, enchanted vibe we've got as thunder booms and the wooden door smacks against the wall.

"Wow, sorry." Grant pulls the hood down on his forest green rain jacket. He closes the door gently and stomps his feet on the welcome mat.

I notice Agnes pop her head around from the back, and I quickly move toward Grant.

"What are you doing here?" It sounds more annoyed than I mean for it to, but try as I might to let it go completely, I'm still pissed about being stood up. About even giving him a chance.

Grant's mouth turns up into an amused smile, and I shake my head.

"Grant, no," I say. "You can't keep doing this. And I mean, like, what—this is your grand gesture? To come into my place of work?" I stand up a little straighter, making it sound really official.

Grant's not fazed, though, as he typically isn't, so I just exhale.

"This isn't— You can't keep doing this," I repeat.

"Well, I'm just here for another good book to read. Figured I'd pop into the little shop around the corner." Grant smirks, taking a step forward and looking around the store. His finger trails the bestseller table's prominent titles. "This *is* your *You've Got Mail* fantasy—isn't it?"

"It is not," I say too defensively. "I just love books."

"Right."

God, Grant really knows how to get under my skin when he wants to.

"If this *were* my *You've Got Mail* fantasy, I don't think my friend Agnes and I"—Agnes smiles at that—we've absolutely become friends, even if we've never said it out loud—"would be very pleased with some self-centered jerk coming into our store when we're trying to... What are you doing?"

Grant looks up from the book he's holding, "I'm reading the jacket copy."

"Why?"

"Because, as I told you, I'm here for a book."

There's silence between us as he scans the inside of a few books, like I'm not standing there across from him waiting for whatever is going to come next. He's going to try to charm me or weasel his way out of the fact that he ditched me the other night. I wait, hardly even blinking, just anticipating his next move.

"Well," he says, drawing it out for as long as he can, I'm

sure. He takes a step toward me, and his scent is too familiar, his lips look too soft, and his eyes are too warm. I'm *mad*
at him right now, not to mention I'm *something* with Logan.
I don't know what exactly, but I'm pretty sure whatever it is
should stop me from feeling this flip in my stomach as Grant
bites down on his bottom lip and turns to the shelf next to
me, reaching up and grabbing a few random titles.

I don't know what he's trying to do, but I shake it away
and pull a book down. "Read this one. She falls for this guy
who constantly lets her down."

Grant doesn't say anything, just takes the book slowly.

"Or this one," I say, my finger running down the bright
yellow spine. "The main character gets her heart broken by
this guy who is a total liar."

On a roll, I pull down another. "Or this—"

"I get it," Grant says, setting all of the books down. "Fine,
you're right. I came here to talk to you. Because you're avoiding me."

"Right," I say resolutely.

"I tried to say sorry," Grant says.

"I'm going to pop back into the office and… Erm. File
some papers," Agnes calls out. "Unless I should get some orange juice?"

"That's okay, thanks." I stifle a laugh, and she winks as she
opens the office door.

"I feel so shitty about it," Grant says. "And I've tried to give
you your space, but I just want to fix things with us. They
were going so good!"

"Right," I repeat, huffing and puffing as I push past him

toward the counter. "Can you put those books back where they go?"

I hear him, behind me, shelving the books and then he takes the few steps to cross the store and join me as I straighten the guest book and run my finger over a spot of dust on the receipt printer.

"Can't you just hear me out?"

"I don't— There's not really anything to say," I admit.

Grant straightens and squints. "Is this because of that guy?"

"What guy?"

"I know about your guy."

"You do not."

"I do."

I swallow, throat tight.

Grant smirks. "I'm stoked for you."

"You don't have to be an asshole about it," I say, unsure of how to navigate this.

Grant leans forward. "So your new guy. Do I get to meet him at the Fourth of July festival?"

"You're going to that?" I say, feeling a little nauseated all of a sudden. Holy shit. It's one thing to tell Logan more about Grant in a controlled environment where I can explain and deal. They can't meet, though. That's a big, huge, resounding N-O.

Grant grins. "Yep. Is he?"

"Um." I wish I could disappear right now. "No, he probably won't. You know. He's busy. He's actually going to Columbia in the fall. He's going to be a cyber...counterterrorist agent for the FBI. Like, a total genius. So he's a pretty busy guy."

"Right," Grant says, his smile widening.

"He *is*," I say, realizing he's taunting me.

"And his name is Logan, right?" Grant says.

I hate hearing him say Logan's name, and I just nod quietly. "Are we done here? Because I don't…"

Then, of course, I see Logan through the glass, holding a giant cardboard box with a six-pack of Dr. Brown's soda on top of it while his other hand grips the handle of an umbrella. I leap up and open the door for him, taking the pizza to free his hand.

Then I remember Grant is here, and my chest tightens because this is actually happening right now.

"Just thought I'd bring you lunch—hope that's okay," Logan says, shaking out the umbrella and stepping inside. He looks up and sees Grant.

"More than okay," I say, nodding eagerly.

Grant steps forward and holds his hand out. "Grant Kennedy."

"Logan," he grins, his typical friendly and warm introduction, looking from Grant to me and back to Grant before taking his hand. "Uh, Logan Waters."

"Nice to meet you, man." Grant nods toward the pizza and pulls his hood up, reaching for the door. "Well, I'll let you guys get to your lunch. Nice talk, Harry."

With that, he's gone, and Logan looks at me like I just told a really funny joke.

"That's the… Um, the guy I told you about before," I say. "He just stopped in. But it's not at *all* like—"

"No need to explain," Logan says, rubbing his hands together and opening the pizza box. "I actually think it's cool you guys are friends. It's, like…mature." Logan nods. "My last relationship—my first, actually, the one I told you about—well, he cheated. So, I never got the whole friends-with-your-ex experience. It was pretty awful."

"I'm sorry," I say, but Logan waves it away.

"No, no." He smiles. "I didn't mean to bring that up. I just mean it's good you can be friends after everything."

I lower my eyes, wondering what he means since I haven't spilled many details. "After everything?"

"Well." Logan's eyes dart around. "He's Jenson? Right?"

And now I'm *mortified* because Logan does know an awful lot about Grant. "It's fiction," I say, hoping it's convincing.

Logan nods. "Look—you don't have to worry. I get it. The Grant and Jenson thing. And I love the changes you made to the script," he says. "The big reveal."

"Wait, how did you—"

Logan winces. "I read it that night. Remember? I asked about the big twist? You had just finished it—I *did* ask for permission, though you were in and out of consciousness."

I cringe, but he just laughs.

"No, I *loved* it. I was actually thinking—I don't know the logistics, but do you have as good of a chance of winning an Oscar for your screenplay if you have, like, Hans Zimmer doing the score? I wonder if they limit how many awards each movie can get. I don't know anything about anything I'm saying, clearly."

"I don't know that Hans Zimmer would be interested," I laugh.

"You never know! I'm really looking forward to attending the Oscars. Anyway, I could be biased, but seriously. Your writing? Award-winning material."

Something is starting in this moment. And the wildest part is it's not just excitement about my future, like it always has been. Logan's genuinely happy for me. He's like this light—bright and radiant.

"You'll probably win a big-deal international math award, too," I say, giving in to the daydream. "Or an FBI one? You chose a very specific career, and I don't know exactly how awards play out there. Do they have them?"

"We'll have so many awards," he says, looking off like he can see it now.

"An entire award room," I say out loud, feeling bold.

Logan beams. "Yes, an entire award room. Honestly, you'll probably have to walk through an award hallway to get to the award room because there will be *so* many damn awards."

My heart is doing all kinds of summersaults and leaps, so I just kiss him.

"All right," he says, pulling back from the kiss, his hands locked together around my back. "Ready for some pizza?"

I raise an eyebrow and smile brightly. "Pizza with Harry. Logan eats."

And just like that, with a Yoda impression, that feeling between us is fizzing and even more thrilling. I can't help but kiss him—once, twice, three times.

Logan's jaw does this cute little flex as he opens the lid of the pizza box, and he ruffles my hair when he catches me glancing up at him with admiring eyes. I call for Agnes to come out and join us as I sit across from Logan and grab a slice of pizza, feeling like an absolute winner.

Nothing can ruin this.

EXT. THE PARK OUTSIDE OF THE UNITED NATIONS
BUILDING

Rory, Skip, and Jenson stand under the trees.

    JENSON
You're The Sting? Skip Stanley?

    SKIP
Is that *so* surprising?

    JENSON
I mean...

    RORY
He just saved you from being locked up by The Vicious,
and that's the best you can—

    JENSON
Fine, sorry. Thanks for—

    SKIP
It's okay, I don't need—

    RORY
Let him.

Jenson notices the friendliness between Skip and Rory, and Rory sees Jenson catching on.

    SKIP
Okay, you know what, this is kind of awkward after all, but... We have a universe to save.

    RORY
(to Jenson)
You're going to have to face off with yourself. And we have no time to waste now that we've breached one of The Vicious's hideouts.

    JENSON
Face off with myself?

    RORY
The other you... From another dimension... He has the same genetic material used to amplify your powers.

    JENSON
Well, we can't face off against each other. That'd lead to, like, a supernova.

    RORY
Actually likely something worse.

    SKIP
What could go wrong?

21

10 THINGS I HATE ABOUT YOU

I do my best to focus on the laptop screen in front of me, my fingers practically going numb and my wrists a little sore from just sitting here and staring at my screenplay with no clear idea of how to revise this damn script.

For a split second, I think I should just turn it in like this and hope for the best. But that's nuts. This is a major deal, and I need to make sure it's my absolute best work. I've already found so many typos and inconsistencies, and there are characters who need way more development. Plus, the payoff at the end honestly needs more work.

Just this morning, I was feeling confident about how I'd *totally* get this entire thing finished within the next three days. Now that I'm scrolling through the pages, I don't know what to keep or cut or rewrite.

I wish, at the very least, Hailey was here to distract me properly if I'm meant to fail, but she's at that wedding, and even Milly and Lottie are both at friends' houses tonight. So I'm all on my own.

Picking up my phone, I remind myself that I didn't ask Logan to come over tonight because I think it's important for him to spend time with his aunt. Then again, maybe he'd be interested in us all hanging out together? Playing Scrabble or watching a movie or something. Maybe he would even prefer it. But then maybe he'd have invited me.

Before I can get too far down a rabbit hole, the doorbell rings, and I perk up because maybe he and I are telepathic and he already thought of this.

"Coming," I yell, though I know there's no way anyone can hear me from my bedroom. I look out the window over my desk but don't see a car in our driveway. Regardless, I run down the stairs, in my white T-shirt and plaid pajama pants.

I slide to a halt in the foyer and check my hair in the giant silver-lined mirror hanging opposite a wall of framed family photos, and I run my hands through my curls strategically and check for food in my teeth.

I quickly open the door with a smile that falls immediately when I see Grant in an old gray button-down and jeans.

"Hear me out!" Grant says when I instinctively bring the door closer to being shut. "Can I just come in for a second?"

If I had an angel and a devil on my shoulder, I think the devil would win as I gesture for him to come inside.

"Alexa, play 'I Forgot That You Existed,'" I shout.

"Point made." He stands awkwardly in the foyer once I shut the door.

"It's just us," I tell him, gesturing toward the kitchen and beginning to walk. "My mom is on a date, and the girls are at their friends' houses."

Grant considers this for a minute, and I can't tell if he thinks this is good news or not. In some weird way, he almost seems disappointed. I wonder if he thought he'd win me over by doing a bit with Lottie and making Milly go all goo-goo-eyed like old times.

I open the fridge while he leans against the counter, and I pull out two sparkling waters.

"Whoa, okay, very civil," Grant says, taking the water with a smile. "Thank you."

"It's a water," I say, unscrewing the top to mine and taking a sip.

Grant nods, and the tension between us feels like a concrete block pushing against my chest. I keep the bottle to my lips, hoping he'll start talking since he clearly is here on a mission.

"Is this about Logan?" I finally say, unable to take the uncomfortable silence any longer.

Grant shakes his head. "No, not at all. He seems cool. Nice enough guy, I hear."

"You hear?" I raise a brow.

"Well, he works with all my old coworkers," Grant says slowly. "And, I mean, people talk."

"I know you didn't come here to tell me people talk," I say, dying to speed this up.

Grant shifts a little and sets his unopened sparkling water on the island between us. "You're right, I came here to talk to you because I can't just let things go to shit like this again."

"There's nothing *to* go to shit." I cringe at how harsh it sounds and offer as apologetic of a smile as I can. "I don't want to sound mean about it. It's just… You were gone for so long and yeah, we kissed a few times, but it's not like… It's not like we…"

Then more silence between us because he and I both know we didn't have to push a start button for things to begin again. For the feelings to resurface—the hope and the desire.

"It never went away for me," Grant says. "I'm trying to say that. And I *know* I screwed up. I promise, I didn't mean to—we were just golfing and… The sun and beer. I just fell asleep. I didn't even mean to, and if I could go back and redo how I spent that entire day, I would."

I don't know what to say, so I just swallow.

"I don't even know what the explanation is," Grant says, laughing and looking around the kitchen. "This is nuts, right? But, like, there's no logical explanation—I just haven't felt the way I felt with you."

Grant runs his fingers through his hair, and his shoulders fall. He looks spent.

"I don't understand why you never texted me," I say.

"I just thought it'd be too little too late," Grant says. "And I always… I always thought or hoped when I came back I'd have the courage to say all of this to your face. Obviously, I didn't think you'd give me another chance and I'd screw it up."

I don't say anything.

"Do you still have your USC sweatshirt?" Grant says with a little smile. "In the top right drawer?"

I feel my cheeks go hot.

"Yeah?" Grant straightens up a little. "I was going to tell you on our date—because I know you wanted to just be friends—but I've been looking at transferring to USC. Which may sound nuts. But, um… I figured if two people are supposed to end up together, then the universe or whatever makes it happen. Remember that movie?"

"*Serendipity*," I laugh, trying to make sure I don't show him how much that means to me. "Did you really think that would work?"

"I don't know," Grant says. "I guess LA is pretty big, but I have a better chance of bumping into you there than if I'm at UCLA."

"That's true," I tell him. "But Grant, I can't just forget everything. You know? You're always great at the apologies. Don't look at me like that—you know you are! You can do the whole charming thing. But I need more than that and now—I really like Logan."

"I know you do," Grant says. "I know you like him, but you don't *love* him."

There's nothing for me to say to that because of course I don't love Logan yet. But do I still love Grant? How am I supposed to know the difference between all of these confusing feelings I have for him? I feel like Grant and Logan both make me feel ways I never thought I could, but I have no idea what these feelings are called or how to interpret them.

Grant crosses the kitchen, around the island, and keeps a few steps between us because he can tell I need them, and then he looks me in the eyes and smiles.

"I love you, though," Grant tells me. "And you don't have to say it back, it's cool. But I do. And I don't want to spend the rest of my time here in Citrus Harbor just miserable without you."

Which is mind-blowing to me, I realize, because he's *Grant Kennedy*. In what reality would Grant Kennedy be miserable without me? Still, he's standing in front of me, in my mom's kitchen with something that looks like honesty written across his face.

"The timing—"

"When you know you want to spend the rest of your life with someone—"

I lightly punch him in the arm. "Don't even try using *When Harry Met Sally*. Off-limits."

"Can you get dressed?" Grant rubs the back of his neck. "Let's say upscale casual. Just in case."

"I can't," I say. "I'm working on edits for my screenplay. I'm running really behind on it."

Grant narrows his eyes. "I could help? After? And my dad is still going to give you that letter, too. So…"

"Grant…" I hesitate. "Things have changed."

"But you said you'd go on another date with me—"

"That was before," I point out, feeling slightly irritated that I have to explain this. "Before you stood me up. And before things changed with Logan. I really like him."

Grant nods. "Just… Okay. Fine, but can you look me in the eye right now and tell me you don't feel anything at all for me anymore? Not a single thing? Because if you do, even a little, then there's still a chance and we'll both regret it if we don't find out."

I don't say anything, because I can't say I don't feel *anything* for him. But what is it, really? Familiarity? Nostalgia? It might just be something like comfort and a guy who knows me like the back of my hand, but Logan is—

"So? Do you? Feel even a slight hint of something?"

I tap my foot impatiently, willing the right answer to come to me, until I just settle for the truth: "I don't know."

Because despite the fact that my entire heart seems to beat for Logan, Grant is standing in front of me right now. And it shouldn't be this way, but he still somehow feels like more than just Grant—he feels like *my* Grant. Even if that part is so small you need a microscope to see it, it's there.

I don't know if I'll ever know. People say you never really get over your first love, and maybe that's true. But how am I supposed to know—at seventeen—the difference between what was, what is, and what could be?

"Then come on," Grant says. "One night. I just want to see if this serendipity thing is real or not."

EXT. DOWNTOWN

A cosmic blast blows through lower Manhattan. Nothing is destroyed, but things seem to bend and alter—almost glitching.

Music swells.

Quick Circuit and Gold Honor are wearing new armor that resists the glitching. The Atomic Soldier and Agent Arachnid join them, both wearing the same armor.

The evil Captain Warp rises above the city. He holds out the canister.

     EVIL WARP
I am so glad to have you all here for this.

MEDIUM SHOT. A nearby alley.

Rory is wearing a headset and nods to The Sting and Jenson.

       THE STING
   It's game time.

22

SERENDIPITY

Grant's face is lit up by the neon lights at Neptune Theater, a pastel-painted wonderland surrounded by palm trees that was probably here long before anything else in Citrus Harbor. It's old as dirt, the lobby is super small, and the concession stand has never replaced the old letter board menus. That said, the place should *never* be renovated, no matter how many times they've duct-taped the roof due to leaks. We're stopped on the sidewalk, and Grant's grinning, reaching into his pocket.

"Okay, here," he says, handing me a ten-dollar bill. "You take this and get a movie ticket from the girl over at the ticket booth on the far right. Any of the seven o'clock movies. And if we get the same tickets to the same movie, then it's fate."

I laugh, accepting the money. "And if we don't?"

"Then I guess it's not fate."

"But then we wasted ten dollars," I huff. "Each."

"No, you're taking the fun away," Grant laughs, taking me by the shoulders and leading me toward the box office.

My feet take me to the girl at the ticket booth on the far right, just like Grant said. "Hi," I say absently, looking over her head at the show times. They're also in the letter boards, which are trendy and cool, ironically.

Grant has either a ton of faith in the universe and fate or had no idea that Neptune is playing two older movies and two new movies at 7:00. All four of which I'd want to see. Two rom-coms and two superhero movies. I just smile at Jules with the blond bob and Neptune Theater T-shirt.

When I've given her the cash for my ticket and let her keep the rest, courtesy of Grant, I step to my left. Hands in his pockets, Grant toes over and looks down at me with a bit of a concerned expression.

"I think I got this one," Grant says and holds out his hand for me to show him my ticket. When I do, he clutches it to his chest and frowns. "Oh no."

I guess fate did its thing.

Until Grant's frown snakes into a smile and he pulls his hand out of his pocket to show me, with a tiny little piece of blue paper, that he also bought a ticket to see *The Amazing Spider-Man* at 7:00 p.m. I can't stop laughing, and I'm still a little surprised as he buys us popcorn and drinks and we sit in the creaky old chairs.

Halfway through the movie, he fake yawns and puts his arm around me. I hit him on the chest and he just smirks while he takes a sip of his slushie.

After the movie ends, I wonder what could possibly be next, but Grant doesn't seem to be wasting any time. He dumps our concessions into the trash can and hurries down the sidewalk, smashing the button for the crosswalk a few times.

As we run across the street, Grant turns to me with wide eyes and points to two electric scooters propped up against each other on a brick wall covered in ivy. Dimly lit under a streetlight, the scooters' screens are blinking, and he approaches them, raising a brow at me.

"There are three minutes left," Grant says.

"Well, maybe they're coming back for them," I offer.

With arms outstretched, Grant turns and reaches for one of the scooters. "I don't see anybody."

"You're nuts," I say, taking a step forward.

"I'm just listening to fate." Grant smirks and lifts the scooter up, gesturing for me to take it. "After you."

Stepping on, I read the instructions and keep one foot on the ground. If Hailey were here, she'd insist we race down to the beach, even though once we got there the scooters' GPSs would disable the maximum speed. In a matter of seconds, Grant has kicked off and has both feet on his scooter and he's lightly pulling on the handle to rev up the speed.

"So *fate* is stealing scooters," I call out as Grant hops off the sidewalk and into the bike lane before turning onto a residential street and heading east.

As we zip under street lights and Grant turns back to stick his tongue out at me, I feel like I should be enjoying this more, but there's no spark there anymore. There's no tug—no butterflies.

When we reach the boardwalk, Grant slows and leans his scooter up against another brick wall, this time on the side of a small chocolate shop. I prop mine up, too, and follow down the sandy concrete until we're walking along the wooden pier.

"I say we ask fate what we do next," Grant says, leaning over the rail halfway out the pier. The ocean roars beneath us and slaps against the wooden beams.

"How?" I lean next to him and look out at the moon and the stars, far across the sky from the bright lights of the boardwalk. I inhale, taking in the salty spray and Grant's woody cologne. Farther up the pier, couples and families order hot dogs and funnel cakes and popcorn, and my stomach tugs me toward them.

"Flip a coin?"

"Fine."

Grant furrows his brow and rubs the back of his neck. "Er—do you have a coin?"

"No." I shake my head, laughing, and begin to turn around when Grant gasps. He crouches down and holds up a shining copper coin.

"Penny for your thoughts?" Grant chuckles.

I roll my eyes, fighting a smile and feigning indifference to all of this.

"So now what?"

"Well, since fate left this penny here for us," Grant says, flipping it with his thumb, catching it, and covering it with his other hand. "You call it. You get it right, you decide what we do. If you want to keep hanging out at all."

I don't know if I do, really. The more we spend time together, the more it seems like despite nostalgia or comfort, things haven't actually changed, which means I was right to question this. And what's worse—while Grant feels like *my* Grant, I'm starting to realize the weight of that doesn't even begin to compare to what I have with Logan.

But Grant flips the coin and I watch it fly up, and so I just call it: "Heads."

"Tails," Grant says, lifting his hand off the coin and showing me the penny. "So *I* say we get pizza."

He's totally doing that thing where he wants to do things we used to do together, but I'm also a complete glutton, and I can, canonically, never say no to pizza. Ever. So I take a moment before nodding and starting back down the pier, toward the shore and a row of crowded shops and restaurants, sights set on the neon sign for Lil Bite's Pizza.

Lil Bite's is a really crappy excuse for a walk-up pizza place with nothing but a red-and-white-tile facade and two barstools under the counter. We get in the line that wraps around the corner, in front of the lilac gift shop building.

Once we get our pizza on thin white paper plates, Grant and I walk up the boardwalk, and he fiddles with his phone for a second before apologizing, shoving it back into his pocket, and taking a bite of the gooey cheese slice on his plate. He stretches the cheese out, offering a goofy smile, and his shoulders fall when I don't laugh.

"Oh, come on, you used to think that was funny," Grant says.

I fake a loud, awful laugh, and he nearly doubles over because I am just *that* hilarious and charming.

"All right, if you're hating this that much..." Grant says, and in an odd moment, I can't tell if he's playing it cool or actually offended.

"No, I'm not," I say. "I'm sorry. It's just... I don't know, Grant. I told you, things have changed. I'm not sure how I feel anymore."

"Well, how about one drink?" Grant gestures toward the bright lights coming from the club a few blocks down. "One drink, just for old time's sake, and then we can call it. Talk through some of your revision ideas? FaceTime my dad, maybe? It's three hours behind in LA, it might be a good time for him, actually."

I don't answer, but we ditch our paper plates in the garbage and keep walking. The night is lively—skateboarders zoom past us, and a party overflows onto the balcony of one of the beachfront condos. There are people snuggled up on blankets watching the stars down on the sand and a guy with a metal detector and night vision goggles clunks along.

Loud music reverberates, getting clearer as we pass the pool gate for the club and reach the gate leading to the courtyard between the hotel rooms and the restaurant. The view is obstructed by palm trees and stucco arches, but I can see fairy lights strung up around the courtyard and hear Ariana Grande. Grant pulls out his wallet and holds it to the keycard reader, pulling open the gate for me.

"Is there a party going on?" I say to Grant, who looks as confused as I am.

We start up the steps, and I see a ton of people in the courtyard, clapping along to the music, kicking and spinning and holding up champagne flutes. It's got to be a wedding—there are high-top tables set up on the perimeter of the courtyard, and it's decorated to look like a sparkling paradise.

Grant taps my arm and points to the set of wooden doors on the far left side of the courtyard, and I nod, knowing he's going to steer us toward the hotel bar. We toe the edge of the party, careful not to disturb anyone.

I wonder if this is the wedding Hailey and Amanda are at. I don't see them anywhere, so I guess not.

The bride, in the center of the party, looks like a real-life princess in a white strapless dress that's tight until her waist, where it poofs out like a Barbie Christmas ornament Milly got one year. I laugh a little as she and her bridesmaids get really into the song, and all of the guests, even the grand-mother, are dancing along with her.

The song ends, and we're nearly to the door when I hear a squeal and feel a rush of wind as a redhead in an aquamarine dress tackles Grant. He catches her, and they spin, her arms locked around his neck.

"It's so good to see you!" she says, falling to her feet and brushing her hair out of her face. She smells like tequila and points to me, blinking slowly and hiccupping. "And you look form—familiar."

"This is Harry," Grant says. "Harry, this is Everly."

"Oh my God, yes! *You're* Harry." She claps and laughs. "You're *Kate Kensington*'s son! My brother, like, loves you. I can't believe your mom is Kate Kensington. I hear I'm going to be TikTok famous. Like, is this the beginning of my Gigi Hadid moment?"

"Everly Billings." Grant smirks at me, connecting the dots.

"You're Foster's sister," I say, though as she wobbles, I'm not entirely sure she can even *fully* comprehend this conversation.

I feel a lump in my throat as it hits me. Everly is going to tell Foster she saw me here. With Grant. And while I'm imagining Foster's line of questions around my hanging out with Grant, I realize the only person I actually care about knowing is Logan. And then I realize I hadn't even thought about telling Logan about this. I shouldn't lie, but how would I ever explain tonight to him without him thinking something was up?

Everly nods. "Too bad he's not here. This is my sister's wedding. I mean we're both in Zeta, not like *sisters*. You guys, come dance with us."

"No, that's okay," I say.

"BEV!" Everly shouts toward the party behind her, and the bride perks up, rushing over to us. Laughing, Everly pokes me in the shoulder and hiccups. "She's Beverly, and I'm Everly. Bev and Ev. Can you even believe it? It's stupid."

Leaning into Grant and thinking I can't hear her she holds her hand up to her mouth and whispers, loudly, "You guys are cute together."

When Bev makes it to us, she's clearly also intoxicated, though she looks even more like a real-life princess up close—with sparkling emerald earrings and glitter dusted across her black chest and cheeks. She offers us a huge smile.

"Bev, this is Grant," Everly slurs. "I used to, like, babysit him."

"Not *exactly*," Grant protests. "You were just the oldest."

"And this is Foster's friend," she says with a high-pitched giggle. "*Kate Kensington*'s son."

"Remember the name—Harry Kensington," Grant says with a grin, pinching my shoulder. "He's going to be a famous screenwriter. We're talking Hollywood Walk of Fame."

I look at him and suddenly feel so strange. That's something I'd normally love to hear. It's everything I've dreamed of forever. It's consumed my summer and woven its way into everything.

But it hits me like a giant wave that Grant could have introduced me in a million ways and *that* is the lead. For the first time, it's not some shining beacon of what could be. Instead, I feel *reduced* to this goal—one that might not ever come true, at that—and it's all my own doing.

Bev only throws her hands up. "Oh my God! You work at Jesse's bookstore. Wow, hi! I'm Bev."

I remember suddenly that Jesse said her nephew was getting married at the club—it all clicks, this is his new wife.

"I told them," Everly says, grinning and hitting her arm with the back of her hand.

"Bev and Ev." Bev nods, eyes bright. "That's cool about the movies. And I *love* your mom's makeup."

"Thanks! We were just going to go in and get a drink," I say, desperate to get away before it's too late. "We don't want to interrupt your—"

Bev holds her hand up, already calling over one of the waiters. "No way, we have drinks for you here. *Duh.* Are you two…?" She wags her finger between us, obviously wondering if we're a couple, but before we can answer, she hands us each a glass of champagne and pulls Everly out to the dance floor.

Grant taps his glass against mine and raises a brow. "Fate?"

"We *cannot* crash this wedding," I say. And I know for so many reasons this is just so far beyond wrong.

"We're not crashing," Grant says, taking a sip and gently nudging the stem of my glass with his finger. "We were invited."

Way too charming and with an attempt at some kind of fancy footwork, Grant leads us into the heart of the courtyard, where he and Everly dance horribly offbeat. I follow, reluctantly dancing with them, with Bev and her groom—who *totally* is related to Jesse with those dance moves—cheering me on drunkenly from a few feet over. I look around for the aforementioned aunt of the groom, but I don't see her anywhere.

One of the bridesmaids makes Grant and me stand together for a Polaroid. I don't really want to, but I don't know what to say. It happens so quickly, and then she's running off, adding it to the table with the rest of the photos and the guest book. Grant insists the photo will look great and gets back to dancing.

Admittedly, after a couple of glasses of champagne, this is mildly fun. Grant and I are laughing, mostly because he keeps reverting to awful moves straight out of the '60s that he's not even doing correctly, and Everly and the rest of the bridesmaids keep twirling us and dancing up on us like we're in a club. Still, being at a wedding with Grant just feels like I'm playing a part in a movie and not even one I really want to star in.

Grant puts his hand on my back and leads me out of the crowd when there's a lull. He wipes at his forehead, and I realize we're both ridiculously sweaty, considering it's at least ninety degrees and we've been dancing for an alarmingly long time.

"This is fun, right?"

I tell him it is, though I just can't stop thinking this should be over by now. It *has* been a lot of fun, but my mind has been elsewhere, and I'm ready to go home. I need to process this entire night. I set my empty glass down on one of the high-top tables.

"Remind me to send Bev a gift," Grant laughs and tilts his head. "What's up?"

"I'm just tired," I say.

There's no part of me that wants to celebrate true love and union with Grant right now. No matter what fate or serendipity has to say about us, no matter how much fun tonight has been, it doesn't feel right, and I just want to go home and get in bed and deal with these confusing feelings and how I'm going to explain this to Logan tomorrow.

I have to explain it just right and hope I haven't screwed this all up like I always screw everything up. Only, Logan's not like *everything*. He's different.

Damn it.

Logan is warm and kind and sweet. Logan is like freshly baked sugar cookies at Christmas or the way your skin feels toasty after being in the summer sun's glow all day. Logan is all the things I never imagined I'd have.

And by some unfortunate twist of fate, as I turn away from Grant, I see Logan is standing on the other side of the high-top table, wearing a black button-down and grabbing empty glasses. His lips are the ghost of a frown as he glances from Grant to me.

"Harry?"

Evil Warp and The Champions Alliance face off.

The Sting and Jenson—not in his suit—get closer, though the city is beginning to become a warped reality.

CLOSE-UP. The Sting taps his ear.

> THE STING
> Rory, we need help—it's all mirages.

We hear static.

CLOSE-UP. Jenson looks at The Sting with wide eyes.

> THE STING
> Rory? Are you there?

23

I KNOW WHAT YOU DID LAST SUMMER

My heart is pounding, and I know how this must look to Logan. His expression seems to shift from surprise to disappointment.

"Um, Logan," I start.

"No way," Grant says. I can see the way his face changes, hardens. "How's it going, bud? Picked up a wedding shift? God, I miss working here sometimes. But you know, bigger and better things."

Logan stiffens. "Harry, I thought you were— I texted you earlier."

I meant to reply. I was in the movie when I saw the text come in. How do I even start to explain this?

"I was just thinking about getting us a room," Grant says, glancing from me to Logan. "We were going to talk through some screenplay ideas. If you want to come up when you get off, we can all get a drink and brainstorm together."

Knowing exactly what kind of mind games Grant is trying to play, I shake my head. "What? No."

Logan purses his lips and points to the empty champagne glass I had set down. "Are you done with this?"

"Yeah," Grant says, handing him his empty glass. "Thanks."

Logan takes our glasses, and I shoot Grant eye daggers as sharp as I can make them before running after Logan, who's speed walking through the courtyard, past the club's French doors and down the hallway.

"Wait, Logan!" I call.

"It's all good, Harry," Logan says, turning around and offering a soft smile. "I get it. Complicated."

"No, it's not complicated," I say, but before I can say anything else, Grant walks up next to me holding the Polaroid and Logan sees it and just sighs, and there's something like sadness washing over him as he offers a silent wave, turning away and pushing the door to the kitchen open. I try to stop him, but I'm too late. I can't stand to see him like that—Logan, with the usually sunny disposition, followed by a storm cloud. And it's all my fault. All of this is my fault. The way *I* handled everything. Grant is making it worse, but I have myself to thank.

I turn to Grant. I wipe my cheek and roll my eyes. "Are you happy? Jesus, Grant. What the hell? What are you trying to do here?"

"What," Grant jeers. "You're crying over that guy? Come on. You and I both know what we have—"

"*Had!* Grant, it's in the past." I start to walk up the hallway toward the entrance of the hotel. "Like I said, things have changed."

"Harry," Grant says.

"And what is all this for, anyway…" It hurts to even say it out loud. "Your best-case scenario? A long-distance relationship my senior year, while you're at UCLA? And I'm just supposed to trust you again after a few nice gestures this summer? It's pointless."

Grant doesn't say anything, just pokes his tongue into his cheek. Then he scoffs, "We were— Things were going good, and now you're really this worked up over this rando?"

"Why are you being such an asshole?"

"It's ridiculous. I mean, at the start of summer, here's this dorky kid from out of town—" Grant laughs.

"At the start of summer?"

"Well, yeah, at the club."

It clicks. Grant was there that day. The day all of Grant's friends hazed Logan and shoved him in a locker.

"It was your idea to mess with him, wasn't it?"

"I didn't even know him. It was harmless fun. The guys always do stuff like that."

I don't even know what to say anymore, and now I am fighting tears, which makes this even worse.

"Well, if the guys *always* do stuff like that…" I scoff. "For a split second, I thought you'd changed, but you're still *exactly* the same."

"What's that supposed to mean?"

"It means you're spineless." I'm slightly surprised at the word as it passes my lips. "You do what the guys want so you look cool. You go along with what your parents say so you don't rock the boat. You can't tell me face-to-face when you're about to literally move across the country—"

"That again?"

"What, it isn't a big deal?"

"Jesus. Let's just get a room for the night, order some room service, and you can talk to me," Grant says. "You just need a little—"

I laugh. "You don't know what I need. What I need is for you to not get involved in my life anymore. I am so confused."

Grant waves this away. "*You* FaceTimed me that night. *You* kissed me at my pool."

"I made mistakes." I blink.

"I know, Harry." Grant pushes two fingers to his forehead. "I know."

"And anyway you knew what you were doing—dangling the letter of recommendation in front of me," I say. "To get what *you* want."

"I wanted to help you," Grant scoffs. "You have no idea how hard it is to make it out there, do you? I have a way for you to get in with the top studio executives, Harry. You think you're just gonna work your way up to success even if you do get in? A random kid from Florida at USC?"

I feel my breath hitch.

"I'm sorry," Grant says. "I didn't mean that."

I don't say anything, just feel the weight of his words.

"Why don't you text me later?" Grant says, brushing off everything that's just been said. "When you've had some time. I'm getting a room, so if you want to... You know where I'll be."

He shakes his head and walks off, and I'm left there, tears streaming down my cheeks in the hotel hallway.

What will I say to Logan? I try to run through it in my head as I pace up and down the hall. The wedding ends, and people are leaving the courtyard, swanky in shimmering pastels and metallics. Smiling drunk couples blowing bubbles.

As I pace, I keep noticing things about the giant framed photo of four elderly women in matching pastel visors and rollerblades from the '90s. It makes me feel like I'll never be that happy again, which I know is dramatic and next-level, but the longer I wait for Logan to come out of the kitchen doors, the more I feel like the smiles in the photograph are taunting me—out of reach and unattainable.

This whole thing just feels like a *Black Mirror* episode or something. Title it *Harry's Worst Summer Ever—Even Worse Than the Last*.

Basically, I feel like shit, and I don't know how to undo the storm that I've brewed up.

Maybe I'm overreacting. Logan and I never said we're *exclusive*, so he might not even care after some time and a talk. He might have just been put off by how much of an asshole Grant is. Who wouldn't be?

After a long while of nobody coming out of the kitchen doors, I start to walk down another hallway, toward the pool and the cantina and kids' lounge. Through the windows, I notice a bunch of the employees from the wedding are laughing, lugging trash bags, and moving equipment from the cantina to the courtyard. Logan is one of them.

He's standing behind the cantina, grabbing a spray bottle from under the counter, and when we lock eyes, he immediately looks away.

Not a good sign.

I don't know what I should do. I don't want to interrupt him while he's working, but this is killing me. I opt for a gesture that comes with a little less pressure—I push the door open and walk out to the kiddie pool, sitting down at one of the tables. He sees me, and I see him, hurrying from group to group and back and forth from the cantina.

The employees are all rushing along the walkways with broken-down chairs and tables and folded-up tablecloths. There's an after-party going on at the adult pool, and I can hear Bev laughing before I see the spray of a champagne bottle opening.

Eventually, Logan is left without anything to do, and he finally looks to me. I can see him sigh as he drops something off at the cantina and heads over to me, head hung.

"Hey," I say, standing up when he gets closer. I clap my hands together. "Are you 45 degrees? Because you're really acute guy."

Logan's frown breaks, but he doesn't belly laugh or tell me it's a job well done.

"I'm really sorry about Grant," I say. "He's a douchebag. We had a thing last summer, like I said before… I know how tonight looked, but—"

"I think it's pretty obvious," Logan says. "He clearly still likes you."

"It doesn't— I told him it's in the past," I argue. "It's hard to explain. He's just used to having his way. And I want you. So, that must be driving him nuts or something."

"Right, just like Jenson. Honestly, I feel like I know the guy. It's just…" Logan is thinking of what he wants to say, I can see it. "You didn't even text me back tonight, and then you're with him, and that picture—"

"No, it wasn't like that at all," I say. "We didn't even plan to go to the wedding or take that picture. There isn't anything there. There isn't. It's only you. And I've only been talking to Grant because he said his dad might have these connections in LA to help me with my application and… Now that I say it out loud it doesn't even sound that much better. But I—"

"So you were using him as means to an end? For LA?"

"No! Well, sort of. But not *really*—"

Logan exhales. "I do really care about you, but it's just too much right now, and I can't."

With that, he sighs and turns toward the cantina. I watch him say something to the girls behind the counter before heading over to the after-party. I can't even move; I can't muster up the motivation to take a single step. My breathing feels shallow, and my eyes feel hot, and my nose is tingling, and then there are tears, like waves, and the swell won't stop.

Everything's flashing through my mind right now. Getting Logan out of that locker and seeing him there, in his soaking too-big T-shirt on his surfboard every morning. Sharing croissants and warm smiles over coffee and the way he and Lottie and Milly were like best friends. How he came into Books by the Sea and dropped that stupid, adorable pickup line. Kissing him on the beach and laughing with him when I wiped out on the surfboard. His compliments and the way his eyes lit up so I knew he meant them.

I started this summer determined not to get my heart broken by a guy like Grant and to keep pursuing my dreams of being a screenwriter. Somehow, I not only repeated old mistakes, I learned there's something even worse: breaking the heart of a guy like Logan.

I sit down on a bench, thinking things can't possibly get worse.

Across the hall, I see Hailey walking through a pair of double doors toward me. She must have been at the wedding after all, though I don't know how we didn't bump into each other.

I've never been so glad to see her. After everything that's happened tonight, I really need her. She's wearing a sparkling maroon dress, and her hair is done up like a princess, but as she gets closer, I see her lipstick is a little smeared and her eyeliner and mascara look like she's been crying.

"Hailey, what're you doing here?"

"I was at the wedding." She sniffs. "And of course Justin just had to post an Insta story—he's bowling with *Zoe*."

I frown. "I've had the worst night, too. First, Grant shows up and does this whole *Serendipity* thing where he was trying to prove fate wanted us to hang out, and then we ended up at the wedding and—"

"No offense, Harry, but just this once, can we not make this about you?" Hailey says, tears falling down her cheeks.

"Just this once?" I say, seeing a little tiny bit of that red mist from the first day of summer. "Are you for real?"

Hailey rolls her eyes.

"All we ever seem to talk about is Justin," I say. "You have no idea about what has been going on with Grant. Or with Logan, even, really. I had to just be there for you—"

"Oh, I'm sorry my boyfriend cheated on me," Hailey snaps. "Was that inconvenient for you? I didn't mean to mess up your summer. Next time I'll ask when it works for you."

I shake my head. "I didn't even—"

"I mean, remember when you had *your* heart broken? Who was there for you then?"

"What happened with Grant was different."

"Right," Hailey says. "Of course. Your heartbreak was obviously worse than mine."

I don't really mean to say it, but it's like I've lost control of my words—they're just flames bursting from the fire, hoping to burn anything they can. "I tried to warn you about Justin, and you didn't want to hear it."

"You tried to *warn* me?" Hailey bites.

"Of course I did! Everyone knew what he did," I say, seething. "But you wanted to have the picture-perfect relationship. You chose to ignore the red flags with him."

"Everyone knew?" Hailey raises a brow. "So you're saying *you* knew?"

I don't say anything.

"You knew, and you didn't tell me?" I can see her anger twisting into disappointment or heartache. "How long did you know?"

I wish I could rewind and take back my words. We were having a fight—one we'd be able to just get over and move on from. But now it's way bigger. Now it's catastrophic.

"How long did you know?"

"Grant told me that first day he was back," I say slowly. "He said you and Justin were happy and I shouldn't—"

Hailey cocks her head and takes a step back. "The first day of summer. You knew *this whole time?*"

No, no, no. I feel my chest tighten, and my eyes sting. I stand up and reach for her, but she yanks her arm away.

"You're supposed to be my best friend," Hailey scoffs. "My very best friend—like my brother. And all this time... I can't even trust you."

"You can trust me," I say. "I'm so sorry, Hailey, I was trying to—"

"Trying to what?" Hailey cries. "Make me look like an idiot? Keep me with someone who didn't value me? Or were you just trying to protect yourself? Were you trying to protect *Grant*? I would have never done this to you. But it's Harry's world, isn't it?"

"It wasn't for Grant or me," I say, starting to feel that defensiveness simmering inside me again. "How can you even say that? You were the one who made it sound like it was Justin or me."

Hailey squints. "I never said that."

"You made it clear," I say. "Your whole entire world revolved around him. You couldn't do anything without him, and he was all you thought about—all you talked about. Ever. It was always 'Justin this' or 'Justin that.' Was I supposed to feel like telling you would just be a breeze? You were so—"

"Stupid." She rolls her eyes. "For trusting Justin, sure, but I was *really* stupid because I totally trusted you."

"Wow," I say. Taking a step back.

"Were you just going to let me stay with him?" Hailey chews the inside of her cheek. "Then move to LA? To hell with me, right? As long as you got your way."

That knocks the wind out of me. Is she wrong? I want her to be wrong, but I'm not even sure.

She shakes her head and blinks away more tears. "I would have never done this to you," she repeats as she walks away.

I don't even know what to say. I stand there, speechless, hoping something brilliant will come to mind, but she's gone, and as soon as she is I feel sorry for how I reacted.

How am I going to fix this? How can I ever fix any of this? I thought losing Grant and Logan hurt, but hearing those things from Hailey was… I sob into my hands. Maybe she's right. Maybe I am selfish and a bad friend.

Gathering myself and straightening up, I pass through the lobby, offering a half-assed wave to the concierge and pushing through the revolving doors. When I'm let out into the humid night, I pass the horseshoe driveway and the valet stand and start down the palm tree–lined sidewalk. There's no music playing anymore. All I hear is the ocean on the other side of the club.

I walk for a few minutes, sniffling and feeling really sorry for myself. I can't believe I messed things up on such a huge scale.

"The hell are you doing, Kensy?"

"Oh my God, Foster, it's *Harry*!"

I stop walking as Foster and Everly pull up next to me in a black Mercedes SUV. It must be Everly's, since Foster drives a station wagon that could be straight out of a Beach Boys music video. Everly hangs out of the passenger window and blows me a dramatic kiss.

"Want a ride?" Foster says, and Everly's eyes go wide as she nods and reaches out to slap the door.

"Sure," I say, because I don't want to walk all the way home right now when I feel weak and defeated. So, I pull open the door and slide into the back seat. "You didn't go to the wedding?"

"He's lame," Everly says.

"So lame that I just picked up my drunk-ass sister," Foster teases.

"Thank you, Fossy," Everly says in a baby voice and then

turns back to me, grabbing a scrunchie from around the gear stick and wrapping up her hair in an extremely lopsided knot. "I look like shit. I need your mom to help me with my makeup. Do you like Taco Bell? We're going to Taco Bell."

Foster laughs and looks at me in the rearview mirror. "Are you okay?"

"Yeah," I say, watching fence posts and palmetto trees and hydrangea bushes as we cruise along the residential drive and turn up a side street, landing in the Taco Bell drive-through.

The line is ridiculously long, of course.

"Wait, so you're famous right?" Everly drawls.

"Nope."

"Grant said— I thought?"

"No, he's just being—"

"Harry's *gonna* be famous." Foster smirks, locking eyes with me in the rearview mirror. "He's gonna be famous, and he'll forget all about us and our Taco Bell run."

Is that really what Foster thinks?

"Not the Taco Bell run," Everly says, horrified.

We finally get to the order box, and Everly leans across Foster and screams into the wind, ordering *way* too much food. I tell her I don't want anything, and she orders me some kind of slushie drink anyway, saying it'll make my frown go upside down.

We wait another lifetime to get up to the window, where Foster hands the girl Everly's credit card and grabs the giant bag of food before offering me a red frozen drink.

"Drink it, Kensy!" Everly says, stuffing a soft taco in her mouth while looking at me with droopy champagne-drunk eyes. "Ugh, my last boyfriend was such a hater—he made fun of me when I ate Taco Bell. Proof guys suck, right? Well, look who I'm talking to."

"Guys do suck," I say. "Especially me."

Except for Logan, I want to say. *And maybe Foster since he picked me up. Maybe.*

"Oh, all right, boo-hoo." Foster rolls his eyes with a grin. "Go ahead and drink up."

I take a sip and feel my head get filled with sugary, syrupy sweet stars and rainbows, all strawberries and Skittles. "Oh my God. It tastes like…"

"I know, right?" Everly cackles. "It's like a magic potion."

So, I spend the rest of the ride home laughing as Everly sings along to Katy Perry with a mouth full of tacos and her hand out the window. When Foster drops me off at my house, I thank Everly for my magic potion from Taco Bell, and Foster blows me a kiss and tells me to text him.

I don't, though. I just brush my teeth and put my pajamas on.

I try to call Hailey twice, but I'm not surprised when she puts me through to voicemail.

ME: I'm really sorry. Please call me tomorrow?

I lie in bed, staring up at the ceiling. There's no magic solution for any of this. I want to be furious at Grant, but really, everything that's happened is my own fault.

I don't get a text back from Hailey, and when I open Instagram, I see a photo of her and Amanda smiling at the wedding before everything was ruined.

Playing the saddest playlist I can find—which I know is the

absolute worst idea since sad music only makes you sadder—
I roll over and pull up my text thread with Logan, though I
don't feel like there's much hope left.

ME: Any chance you want to talk?

ME: Of course I understand if you need more time but I'm
here

*Remember the name—Harry Kensington. He's going to be a fa-
mous screenwriter. We're talking Hollywood Walk of Fame.*

I feel sick remembering what Grant said. I don't know if
it's because it's what I've become or because it's what I wanted
to become.

You know, life is not all about success.

*I hope you have time to do Donna and the Dynamos on Face-
Time when you're gone.*

I look around my room at the movie posters and the pictures of Hollywood I've stuck on my walls. They're eclipsed
by the smiles radiating from the photos I have with Hailey.
The memories I have with Lottie and Milly. The torn photo
booth pictures of Logan and me. Even the movie ticket from
tonight—crumpled up with the other contents of my pockets
on my desk—because all those moments with Grant, good
and bad, are part of me.

So you were using him as means to an end? For LA?

I open my laptop and scroll through my screenplay, smiling
to myself at some of the moments between Skip and Rory.
I look at the page count and think of how much work went
into this. How much it took over me and became everything.

Maybe I've been trying to force it all along. Maybe for someone else, becoming an Oscar-winning screenwriter wouldn't cost them love and friendship. It's like the signs have been here all along—the costs, the things I'd have to lose to *maybe* get a shot at my dreams—and I ignored them or pretended they weren't right in front of me.

For someone else, dreams and friendship and romance and family can all exist in harmony. Not a constant fight or struggle. Not a *reach*. For me? It's been an uphill battle all along, and for what?

I get up and go over to my dresser, opening the top right drawer. My USC sweatshirt is folded there, just like it always is. Like it always has been. A tangible reminder of where I'm going. A physical object that signified the first major step to being a celebrated and famous Hollywood screenwriter with Oscars and everything he ever wanted.

Were you just going to let me stay with him? Then move to LA? To hell with me, right? As long as you got your way.

My vision goes blurry, and I wipe away the tears, but they keep coming. I close the drawer and find myself back at my desk—faced with that photo of Hailey and me on that first day. The picture of us all screaming our heads off on the Tower of Terror, Mom clutching Lottie like she was going to fly away; Nana's terrified, wide eyes with her arms up; and Milly a mess of tears as I laughed in her direction. Even the cast and crew photo from our last production, where Penny and I have our arms over each other's shoulders, surrounded by friends.

I open my browser and take a deep breath as I type.

Harry's gonna be famous. He's gonna be famous, and he'll forget all about us and our Taco Bell run.

Impulsivity has sort of always been a problem of mine. So now, I think, I'll put it to good use. Because if I've learned anything, it's that there are a hell of a lot more things that matter to me more than where I go to college.

I have plenty of time to figure the rest out, but for now?

I click once, twice.

Are you sure you want to withdraw your unfinished submission to the Reel Sunshine's Young Screenwriters Competition? Please note, due to volume and the nature of the review process, new applications are no longer being accepted.

Getting what you want can't be worth it if you have to go full Thanos to make it happen. My finger hovers above the trackpad for one split second before I commit to it and press the confirmation.

EXT. DOWNTOWN—ALLEY

Rory taps his earbud.

>RORY
>I can hear you. Can you not hear me?

Evil Warp and Quick Circuit fight. Blasts from Quick Circuit's suit just reflect off Evil Warp, and Quick Circuit realizes he can't win with his usual combat style. There's no time to reevaluate, though. Evil Warp twists reality—the sky falls like puzzle pieces, and The Champions Alliance members all shield themselves, though Evil Warp only laughs as they realize it's an illusion.

In the confusion, Evil Warp uses his powers to magnetize Quick Circuit's suit as Volt approaches.

We cut to The Sting and Jenson, now hiding behind a flaming upside-down taxi.

THE STING
Rory, we're in big trouble.

JENSON
Big trouble. All The Vicious are here.

MEDIUM SHOT. Rory in the dark alley as a large shadow
appears behind him.

THE PYTHON
(*hissing*)
Long time no see.

CLOSE-UP. Rory's eyes widen.

24

SHE'S ALL THAT

My whole life is ruined.

A time machine would be exceptionally useful, I think, for a handful of reasons.

I don't necessarily regret withdrawing my application, because the good intentions were there in the moment, but *maybe* I threw the baby out with the bathwater on this one. I could have just made better choices moving forward—prioritized differently, been less obsessive and insecure.

But it is what it is.

I lost my best friend, the guy I liked, and my chance at my dream all in one night, and it was literally all thanks to me.

There are a few things helping right now: the smell of sunscreen and coconut, the kids having the time of their lives playing and splashing in the pool, and the burning warmth on my skin. Plus, they're playing Top 40 today. I sit on the edge of the pool, sipping a sweet tea that somehow doesn't taste the same as when Logan makes it, and kick my feet every now and then, splashing the water up to my shins and making sure my bottom half doesn't start to feel like TV static.

"Hey, you know, my sister won't shut up about how much she loves you, Kensy."

Foster sits down next to me, flashing a smile. He's wearing black sunglasses. I can't see his eyes, but I imagine they're blue and happy like always, which is funny because at the start of summer they were endlessly annoying, but now I just want to see them.

I bite down on my straw and force my mouth to do its best fake smile. "Hey, Foster."

A silent beat, then Foster sits up a little straighter. "Um, want me to... I won't call you that anymore, I'm sorry."

"What?" I look at him and feel my chest tighten. Foster hasn't changed—he's still got long blond hair to his chin, and it's wet and stringy like always because he's in the ocean, rain or shine, hot or cold. His face is tan and pink from the sun, and he's lean with the annoyingly perfect build of a surfer and now he wants to change. Suddenly, I realize Foster is the one thing that hasn't changed and that if he does, I don't know how I'll handle it.

Before either of us can say anything, I'm sniffling, my lip is shaking, and I feel my brows furrow as my eyes well up behind my sunglasses.

"Whoa." Foster pats my shoulder. "Um, I didn't mean to upset you. I know things... I heard what— I just— Anyway, I won't call you that anymore."

That's when the waterworks start, and I might even blubber a little because if there's anything I don't want, it's for Foster

Billings to be different, too. If there's anything I don't want, it's for Foster to stop calling me that dumbass nickname.

"Jesus," Foster says, putting his arm around me as his forehead wrinkles and he chews on the inside of his mouth. "Um."

I keep my sunglasses on, of course, and try to silently regain my composure.

"I just don't know *anything* anymore," I manage, pulling it together a little. I don't even want to get into the college conversation out loud. I tell him what happened at the wedding with Logan and Grant and Hailey.

"Grant is kind of a jerk," Foster offers.

"I'm kind of a jerk, too." I frown. "I was always a jerk to you."

"But we're friends," Foster points out. "It's, like, our thing, Kensy. Sorry, habit. I *will* stop calling you that."

"No, don't." I smile and pat Foster's leg. "You really don't think I was a jerk? Not even when…"

Foster beams. "You were involved with two guys?"

"It sounds awful out loud doesn't it?" I wince.

"It's complicated." Foster nods toward the ocean, past the pool and the gate and the dunes. "I get how it was a hard situation. You and Grant go way back. And Logan's a super nice guy. But the thing is, no, I don't think you're a jerk. We all make mistakes."

"Right." I don't know what else to say, so I just watch the sun bounce against the pool water for a moment.

"Speaking of Logan—you don't want to try to fix it?" Foster says, like he doesn't know the answer. "It's not like you to give up."

"Really?" I say.

"I don't think so," Foster says. "I couldn't have written a whole screenplay. And you never gave up on Hailey, even when you didn't like what was going on."

"I withdrew my application," I say finally. "You said it yourself—I kept acting like I was going to become some Hollywood big shot and leave this town behind. But I was all wrong."

Foster flinches at that. "I was only kidding. I don't think that at all."

"Well, everyone else did," I say. "They weren't wrong. I kept thinking I wanted to get out of here and move on to bigger, better things. I didn't even realize how great I had it."

"You can fix all this stuff," Foster says. "You can!"

Obviously, I want to fix things with Logan. But I think that ship has sailed. He made it pretty clear, but I don't have the heart to say that out loud right now, so I tilt my head and shrug.

"Oh, okay. So if you're fully single again, you wanna rent one of those cabanas?" Foster smirks, raising a brow and winking, and I shove him, finally feeling laughter bubble up in my chest.

"When it comes to Hailey," Foster says. "I think it's fine you had your first real fight. All relationships go through ups and downs; they make you stronger. Ask my parents."

I laugh—both of Foster's parents are psychologists. I'd imagine their house is interesting.

"I shouldn't have kept it from her, though," I say. "If she had done that to me, I'd feel the same way. And she's right. It's always about me. I only *really* think about myself. I don't want to be that person."

ROBBY WEBER

"Did you do it on purpose?" Foster asks, point-blank. "Hide it to hurt her?"

"What? No."

"Then you just need to accept that you made a mistake and move on," Foster offers. "Gotta grow through what you go through, right?"

"Foster Billings, when did you start talking like a Pinterest board?"

"Since you started listening?" Foster smirks. "Nah, Everly is really into her vision boards right now."

That makes me laugh, and I take a deep breath. "So how do I get her to forgive me?"

"I dunno." Foster bites his lip. "I mean, I'm sure it's just a matter of time. You guys are, like, the two closest friends in our entire senior class."

"Oh my God," I say. That's it. "Foster, you're a genius."

I can't believe the source of my biggest epiphany this summer was Foster Billings, but here I am, at Hailey's front door. I know she's home, and I'm not sure if she's jamming out with her headphones or if she saw me in the peephole and decided I should eff off, but I've been waiting for a couple minutes.

I knock again, and when nobody comes to the door, I assess my options. The door is locked, so I walk around to the back gate and let myself in her backyard. I cross the yard to her window, and there she is—headphones in, just like I suspected—lying on her bed with a bag of chips, flipping through an issue of *Cosmopolitan*.

I tap on the glass, gently at first, but she doesn't notice, so I finally knock harder, and she screams, throws the chips across the room, and jumps out of bed.

"Harry, I swear," she says as she pulls the window up.

I climb into her room. "I tried to knock on the front door, like, a dozen times."

"You almost gave me a heart attack," she says, closing the window. "Why didn't you just text me? I would have let you in."

"I didn't know if you would," I admit.

Hailey is quiet and crosses her arms over her chest. "Harry, look—"

"No, wait," I say. "Listen to me. I know there's all this crap that has happened. Crap *I've* done. And we both have a lot of things going on in our lives, things that feel important. But there's one thing that's *actually* important. Like, more than any of the other stuff. It's my fault, really, for not realizing it or for taking it for granted."

Hailey narrows her eyes, and I turn around and grab our junior yearbook from her desk.

"You did *not* come here to—"

"No, look," I say. "Of all the crap. The mistakes I've made. The secrets, the boys, and the breakups, and the parties... There's only *one* thing that matters."

I open to last year's seniors and, flipping to the superlatives, point to the middle of the page.

Hailey glances down, and I see it on her face—she smiles softly. "'Attached at the Hip.'"

"You are my *best* friend," I say. "You have my back through everything. You support me and cheer me on, and I am so sorry. I promise I didn't mean to hurt you. You were right, honestly. It's always about me. Maybe if I stopped to slow down and think about someone other than myself, I would have realized what I was doing."

Wiping at her cheeks, Hailey shakes her head. "No, you're a great friend. I'm sorry I said I couldn't trust you. I know I can. I was just so hurt. This whole thing with Justin is so awful and so embarrassing. I keep trying to tell myself I'm okay and I'll get over it, but everywhere I turn in this town— there are his friends or there's a spot we used to hang out. Every song on my phone reminds me of him somehow. Remember when you couldn't even listen to 'Cornelia Street' after Grant?"

I wince.

"I exploded at you," she says. "But I know you'd never hurt me."

I hug her. "I'm really sorry. I might not have ever had what you and Justin had—like, a real, genuine *love*, but... I know how it feels to be heartbroken. And it sucks. I can't believe he'd... You're amazing."

I look at Hailey, and I see someone special. Any guy must be completely out of his mind to cheat on her. I look at Hailey and see this funny, outgoing, and wild ride of a best friend who is always down for whatever and looks out for me like family. She's the feeling you get flying down the avenue on a beach cruiser in the rain, and she's sunburns because we fell asleep listening to Olivia Rodrigo and drinking Capri Suns on the roof.

Hailey is sunflower picking and impromptu, makeshift root beer floats.

Hailey's more than just fun, though. She's caring, and she's kind, with this big heart. She deserves the world, including a best friend who's honest with her.

"I won't ever lie to you again. I promise," I say, sitting on her bed. "And you won't have to hear about USC or the competition or any of it. I withdrew my application."

"What?" Hailey gasps. "Why would you do that? What about LA?"

"You know how the Biebs says, 'what if you had it all, but nobody to call?' It was like I was heading there."

"That's deep." Hailey frowns.

I nod. "Plus, I need to figure out what I'm passionate about and why. From scratch. But I don't know. Weirdly, the more time passes, the less I feel like I gave something up and more like I opened up the future for new possibilities."

Hailey smiles. "We can always ask the stars."

"True. And, anyway, here's how I see it: We'll always have each other. To get through whatever comes our way. And we don't need guys, really."

Hailey grabs a scrunchie and does her hair up. "Easy for you to say with the totally perfect boyfriend."

"Well…"

"Oh, no," Hailey winces. "What happened?"

I'm trying this new thing where I take responsibility for my actions, so I hang my head. "I was with Grant, and he saw, and… Logan and I are done. He's going through a lot, you know?"

"But he's totally in love with you," Hailey cries. "I mean, what you said? About not having something like Justin and me? Sure, we were together for a long time, but it clearly wasn't *real*. You and Logan have an amazing, real thing."

"This isn't about me." I smile. "I came to apologize to you and—"

"Apology accepted." Hailey grabs my hands and pulls me up off the bed, marching me to the front door. "You and I are fine, Harry. Now go and fix things with Logan. Or else I'll be actually mad at you."

EXT. ALLEY

Rory runs from The Python. He ducks into the closest door at the end of the alley.

INT. EMPTY RESTAURANT

Rory hides behind a table.

CLOSE-UP. Rory scans the restaurant. As much as he can, anyway—it's nearly pitch-black, and we can only see the blinking of his earpiece.

> THE STING
> Rory—hello? Are you okay?

The Python picks up the table Rory is hiding behind and throws it across the restaurant.

Rory bolts, this time with purpose. He knocks chairs off the tops of tables to slow down The Python behind him.

> RORY
It's The Python!

> JENSON
We'll come and—

> RORY
No, I got it.

He runs through the kitchen, and we hear metal clambering as he cranks a knob and opens a door. Hurrying inside, he ducks as The Python swipes at him.

Meat hangs from the ceiling, and Rory pulls off his earpiece and jabs it onto a hanging carcass.

As quietly as possible, he ducks again, walking slowly around the perimeter to the open door.

Falling for the trap, The Python attacks the carcass with the blinking earpiece before realizing he's been set up. It's too late—Rory closes the door on him.

CLOSE-UP. Rory cranks the freezer to the coldest setting.

The Python bangs against the door.

> RORY
Zoology 101. Pythons don't last long in the cold.

EXT. ALLEY

Rory walks out slowly, and the city is descending into more chaos.

We see Rory's reaction as The Sting gets shot by Dr. Dreadworthy.

25

STUCK IN LOVE

I lay out all the possibilities, hoping to find some of them less awful, but truthfully it seems like losing Logan will feel like heartbreak forever. How many chances at a *real* connection does someone get anyway? What if the universe has decided I've wasted too many shots? I'll be totally barren of emotional connection for the rest of my days.

I remember something Logan said: *positive thinking creates positive results.*

In my head, I decide Logan and I will have a totally magical long-distance relationship for a few years, depending on where I end up. We're always there for each other to have Chinese takeout on FaceTime and send each other encouraging texts throughout the day.

In my head, none of the stuff that happened this summer affects us. We're strong, and we trust each other and support everything the other wants to do. I can already see it: he'll accept my apology, and we'll start to move past all the other crap that happened.

I count my steps from one end of the sidewalk, across the street, and back onto the sidewalk. At the crack in the pavement, I know I'm almost to Logan's. My steps and my mind are steady, but my heart isn't. I stop for a minute, wondering if I should turn around, but I know the future I want will never happen if I don't try and make this work. I have to tell Logan how I feel.

Pacing myself, I start toward the house. As I turn past the hedges lining the fence, I find I have no time left at all to conjure up some magic speech or perfect apology.

Logan kicks his foot up on the skateboard, attempting to do a trick, but it just flops around under his feet, and he lands awkwardly, mumbling under his breath. He's wearing a pair of gym shorts that say FBI and fall right above his knees with those tattered Vans and a white T-shirt that reads STAT WARS. Again, he brings one foot up across the board and pops it. I'm not even sure what he's trying to do with the damn thing. His other foot kicks it from the bottom and he is back to square one, with the board lying wheels up, taunting him.

He sees me and pouts, letting his hands fall to his waist. "Oh, no. This isn't— You should have come a few minutes ago, I was doing pull-ups."

"I'm not judging you," I say. "It's not like I could do a trick on that thing."

Logan stays quiet, just wipes sweat off his forehead.

"I'm really sorry," I offer. "Specifically, I'm sorry for not just being open with you about the Grant situation and I'm sorry for not making the right choices. I'm sorry for hurting you in any way and for all the wasted time, and I just… I don't know what I can say or do to make any of it up to you."

Maybe I can't make it up to him, I think, *but I can at least explain better.*

"What happened with Grant was just… It was confusing. And I don't know why it happened, and it maybe shouldn't have happened." I consider the words before I say them. "But it's over with Grant. It's way over, Logan. You're the one I want to be with. I want to surf with you and eat pizza with you and have coffee and… I want to do everything with *you*. And I'm sorry if I didn't make that clear or made you feel like that isn't true, but the entire thing with Grant is over. I promise."

Logan steps toward me now and smiles gently and sincerely. "Harry, I believe you. I don't want to make you feel bad about anything—we're still just kids, really. And it's okay to figure stuff out. And I think it might be over for you, but I don't know if it's over for him. And that's important, too."

"I used to think that," I say. "That we're just kids. That I didn't want to deal with romance or dating until I was 'all grown up' and out of Citrus—living my big LA life. But then you came around and suddenly…"

"Harry—"

"You changed everything. And… I really care about you, Logan. A lot," I say.

"I know, and I care about you, too, Harry."

"But?"

"I don't know."

We don't speak for a minute, and Logan frowns. And I feel like *now* it's the end of the world.

"After everything I went through with my ex, and with everything going on with Jane, I just really don't want to… I can't get involved in something that's gonna hurt anymore," he says. "I just can't, Harry."

"But I—"

"I know you wouldn't hurt me on purpose," Logan says. "And I don't want you to feel like it's just that—I mean, when the summer ends, I'm going back to North Carolina and then to New York. And you're going off to California next year."

And I want to tell him I don't know where I'm going now. I want to tell him all about my new brilliant plan for us. But now it all feels too far away. Suddenly it's caught in my throat.

"I'm sorry, Harry," he says, his shoulders rising.

And with that I nod, wiping at my cheek before a tear can fall, and I swallow, hard. "No, you're right. So, I guess that's it, then."

"No hard feelings. Friends?" Logan says, his hand almost coming up to comfort me before he stops himself. He looks sad but sounds hopeful, and it feels like a knife has been shoved into my chest, even as I continue to nod.

"Yeah, of course," I say. "I'll see you around."

And I walk away, with a smile and all the willpower in the world keeping me from crying until I make it home.

EXT. DOWNTOWN

In slow motion, we see the bullet pierce The Sting's suit.
Quick Circuit and Gold Honor see, too, but everyone is too
late.

The Sting falls to the ground, hard, as Jenson uses his
powers to turn Dr. Dreadworthy to vapor.

The streets glitch, and there is a loud rumbling.

WIDE SHOT. Rory runs to The Sting, with tears falling down
his cheeks.

26

HOW TO LOSE A GUY IN 10 DAYS

A flying croissant marks a new day in the Kensington household, and I watch as golden-brown pastry is sprinkled across the marble countertop and droplets of Nutella shower the kitchen.

It's been a few days since I went to Logan's and got a hard rejection. Self-help YouTube videos say to focus on the positives and stay busy, so that's what I've been doing—trying Pinterest crafts with Hailey and forcing my family to have movie nights so I don't start listening to sad songs alone in my room. This morning, Mom planned for us all to wake up and convene in the kitchen for a breakfast together. She just sighs at the destroyed pastry, rubbing her temples.

"Real nice, girls," she says, closing the magnetic case of her iPad.

Lottie, sitting at the counter in her pale pink polka dot pajamas, frowns. "Sorry, Mom. I didn't mean for it to go every-where!"

"I thought a family breakfast would be a *nice* thing," Mom says, though we're all just scattered around the kitchen and in various stages of waking up. It's a Saturday, so Mom doesn't need to get ready for work and Milly and Lottie would nor-mally be sleeping right now.

I take a sip of my coffee. Even with the chocolate syrup I added, it needs a little more sugar, so I cross the kitchen to pick up the porcelain canister—one gifted to my mom by one of her clients in Paris. It would be nice to escape to Paris right now, escape any reminders of how I screwed up every-thing with Logan.

"Listen, girls," Mom says, walking back to the pantry. She's wearing silky pajamas that are covered with sock monkeys dressed like Santa Claus. "I read a study this morning—"

Milly drops her head, her phone dramatically crashing out of her hand onto the counter.

"Okay, listen!" Mom closes the pantry door and places her hands on the counter across from Milly. I sit next to Lottie. "They're saying if you look at your screens too much you might completely lose your sense of color."

"Who told you that?" I raise a brow.

"It was on one of my apps," Mom says. "And they also had something on there about making sure you're wiping down, not up." She looks to the girls, who both stick their tongues out and make gagging noises. "I mean I didn't think I needed to say it, but just making sure."

"Gross," I say. I wonder if she and Mark bond over these weird parenting tips. They're basically going steady, but I don't know when in a relationship you start talking about your kids' wiping habits.

"It's *very* bad," Mom says, nodding slowly. "If you wipe things up, you get all kinds of guck in your hoo-ha, and that's just not what we want."

Milly continues scrolling. "Mom, honestly, I'm *fifteen*. Do you think I need my mother to tell me how to wipe? None of the other girls' parents pull this kind of crap. Why can't you just tell us funny stories in the mornings instead of talking about weird studies about vaginas?"

"Is she allowed to say vagina?" Lottie quickly says.

"Yes, Lottie," I say. "It is what it is."

"I'm looking at you, Lottie," Mom says, pointedly, strategically ignoring Milly.

"I know how to wipe," Lottie whines. "I'm five."

"Okay, that tone sounds a little—"

"Hello, hello!" Nana slams the front door, and Mom winces.

"Mom, please," she says when Nana comes into the kitchen with two baskets full of fruit. "Don't slam that door, remember?"

"Oh, right." Nana is wearing a shibori caftan, her gray hair pulled into a thick braid that falls over her shoulder, and she pulls her sunglasses off her face. "Your poor old mother had better watch how she treats the shiny, expensive door."

I laugh, and Lottie throws a Fruity Pebbles my way.

"Hey, we don't throw food!" Nana narrows her eyes.

Milly looks up. "Who doesn't throw food? Have you ever met Lottie?"

"In an ideal world," Mom says, "nobody throws food in this house."

"Do you want one of these nectarines? They're fresh," Nana says, pulling one from the basket and dangling it in front of Lottie's face.

Lottie blows a raspberry.

"Hey, be nice to your Nana," Mom warns.

Nana hugs me before pouring herself some orange juice and then pointing my way. "Harold, why don't you invite that cute boy over? Jane's nephew?"

I have to physically fight not to flinch, but I just smile, looking down into my coffee mug.

"They broke up," Lottie says flatly, her face lit up by her iPad.

"Mom!" Milly squeals. "You were supposed to tell Nana."

"We didn't *break up*," I say, waving them away.

"I'm really gonna miss Logan," Lottie says, poking out her bottom lip and locking her iPad.

"You'll see him at the club," I offer.

"But he won't be coming over." Lottie groans and looks at me like she's disappointed in my choices. "He's *very* nice, Harold. Very!"

Milly and Mom both exchange looks, and Nana is clearly questioning what to say next.

"Lottie, you know Logan is going away to college, right?" I say. "At the end of the summer, Logan isn't going to be here anymore."

"I know what going away to college means!" Lottie says. "But what about Christmas?"

I smile softly and lean down to her level. "Lottie, we don't know what Logan's Christmas plans are, so there's no reason to get upset over—"

"He said! He said he'd come see us for Christmas." Lottie throws her hands up. "He told me he was going to talk to Santa for me! And Milly too, for her record player. He's closer to the North Pole when he's at college, so he can talk to Santa."

I feel my chest get heavy, and I stand up. Logan talked to Lottie and Milly about coming back for Christmas. He told them he'd be here, and he thought he would. He thought it'd be hot chocolate on the back patio with my family and singing the classics while he probably gave Lottie and Milly and my mom super thoughtful gifts with adorable wrapping paper he chose himself.

"I'm sorry," I say finally.

"It's okay, Harold," Milly says, raising her eyebrows at Lottie. "Lottie is just being a brat."

"I am *not*," Lottie says before she bursts into tears and throws a banana at Milly.

Mom rubs Lottie's back while Nana grabs the banana off the floor and Milly just blinks. I feel like Lottie right now— like I could cry at any moment.

"Lottie, I'm really sorry," I say and she looks to me, sniffling and pulling it together.

"I just will miss Logan," Lottie says. She wipes at her cheeks and tells Milly she's sorry for throwing the banana.

"Me too," I say slowly. "But, you know what? Sometimes people come into our lives for a little bit, but they don't stay for a long while…or at least not for forever."

I feel like I totally destroyed Lottie's hopes and dreams here. I mean, I know realistically it's just because she's five and she really does like Logan, but I wish Logan could be here right now and then he'd come for Christmas and Lottie and Milly wouldn't feel like I took him away.

"It'll all be okay," I say.

After Milly and Lottie run off to the living room to face off in *Super Mario Kart*, Nana starts doing the dishes, and Mom pours herself coffee.

"How are you feeling?" Nana says.

"Not the best," I say.

Mom rubs my arm. "It really, *actually*, will all be okay. Are you sure things with Logan are completely done? I mean he obviously loves the girls, and he cares about you."

"It's complicated," I say. "But I'm sure. Maybe in a Nora Ephron movie he'd be here, and things would be different."

I wish, more than anything, life was like movies and a killer piano score and a grand gesture could fix things. I wish we'd kiss in the rain or meet at the top of the Empire State Building and make everything better. Regardless of how it happened, I just wish I could hear one more goofy pickup line or sit on the beach and watch one more sunrise with Logan.

"But life's not a movie." I shrug, a little too devastated to do much more.

And I know it's not the ending I want for my story with Logan, but it's the one I have.

Then there's a knock on the front door and Mom just gives me a look that tells me exactly who it is.

EXT. DOWNTOWN

Rory and The Sting are hidden behind debris.

>   RORY
> (sobbing)
> You're going to be okay.

>   THE STING
> (coughing)
> I don't think these are regular bullets.

>   RORY
> Just hold on, okay? Once we stop all this, Mr. Wilson
> can figure it out.

>   THE STING
> There's no way to stop all this, Rory.

>   RORY
> I still have a secret weapon.

THE STING
What?

RORY
(laughs, through tears, rolling his eyes)
It always comes back to Jenson.

27

THE WAY WE WERE

The ocean is a green-blue that's nearly too beautiful to be real. Most of the sky is just squished marshmallows, but way off, distant from the rest, these clouds are illuminated in the most perfect oranges and yellows, and they're stacked so perfectly just like a fluffy mountain.

I look at Grant against the pink cotton candy sky. To my left, a couple runs with their dog, and a grandfather and a child race each other to my right.

"I'm sorry," Grant says.

I exhale. "I'm surprisingly not as pissed at you as I thought I'd be."

"Really?" Grant sounds surprised.

I'm taking ownership for my part in all this.

I *sort of* still want to punch him in the face, but I'm mostly trying to be a better person right now.

"Look, I apologize for being a jerk to Logan," Grant says, eyes on the water. "I shouldn't have. I just got jealous."

"Grant Kennedy admitting he got jealous," I laugh, and Grant rolls his eyes, though now he's smiling. "I'm sure I'll forgive you for being a dick to Logan at some point. In the very distant future."

He reaches over and sweeps away some hair that's fallen over my forehead, and I watch the glimmer in his eye, wondering if it really has always been there. Did it really never leave? Even when he was in California? Will it leave when he goes back?

"Anyway, I can't wait for you to get to USC. You're really gonna love it," he says, biting his lip. "I actually met this girl who does screenwriting there. She writes super weird indie films, and you guys may be friends, you never know. You'll just love the weather, too, it's like here but without the humidity. Though, you know, you have to have a hoodie for nighttime."

I just watch him talk, and he laughs, back in true Grant mode, pushing off the ground to swing higher. "We can go to the Santa Monica Pier together. It's so much fun. There's even a roller coaster. Oh, and Catalina is really awesome—there's a ferry and camping. It's not just the wine mixer thing or whatever. I don't even know if that's real."

Once upon a time, it wouldn't be too hard to picture us taking Instagram photos in Venice Beach and hiking the hills and us lying on a green campus lawn as I write a screenplay.

But I can only see those things in my mind. I can't *feel* them like I could imagine my future with Logan.

Beside me, Grant looks out at the water, and he looks different to me now. His sharp features, lit up by the bleeding orange and pinks of the sky, are like that of an old friend. For the first time, I notice the darkness under his eyes and the stubble on his face—imperfections, things that make him human that I never paid attention to before.

Grant smiles. "And my dad will still get you that bomb letter of recommendation."

"Grant." I shake my head. "I'm not going to USC."

He looks to me, his smile fading and his eyes falling. "What?"

"At least I don't think I am," I say. "I don't really know. I don't know what I want to do or where I want to go. I'm going to spend some time figuring it out."

"But you *can* get in, you know. I'm sure my dad can—"

I shake my head. "I have a lot to work out. Who I am, what matters to me. It's more than just where I go to college."

"Well, you still could go to a school in LA," Grant offers. "There's Loyola, CalArts... Or even, like, San Diego. It's a two-hour drive, and then you can transfer after a year and—"

I shake my head slowly, and Grant frowns.

"What we had this summer was amazing in its own way," I say. "I don't regret anything with you, Grant. But I think we had our chance—"

"But I told you, I'm sorry—"

"It's not just you," I say earnestly. "It's me, too. I'm not the same person I was last summer. This thing between us is over, it has been—it already was. And these past few weeks have been us grasping at things from the past—memories and things that are familiar to us because the truth is growing up is scary. It means a lot of unknowns and leaving things behind, and there's nothing wrong with wanting to be around someone who feels familiar and makes you feel loved. It just doesn't mean we should *be together*. We're so young, and we have so much ahead of us. Too much to be clinging to the past already."

Grant doesn't say anything. He just watches me.

"I'll always have love for you," I admit. "And that's why it's so easy for us to pick things up and dream of a new future, but the truth is I don't feel the same way I did before. And I don't really, *honestly* think you feel the same way about me. I just think the idea of *us* is comforting. And that's not a bad thing, as long as we recognize that's what this is."

After a few seconds, Grant smiles, soft and delicate. "Yeah."

"Yeah?"

"I know you really like Logan." Grant sucks his teeth. "And I tried to change your mind or whatever, but I know you're right. I was a dick. I just will always love you, too. I know you didn't believe me before, but I will. I know we have to move on, though. I have to let you go."

"Look at us." I throw up my hands. "Last summer, if you told me we'd be here, having this conversation, I wouldn't have believed you."

"Like total grown-ups," Grant agrees. "I do hope you'll always be part of my life somehow. You know, when we're both ready for that."

As the waves harmonize with the gulls, the oranges drip into purples, and the stars start to shine, I smile and turn to

Grant, but before I can say anything he flashes a bright grin, in typical Grant fashion.

"And Harry? If you're going to write me into one of your screenplays, at least give me a big part."

EXT. DOWNTOWN

The city has become a glitch.

The Champions Alliance have all fallen.

Evil Warp crushes the canister in his hands, but when the DNA spills out, nothing happens.

MEDIUM SHOT. Rory leaps from behind the debris and reaches into his jacket. In slow motion, we see a canister in his hand—the real canister. He throws it at the ground next to Jenson.

Evil Warp shouts and blasts Rory.

     THE STING
 Rory!

As the canister shatters, we see a detonation of prisms and code and diamond-like light.

Jenson kicks off the ground.

We scan The Champions Alliance's reactions as they see his transformation. Rory covers his eyes. Jenson is burning like a supernova.

      EVIL WARP
  No, it can't be.

CLOSE-UP. Jenson's eyes have a galactic look to them.

MEDIUM SHOT. Jenson brings his hands together, and the glitches even out.

CLOSE-UP. He pulls his hands apart.

WIDE SHOT. Everything goes white, and Evil Warp dissipates into fragments.

The city is still, and Jenson slowly rebuilds with his reality magic.

28

AS GOOD AS IT GETS

It's been two weeks since the night I was metaphorically body slammed by the god of disaster at the wedding.

Today was my last day working with Agnes, which was bittersweet. Turns out she got an amazing internship in London, after all, so she's moving to be with her sister. She told me I could come visit and she'd take me to Notting Hill and Trafalgar Square and Kings Cross Station. All the best movie spots (at least to me—the stereotypical American moviegoer). I couldn't believe, considering how we started off the summer, when she hugged me goodbye, I actually didn't want to see her go.

After my shift, Milly and Lottie made a point of blasting *Mamma Mia* and showing me the new outfits they put together—bell-bottoms and '70s scarves from Mom's closet— a major upgrade and one I'm trying to one-up whenever I get the chance.

Now I'm out at the shops with Hailey, and there's a scarf

on one of the mannequins by the window that looks like the most perfect oceanic blue-green with psychedelic orange diamonds and yellow eye patterns.

"I think I need this," I say.

She eyes it for a minute and frowns. "Are you going through a crisis?"

"For our *Mamma Mia* costumes," I laugh. "Milly and Lottie both have great getups, and I can't compete."

"It's on sale," Hailey points out and returns to the dress rack. "I wonder if I should just get cover-ups since I'll pretty much be on the boat and at the beach this whole weekend. Kylie's sister is going to stock the fridge with White Claws."

Suddenly aware, her eyes meet mine, and she winces. "I'm sorry, I know you wanted to come."

"It's fine," I say, unwrapping the scarf from the mannequin and tying it around my neck. "It's a girl's trip. I completely understand. Besides, you need to bond with your teammates."

"I'm checking your horoscope," Hailey says, pulling her phone out of her purse. "'A lover is set to return from a sea voyage.' I wonder who it could be. God, that reminds me of Jack. Poor Jack."

"What did you say?"

"Jack, from *Titanic*." Hailey furrows her brow and stuffs her phone in her bag, making her way into her dressing room.

The scarf looks absolutely ridiculous on me, but it's great for the purposes of concerts with my sisters, so I decide to commit to it.

I sit down on one of the pink velvet couches as I wait for Hailey to show me her outfit choices and stare outside. It's a beautiful day. The sun is out, and we're a block from the ocean, so there are families walking in their swimsuits. When a skateboarder flies by who looks too much like Logan, I look down at my phone.

Scrolling through Instagram, I pass a photo from Beverly's wedding and a few pictures of the sunset last night. Summer Mancini posted a photo at In-N-Out—she's actually dropping out of USC to be a full-time influencer. Before I can get too far down the rabbit hole, Hailey huffs and pulls open the curtain of her fitting room, holding only one top that's white with embroidered flowers. She tosses it on the counter, and I get up to join her.

"Shopping is hard," she says to me and the blond girl at the register simultaneously. She's absentmindedly toying with some of the Kate Kensington lipsticks that are arranged in a pink seashell bowl when she leans to me and whispers, "I cannot afford this place on Peach's salary."

A group of kids about our age walk in, and I notice how they're all giggling and having the best time. I haven't been able to get back to that. Haven't felt one hundred percent yet. I know it'll come back—positive thinking leads to positive results. Or so some say.

I just need to give my heart time to heal, according to all the great rom-coms. I guess I haven't found my opposite lead yet, after all. Just the stories that play in the beginning montage.

"Harry?" Hailey says, knocking my shoulder.

"Did you want the scarf?" the cashier says.

"Yes, please," I say, handing it to her.

She scans the tag, and the price is even lower than I thought. Win. If anything, Milly will probably actually wear it to school, so I give her my debit card. I watch her insert the chip, and I wish Logan were here to make the *erk, erk, erk* noise.

"Do you want to wear it out?"

I start to laugh, but Hailey just nods, grinning as she takes the scarf and wraps it around my neck. Normally I'd protest, but my give-a-fuck meter is a little lower than usual right now. Hailey holds a finger up, accepting a call before stepping outside.

I take my debit card back, turning around and bumping into someone, causing him to drop his phone.

"Oh my God," I say, crouching down to grab it for him. I hold it upside down in my palm and hesitate to flip it, but when I do we both sigh, relieved to see the screen isn't cracked. "I'm sorry."

"No worries. That's a cool scarf," says Tall, Dark, and Handsome, putting his phone in his pocket and grinning. I reach up to yank it off, but he laughs and shakes his head. "No really!"

I fake a laugh and start to walk again.

"Wait," he says, lowering those striking emerald eyes. "Um. Don't you go to Citrus Harbor High?"

"Yeah," I say, feeling even more embarrassed than before.

"Nice, I go to St. Martin's, but I thought you looked familiar," he says. A beat. I expect him to say something else, but he just stares into my eyes and then smiles. "You going to Stivender's tonight?"

Hailey opens the door but stops, holding it open and mouthing O-M-G.

I shake my head. "I don't think so. But I'm sure I'll see you around."

"Okay," he says with a flirtatious grin. "Well, if I see you there, I'll promise not to knock your phone out of your hand."

Forcing a smile, I nod and apologize again, quickly walk outside, past Hailey and onto the sidewalk.

"He was *cute*," Hailey says. "Doesn't he go to St. Martin's?"

"Yeah, but I'm waiting for my lover to return from sea," I tell Hailey pointedly. "Astrology never lies."

"Right," she says seriously. "But are you sure you don't want to go back—"

This time, I'm *really* over hot guys.

For the rest of the summer, I'll be content with just spending my days with Hailey and my nights with Lottie and Milly, binging on Nutella and watching whatever dumb movies they put on.

"Can we get ice cream?" I change the subject quickly and point down the avenue.

Hailey nods as we cross the street. "You might notice the girls' shorts are *not* all hitting just above their knees."

I don't point out that I *wouldn't* notice that—because I'm not looking at girls' shorts and because they're behind a counter—but I squeeze Hailey's arm all the same. "No way! Are you saying what I think you're saying?"

"You were right." She beams. "My mom and Mimi helped me write a letter to the managers about how it was sexist for the boys to do and wear whatever they want and then I got all the girls I work with to sign it."

"Amazing," I say.

"Yeah, some of the girls added their own two cents. And a few of them are on swim team with me, and we're going to try to address the school's sexist dress code, too, once senior year starts," she says. "I'm going to get Penny to help 'cause she's all into student government. I mean, it's not like any of us are trying to wear anything inappropriate. It's just a million degrees outside—it's summertime in Florida. We wanna wear shorts."

"Wow, Hailey, good for you."

She grins and points to my scarf. "This is kind of great."

"I look silly," I say, but she won't let me take it off, swatting at my hands.

"No, it's amazing," Hailey cries as we reach the boardwalk. "I think it's what you've been missing all along."

"Maybe *you* need to check *your* horoscope to see if an ice cream cone is about to magically fall into your lap," I tease.

Her phone buzzes, and I catch a glimpse of all the notifications.

"Are those all guys from camp?"

Hailey smirks. "I'm not looking for anything serious, but it's fun to flirt."

She and Justin are slowly becoming amicable. Very slowly. It's a lot of effort on Justin's part, and Hailey maintains she won't ever get back with him. Still, I understand her wanting things to eventually become less awkward since it's a small town and senior year is quickly approaching. She's making him work for every ounce of forgiveness, though, and it's kind of awesome.

Hailey pockets her phone and gets in line for Peach's, waving to the girls behind the counter.

As she starts to yell over the line, laughing with her coworker, I see Logan, skating toward us in the green-striped shirt I lent him the day we met.

I nudge Hailey and take a few steps toward the sidewalk as Logan hops off the skateboard, holding his hand up in a friendly wave. He looks like a daydream against the row of pastel shops on the boardwalk, accompanied by a soundtrack of the ocean waves and gulls and Elvis coming from the patio of the restaurant behind him.

"Nice T-shirt," I say when we're a few steps apart.

"Nice scarf," Logan says, and I remember I'm wearing this stupid scarf and yank it off, stuffing it in my pocket.

"I got it for Milly and Lottie," I say, knowing he won't need much more of an explanation.

This feels familiar and different, emotional and charged but also—and this is the weirdest part—calming and comfortable. I expected to clam up and flip out the first time I saw Logan since that day on his driveway, but it's the opposite. It's like I can finally breathe.

"How's Jane?" I say.

"She's good," Logan says with a laugh. "We've been watching *House Hunters* on mute a lot—providing our own voiceovers. She's really nailed the 'it would be so nice for him to have a home office' and 'wow, this open floor plan is really great.'"

We laugh, and there's a beat of silence between us, with locked eyes and caught breath.

"Yeah, I'll give the shirt back, sorry," Logan finally says. "Some of the guys from the club went out sailing this morning, and I thought this was, like, the vibe. I looked like a dork. Not because of your shirt. But it turns out you're not supposed to dress to a theme for sailing."

"You went *sailing*?" I cover my mouth and stifle a laugh.

"Hey!" Logan blushes. "It was fun. I mean, will I do it again? Maybe not."

I feel something like sadness wash over me for a minute, thinking this is it. This is who we are now.

"You know, Harry, this isn't just a coincidence—us running into each other here," Logan says slowly. "I tracked you down using state of the art federal investigative equipment."

He holds up the Snapchat map, which shows my little character with Hailey's at Peach's Ice Cream.

I start to laugh, but Logan narrows his eyes, so I straighten up. "And what?"

"There are two dozen French police around the block if you try to run," Logan says. "They're in France in the movie," he whispers before straightening back up. "Anyway, gig's up, I know what you did."

"What did I do now?" I cross my arms.

"Intel from a field agent—Kennedy," Logan says, and I feel my chest tighten. "We know you didn't submit your screenplay. Seems you were planning to fly under the radar, get 'ice cream'"—he holds up his fingers for air quotes—"with your friend. And the question I have is... What's next?"

"I thought you'd have it all figured out," I say, "Special Agent."

Logan furrows his brow. "You can try to run away from it all, but you're Harry Kensington. You're too talented to just give it all up."

"I'm not going to give it all up," I say. "I'm just... I'm going to live in the now, not in the future."

Nodding, Logan puts his hands in his pockets. He does a fine Tom Hanks, I think.

"Right, okay," he says. "That doesn't sound so criminal.

Well, when you *do* want to think about the future, I happen to know another agent located out of our New York office. In the Cinema Studies department at NYU. Someone to talk to, at least."

New York? Mom always said I should look at New York, but I never did—I was too stubborn.

But New York... It takes less than half the time to get to New York by plane than it takes to fly to LA, and there are lots of creatives there. It's fast paced. It's cutting-edge. It's exciting. I can't believe I never really gave it more thought. I've always enjoyed going there with Mom and the girls— the restaurants and shopping and Broadway shows. Lottie's old enough to appreciate the American Museum of Natural History, and I bet Milly and her friends would want to stay with me and see concerts at Madison Square Garden.

And Logan will be in New York.

"Huh," I say, playing it cool. I'm not going to focus on where the grass might be greener again. My grass is green here. Still, New York... "Really?"

"Producing, directing, writing." Logan shrugs. "You name it."

Producing... Directing? I've always been so one-track minded—writing screenplays and going to USC. Living in LA was my end all, be all. But what if I did other things? There are so many parts of filmmaking I could explore along with writing. Now that I'm not limited by my tunnel vision, the possibilities seem endless.

"I wouldn't want to waste the years of research and hard work." I shrug, pretending this isn't a major revelation. "I'd guess there would be *something* in New York that could interest me."

"Or maybe many things," Logan offers.

And it's then that it hits me: My future doesn't start and end with USC or LA. It starts and ends with me. If I want to make something that means something to someone—a rainy day comfort film or even something inspiring—I can. Because my ideas don't die if they don't blossom in LA.

NYU is still not an easy school to get into, but there are others in the city if it doesn't work out. It's exciting, regardless, to feel like I have more of a blank canvas to work with than a narrow pigeon-holed dream that would crush me if it didn't work out.

"I'll think about it," I say, feeling a newfound excitement for the future burning in my chest. I narrow my eyes on him. "So, you tracked me down—using your FBI tech," I say very seriously. "Just to tell me that?"

Logan blinks. Maybe he hadn't thought this all the way through. Only, that doesn't sound like Logan. I think he might want something else—I hope he does, at least. There's only one way to find out:

"Well, thanks," I say, offering a tight-lipped smile and turning on my heel to walk back to Hailey.

There's a beat, and I try to walk slowly, but nothing seems to be happening. Was I wrong? Was he really just trying to be friendly?

But then I hear him clear his throat and follow after me.

"Hey, where do you think you're going? You're still a suspect in a—"

I look back, not at Agent Waters, but at *Logan*.

"You're going to have to catch me."

And with that, Logan grabs my hand, pulling me toward

him and lowering those smoky-blue eyes. He brings a hand up to my jaw and brings my mouth to meet his, our lips melting into each other. His tongue slides over mine, and I wrap my arms around his neck, feeling like I could never be close enough to him, like I want to feel his lips on mine forever.

The kiss is electric—my lips buzz, and my heart quickens, and Logan's hand finds my back. Slowly, our lips break apart, and Logan looks down at me, the sunlight golden on his lashes and reflecting in his eyes.

There's no stopping the grin that lights up his face, and my own smile feels bigger than normal.

"Are we still in character?" I whisper.

Logan barks out a laugh. "I think that was all us."

"I think you're right," I say, nodding and looking down at my feet. "So, wait, you— I thought you didn't…"

"Grant explained everything," Logan says, nodding slowly. "He actually tried to *pay me* to forgive you…"

I cringe. "That is Grant for you."

"I could tell he meant well," Logan laughs. "Plus Hailey wouldn't stop sending me horoscopes, so I figured…"

"You can't argue with the stars. So," I say, already desperate to make up for lost time. "What are you doing tonight?"

Logan smiles. "True crime doc and leftover lasagna. Ron always makes way too much food." He sighs. "And I need someone to help me finally beat Jane at Scrabble…if you're free."

"I'm totally free," I say too quickly, and Logan laughs. He opens his mouth, rubs the back of his neck, and points behind me to Hailey, who is sitting at the bench closest to us and *totally* not eavesdropping.

Caught, she creeps over and puts a hand on each of our arms. "Logan, you were *sailing*? You mean, you were out at sea?"

As I laugh, burying my face in my hands, Hailey hugs Logan, who offers a confused smile and hugs her back.

"Hailey *loves* New York," I say to Logan. "We always go to Dylan's Candy Bar."

Hailey blinks. "Hailey is right here. And what does New York have to do with anything?"

"Hello." I raise a brow. I can picture it already. Brunch on the weekends in Chelsea—Hailey and I are close by since we're downtown while Logan takes the train from Columbia—and we probably have a bunch of new, like, artsy friends or something. "We can move together, and you can go to The New School, and get your dream internship at Cosmo."

Narrowing her eyes, Hailey just nods slowly. "While that does sound amazing, I will *begin* to think about college on the first day of school and no sooner."

"Fine." I nod and as quietly as possible whisper, "Cosmo!" Then another idea strikes. "Maybe I can write for Broadway, too. I wonder if I'd be any good at songwriting."

"What have you done?" Hailey says to Logan.

He takes my hand, and we follow Hailey back into line. After she orders, I shrug and say I'll have whatever their most popular flavor is.

Logan raises a brow.

"You always get the same flavor," he says.

"I'm letting *whatever* happen these days," I tell him with a smile. "Just going with it."

As we wait for our ice cream, Lottie and Milly run over to

us. Lottie bear-hugs Logan and tells him how happy she is to see him, and Milly gives me a look like *finally*.

"Told them we'd get ice cream," Mom says as she and Nana reach us. Mom lifts a brow and gives us a totally obvious smile. "Hi, Logan."

"What's this?" Lottie says, pulling the scarf out of my pocket. She wraps it over her head like Jackie O. "Lovely."

"Very 'Super Trouper,' Lot," Milly giggles.

Hailey nods. "So your look."

"Nana was singing 'Fernando' just like Cher," Lottie whispers to Logan and me.

"Shh!" Nana holds her finger to her lips.

"Mom, I think we should go see how things are going at your Madison Avenue boutique," I say very seriously. "You love Tavern on the Green in summer."

Logan just laughs, and Mom gives me a confused look.

I sit with all of the people I love and watch the cerulean waves, each spoonful of lavender lemonade ice cream completely life-changing, as "Pocketful of Rainbows" plays along the boardwalk. For now, everything feels right, and I don't need a horoscope to predict that real life could be even better than anything in the movies.

EXT. CITYSCAPE—DAY

We hear the busy city and a newscast.

>   POLITE NEWSCASTER (V.O.)
> Three days ago a blast from downtown was contained.
> The Champions Alliance, along with Captain Warp and
> The Sting, have secured all civilians, and we are assured
> levels of radioactivity are low enough for this area to
> be cleared.

EXT. UPTOWN MARKET—A FEW DAYS LATER

We see Rory unscrewing the cap of a water bottle. He puts
sunglasses on as he walks out of the market and smiles softly
as his elderly neighbor and her Maltese pass him on the
sidewalk.

Rory walks down the street. We hear light instrumental
music. The city seems quiet.

Behind Rory, we see Skip running up, disheveled. He's out of breath, and when Rory hears him coming, he turns around, and they smile at each other. Skip has a black eye and a cut on his nose and lip.

> RORY
> I thought you were at The Champions Alliance Campus?

> SKIP
> I just got back.

> RORY
> What about Jenson?

> SKIP
> He's recovering still. But he'll be okay.

> RORY
> That's good. How about you?

> SKIP
> Doing much better. I'm still curious what the hell kind of bullet The Vicious used. I wonder if some of their weaponry was from another dimension, too.

> RORY
> I'm hoping we can focus on one dimension for a while.

> SKIP
> Me too.

They smile and take a step closer to one another.

    RORY
You know, I thought for a second there you were
going to...

Skip grabs Rory with his free hand. Rory wraps his arms
around Skip's neck, and Skip kisses him. The music swells,
and the camera circles around them—finally together for
good, in the sunshine on a flower-lined sidewalk.

Skip breaks the kiss. Beaming, he stares into the other boy's
eyes.

    SKIP
So, I wasn't actually a Future Defense intern this whole
time. I thought you'd figure out I was The Sting if I didn't
have some story for how I knew The Champions Alliance.

    RORY
I see.

    SKIP
But Mr. Wilson got me promoted to *actual* junior agent
for The Champions Alliance. I'm officially in training.

    RORY
What? Are you surprised?

    SKIP
Kinda. You know what else was surprising? The fact that
you switched the DNA canisters and didn't tell anybody.

    RORY
I know. I just— At first it was for Jenson's safety. I
figured we could let him have the fake one until we

figured out a safer way to test the proximity. But then we found out it wasn't really him, and I knew it was the only way and that The Champions Alliance wouldn't willingly expose the real Jenson to the enhanced DNA.

SKIP

All very smart. But you could have told me, you know.

RORY

Mr. Fate made it clear I could *not*.

SKIP

Wait, you know Mr. Fate?

RORY

No, he just stopped me at The Champions Alliance Campus after you lost your suit.

SKIP

Of course he did. So that *was* his card I saw in your dorm!

RORY

He wasn't exactly forthcoming with details—all I knew was "it had to be me."

SKIP

That's totally how he works. Like, why can't he just have a conversation like a normal person?

RORY

That would have made things easier. I knew if I told you, you'd want to do it to keep me out of danger. And I felt like one of us should probably listen to Mr. Fate, anyway.

SKIP
Well, Rory Woods, I'm glad you did. You saved the universe.

Skip rests his forehead on Rory's.

SKIP
You're my hero.

As they kiss again, a police siren wails and we see the red-and-blue flashing lights. Skip's left eye opens and he looks to the street.

Rory laughs and pats Skip on the chest. Smiling—

RORY
Go ahead, Skip Stanley. Save the day.

FADE OUT.

★ ★ ★ ★ ★

ACKNOWLEDGEMENTS

First and foremost, thank you to my family for supporting me—Mom, Gabby, Reagan, Hola (I mixed up *Abuela* and *Hola* as a baby—it's a thing now), Dad, and Erica. I am so grateful for your constant love, guidance, and encouragement. To my friends who have been by my side all along—Lizzy, Ashley, Carson, and Macy—thank you for loving me and for dealing with me when I was obsessively drafting and editing, rinsing and repeating, and bringing up the publishing process every time we spoke during submission.

Thank you to friends who read early pages and offered thoughts—Jenna, Maureen, Kevin, Shawn, and Kat. To those who provided wisdom and guidance—Siobhan, Adam, Emily, and Austin—thank you for your friendship and advice! And a thank you to Natashya Wilson for seeing something in this story and giving it a chance.

My agent, Kristy Hunter... How long do you have? She truly deserves a novella titled *Why Kristy Hunter is the Perfect Agent*. Not even a novella—a multivolume leather-bound boxed set, chronicling all the time she spent working with me and making this book the best it could be. Kristy is a rare human being. I can't imagine having a better advocate for my books, and I am beyond thankful for her wisdom and guidance and for telling me to treat myself to rosé whenever anything good happened—we all need that kind of support in our lives. Kristy, thank you so much. You believed in the story from the moment you read it and loved it as it was. It means everything to me. My gratitude for your hard work, commitment, and friendship is unending!

Connolly Bottum, my editor—thank you so much for loving Harry and his friends and family and world, and for translating that love into thoughtful notes and a fantastic working relationship. I always knew the story was safe with you—more than that, I knew you totally got it and were going to make it even better, and I'm so appreciative of the time and dedication you put into this book. Thank you for helping me tell this story.

Thank you so much to Gigi Lau for art directing the cover of my dreams and the amazing artist, Andi Porretta—just wow. You are both so talented, and I couldn't have asked for a better cover! Harry, Grant, and Logan would thank you both, too, I'm sure, for painting them in such a fantastic light. Big thank-you to Brittany Mitchell and the marketing and publicity team for all their hard work! And to the rest of the Inkyard Press and HarperCollins family for everything.

And last, but absolutely not least, thank *you*, reader, for spending time with Harry & Co. I hope you enjoyed your time in Citrus Harbor as much as I did.